BOOKS BY ELIZABETH SIMS

Nonfiction:
You've Got a Book in You: A Stress-Free Guide to Writing the Book of Your Dreams

Fiction:
(It's not necessary to read either series in order.)

The Rita Farmer Mysteries
The Actress (#1)
The Extra (#2)
On Location (#3)

The Lillian Byrd Crime Novels
Holy Hell (#1)
Damn Straight (#2)
Lucky Stiff (#3)
Easy Street (#4)
Left Field (#5)

Crimes in a Second Language

I am Calico Jones: Four Short Stories

For up-to-date everything about Elizabeth and her books,
visit **elizabethsims.com**.

CRIMES IN A SECOND LANGUAGE

Elizabeth Sims

SPRUCE PARK PRESS

COPYRIGHT

Crimes in a Second Language. Copyright © 2017 by Elizabeth Sims. All rights reserved.

ISBN: 9781520300443

elizabethsims.com
Spruce Park Press

Cover design by TreeHouse Studio

1: The Dog Does Not Answer

A white woman with her hair in a bun and perspiration spangling her upper lip disembarks a bus in a Los Angeles neighborhood she's never been to before. Her stomach jiggles but not in an uncomfortable way. She is old enough to know the rewards of daily fiber supplements, sensible enough to be undaunted riding a bus into this place—in the daytime anyway—and desperate enough to do what she is about to do. The bus driver glances sideways with a molecule of curiosity as she hops down.

Desperation breeds nerve.

Nerve breeds action.

And this woman must act. Today. Lethally.

She walks one block in a random direction, her dusty white Keds rolling over the craggy sidewalk, her head swiveling as she frankly scrutinizes the storefronts. This is the right neighborhood, or really it is *a* right neighborhood.

Liquor-Lotto-Meat.

Pawn Town.

Ned's Bar-B-Q and Sons.

Suellen Beauty.

Dangerous-looking characters drive past, their arms flexed sternly over their steering wheels. A baby wails in a loopy rhythm.

Not long ago, for sure, this woman would have been frightened to be here. But she's got a grip on this city now—all of it. She belongs here.

A stray dog emerges from between two parked cars and humbly approaches. The woman perceives that the dog, half pit bull at least, is a female who must be nursing puppies somewhere; her teats are pronounced and low. It follows her, licks her hand from behind, circles around and looks up at her.

"What do you want to tell me, little dog?" Her voice is slender and clear, in contrast to her fat belly. Her words originate at the root of her tongue, not quite throatily; hers is an earnest voice that would be appropriate for a simultaneous interpreter or a documentary narrator.

Her name is Elnice M. Coker and she was married to Arthur T. "Bullet" Coker until yesterday, when he died before her eyes. His death was inappropriate and ghastly, but chosen. "Elnice" had been his last word.

She wishes people wouldn't mispronounce it. Elnice rhymes with Elvis; in fact the names share a Teutonic root.

Elnice is feeling desperate, nervy, and lethal because she has learned that slow death is not the worst thing that can happen. Her shadow swings along beneath her, keen in the caustic light of the city today.

A cluster of needle-eyed little boys in pyramidal pants give her and the dog a once-over. They can't finger it but she looks different. Not because she's white and wearing dirty clothes—other soiled white people live in the neighborhood. Perhaps it is her purposeful manner. Not acute enough yet to perceive or care, the boys go back to their boasting.

"I'm serious."

"My butthole."

"Did too. I am serious."

"My sweet butthole."

The dog does not answer Elnice's question. She cocks

her head at the animal—just in case—but it remains silent. Everything is all right; Elnice has made her deal with God, and everything is all right.

Another liquor store presents itself. She examines the exterior and, evidently finding something favorable, walks in. She pretends to shop for pretzels until her eyes adjust to the stale light. She turns to the man behind the smeared plexi barrier. He is a Korean with a pencil-line mustache, close to her in age, whose years of running this liquor store in South Los Angeles have given his face the look of a tombstone made of old wood.

"I want to buy a handgun," she tells him, "off the street. Do you know someone who can help me?"

The man's eyes scan her from bun to Keds. She is wearing a Joel Hannaberry top with yellow anemones in a diagonal burst and pink seersucker slacks from Stamenhill Creek, and these clothes when new and clean would place her in a certain category of person, but the clothes are fouled with dirt, badly fouled, even torn in the left knee area, as if she had kicked her way through a snarl of barbed wire.

Her arms bear scratches, not fresh new ones, but jaggy small cuts acquired perhaps a day or two ago, cuts that have stopped bleeding and been cursorily washed.

She carries nothing in her hands. Her eyes are certain and her hair, the color of a gently overcast sky, sweeps tightly upward from her temples.

The Korean hesitates impassively.

She draws a fifty-dollar bill from her front pocket and lays it on the plexi commerce wheel. The store is tiny and smells of beer and herbs and there is only one other person, a very old man sitting on a box in a corner peeling garlic cloves into a bucket.

The storekeeper reaches out and rubs the commerce wheel with his middle finger and the money revolves to him. His fingernails are clean. He picks up the bill, strokes it with the special pen storekeepers use, holds it up to the light, pockets it, and picks up a cell phone.

He looks at Elnice. "Right now?" The plexi barrier muffles his voice but she can hear him.

"Yes."

"You are not a policeman."

"I am not a policeman."

"What kind of gun?"

"A large-caliber handgun. I'd prefer a revolver."

"Three-fifty-seven magnum?"

"That would be fine."

He turns back to the phone. Elnice chomps her lower lip to confirm herself.

2: First Impressions Count

Six months earlier

Elnice pretends she's merely straightening but in fact she's sneaking in a little cleaning too. She rubs at a coffee ring on the kitchen countertop with a damp towel, moving her hand deliberately carelessly as if she could give a damn, really, whether the ring came up. She hadn't even moistened the towel for the purpose of cleaning the stain; it got damp because she'd dried her hands on it, so using it to rub the coffee stain doesn't carry the same weight as it would otherwise.

"You're cleaning." Arthur's voice cuts at her from his recliner across the family area. His emphysema's getting worse by the month, yet that voice still slashes through the household's ambient sounds—refrigerator compressor, ESPN on low—like a little hatchet.

"Why're you cleaning now? Ten minutes before she comes?" He's not just irked once again at Elnice's pathological concern over what other people think, he's furious about his breathing, which trumps everything. The doctor always asked him how he felt on a scale of one to ten, one being death and ten being Clark Gable, and Arthur would be forced to tell him to shove it. The breathing was going shitty-four today, but he hadn't said anything.

Between men and women there is a chasm, Elnice thinks, as with guilty quickness she snatches the towel away from the coffee smear and turns to hang it on the oven door. A rift of geologic, no, Biblical proportions, and on one side of it stand those who get it, who had learned Fels-Naphtha and lemon oil and borax and elbow grease at mother's knee, and on the other stand those who have never been expected to clean a toilet in their lives.

"If you don't pick up *first*," she rhetorically asks the stove loudly enough for Arthur to hear, "how's the cleaner supposed to *clean?* She's not supposed to pick up the whole house."

First impressions count. She simply had not wanted that damn coffee ring on the countertop. It was sticky to boot, from Arthur's coffee-with-honey-and-cream. Some people, she had heard, stopped doing the dishes days before the cleaner came. Appalling.

Never in almost forty-six years of marriage had Elnice wanted help around the house; it isn't even her idea now. Her nervousness creeps around the edges of panic as she fixes her eyes on some fingermarks on a cabinet door.

"But you were wiping there, I saw it. Elnice."

Twenty years ago, maybe even ten, he would have stripped off his own skin to save hers. But since the onset of his lung troubles he's come to realize how unimportant Elnice is compared with his struggle to survive. It isn't that he's made a *decision* to stop loving her, and it isn't as if he doesn't care for her at all. This is not something he's engineered on purpose. The lungs are getting worse fast. Who planned on that? He and Elnice are only sixty-eight.

His sole responsibility now is to get ready to die.

After just a couple of years' worth of retirement in their old house in Reamus, Indiana, Arthur had inherited a split-level pad from his homosexual uncle in the Hollywood Hills. The uncle, who had done props for the movies, had crammed a toe-stubbing oddity of a house onto a steep slope way above Tinseltown. At least it was an oddity to

Arthur and Elnice, who soon discovered how normal such a house is in that neighborhood: only three bedrooms and bath-and-a-half, the same as their house on Cherry Street in Reamus, but the way the thing's put together! Given the essentially vertical lot, the rooms had to be stacked and bumped together up and down half-steps, whole steps, little sets of three steps. Lots of windows and lemon-limey sunshine colors everywhere. The kitchen features a brittle tile floor that runs right out beneath a set of French doors to a patio, which morphs into a curved teakwood deck that hangs out over the canyon like a snared UFO.

Before they moved in, the house smelled powerfully of bleach and Windex, but these, it turned out, were merely topnotes over cat piss and an old queen's Chanel No. 5. Now it is beginning to smell more of Arthur and Elnice: their coffee, their bodies, his aftershave (Mennen Skin Bracer), her cologne (Norell), and well to be frank their little dog Fresco, whose scent is at least lower-pitched than the cat who'd lived and, they'd gotten the feeling, died here.

Anyone's house back in Reamus was accessible from anywhere in the world by a few precision ninety-degree turns from the nearby I-70 exit. But this place, you have to start from one of the hundreds of main-drag-looking streets in Los Angeles—throbbing veins of humanity—so you have to know which tiny little snaky street to take up from Cahuenga Avenue (which they at first pronounced in a sneezy fashion but soon learned "Cawenga"), and go up and up in low gear, watching for another tiny little street that creeps off at an angle, then another, hairpinning this way and that, narrower and narrower like the crudest of ranger trails. No sidewalks, no curbs. Lanceolate trees and bushes stabbing at your car. Up and up, this way and that, in low gear.

One thing, though: the Cokers are the kind of people for whom shifting into D-2 or D-1 is no sweat.

When they were younger they took initiative. They fondued. They recarpeted. They opened accounts. In middle age, Arthur mowed grass for widows, Elnice baked for charity, they attended luau-themed summer cookouts without complaint, they returned phone calls. It all got to be one big habit, and it was OK.

But something about the idea of owning a place in Hollywood made the Cokers frightened of Reamus's familiarity. Reamus, they suspected, was making them tired. The Hollywood house reminded them of the bigger world out there, which they decided it would be dangerous to forget just yet. The idea of a Hollywood house was invigorating.

And Arthur's condition required invigorating. He felt better just thinking about moving to California. He didn't like his Indiana doctor, and he knew if they didn't jump now they never would.

So they brought their stuff and little Fresco to Los Angeles in what they presumed was spring—center of April—just in time for the start of the smog season and wave after wave of heat. Now it's an August Wednesday and it happens to be bull-blood hot and here they are, still not feeling at home.

Not home, but not Outer Mongolia either.

"Fresco, do you need to go out before Solita comes? Because if you don't you'll get too excited and then you know." Elnice always explains more to Fresco, a blond toy poodle with glassy black eyes, than necessary.

The dog jumps down from Arthur's lap readily enough and scampers to the French doors. Elnice picks him up and carries him out. She stoops and attaches a red cable to his collar, the other end of which is anchored to the iron leg of a patio bench.

In the Hollywood Hills the whole canyon is your unfenced backyard. Given the chance, Fresco would surely bolt into the vegetation and be eaten by whatever wild animals were left unslaughtered by the first settlers, so the Cokers had devised the cable setup.

Arthur figures if you start at the French doors and keep going as the crow flies you'll end up in Paramount's back lot.

And that is magic.

They'd begun spotting movie stars at once. Elnice saw Link Meachum buying a cup of coffee at a bookstore in Westwood. Arthur observed Barbara Hatoro ignore a yield sign on a ramp up to the I-5.

On Fourth of July they'd decided to go down and take a dip in the ocean. What fools! Not a parking space to be found in the whole city of Santa Monica. As Arthur patiently inched the car homeward through the traffic jam each silently remembered the quiet beaches on the inland lakes they'd picnicked upon in the past.

Los Angeles. Why do people tear around as if they've got half an hour to live? Waitresses tap their pens anxiously, eyes darting. Customers in line at the dry cleaners swing their keys like aboriginal weapons. Maybe it's the atmosphere of opportunity in Los Angeles. Something advantageous might be waiting just around the corner. You miss it, the chance goes to someone else.

Elnice walks the deck and looks over the hills to the low parts of the city. It is clear that Arthur will die here. And it is growing clearer to her that out there, in the city, lay something for her. She is unexpectedly restless, moreso the sicker Arthur gets. He will go and she will stay, and meanwhile she must find a way to be alive. Sixty-eight is young for a woman now. Los Angeles is the differentest city she has ever seen. She is not repelled by the movie billboards; she likes the cheesy hustle of show business. Hope! Achievement! Expectancy! It is new to her and she likes it. *But how to get at it?* The Cokers have no attachments to the film industry. They cannot work their way into a fascinating circle by throwing money around; their means are ordinary.

But they had met the Hollywood guy next door, Ty Brandewine. Arthur judged Brandewine a put-on name until Ty mentioned how many Brandewines there were in the world. Ty had slouched over as soon as the movers had zipped up their truck and rumbled back down the canyon in reverse, there being no place to turn around even if they crawled all the way up to the headwaters of the street, another half mile. Ty Brandewine had pronounced their new home "darling", as if he'd never seen it before. "A darling farmhouse kitchen," he said. A lovely *divertissement*-room."

"A what?" Arthur had said.

Ty pointed to the family area.

"Oh."

Ty, they learned, had written the pilot for Choose Up Sides, then co-wrote and directed more than a hundred episodes of the sitcom, which became the hottest television show of the early 1970s. In case you were unborn in the early 1970s, "Choose Up Sides" was about a coeducational recreation center in an unnamed seedy part of L.A. where interesting young people congregated and fell into and out of love and trouble. They were disadvantaged but spunky kids who talked tough but had hearts of gold.

In addition, Ty had written ten movie screenplays, all of which had been optioned or bought outright by various studios, but none of which had ever actually been made into a film. This was typical, Ty told them.

Arthur figured out pretty quickly that Ty had been out of work for a while, but the Cokers assumed that Ty must have millions of dollars socked away somewhere in wise investments. His lifestyle is modest, his home smaller than theirs. He doesn't talk about flying around the world to sportfish or ski. He stays home and orders in from the one Chinese restaurant that still delivers all the way up the canyon as a special favor to him. He told them he spends most of his time lying in bed, smoking Chesterfields and thinking about the next project.

"Drinkin', too, no doubt." Arthur's morbid curiosity was aroused by Ty. "You suppose he's been married a few times? You suppose he knows a few secrets about—?" and he named a very big star who'd died under scandalous circumstances years after working on Choose Up Sides.

When Ty mentioned Solita, the woman who had begun cleaning his house after the last one got picked up by Immigration, Arthur jumped on it.

"We need a cleaning lady too," he'd said.

"No, we don't," Elnice countered.

Arthur made a hand motion to Elnice.

Ty parted his lips, his own morbid interest just as aroused by the Arthur-Elnice dynamic.

Arthur said, "I want someone to help Elnice around the house. Let her enjoy more of her own retirement."

Solita did a fine job of cleaning Ty's house, he told them, she was a nice kid.

"She's young, then?" Arthur asked.

When Arthur and Elnice were alone she asked him what was up with the cleaner deal.

"I don't know," he answered, then pretended to think

hard, pinching his lip. But the last thing he wanted to do was think about it.

"Aren't you afraid she'll steal your Anne Murray CDs?"

In a crevice deep in Arthur's mind lurked the awareness that before long Elnice would be helping him into and out of his clothes, on and off the toilet, squeezing his toothpaste and trimming his toenails, and the plain fact was he wanted to save her up. He'd rather pay a Mexican stranger to clean his house now than wipe his butt later. He would trust only Elnice to do that, he would insist that only she perform that task because they had that kind of intimacy. This concept was boarded up in a dank nook of his mind but he never acknowledged it, dear God no, never let it out to run free in the open. He had half expected Southern California itself to clear up his emphysema for good, but no way, really, he had to be realistic. For Arthur, Los Angeles is so feral that he can more readily disengage from it than from a tamer place.

She saw that there was an answer to her question and that she wasn't going to get it.

Fresco yaps and strains at his cable.

Elnice smoothes her slacks over her hips and goes to the front door. "Solita?"

For a millisecond she thinks a trick has been played on her. She stares at a life-sized statue of a startlingly pretty young woman. The statue is staked down by a shining tent of black hair. A plain blouse of vivid white, an unnoticeable woven skirt, run-down espadrilles that had once been bright pink, now faded to a watery salmon color. The face is the face of a postulant in a Sevillean cloister, smooth and full and young, so very young and pretty and unlined and solemn. The eyebrows would have looked ludicrously heavy on anyone else, especially for example Elnice, whose pale blue eyes roost under peaked brows almost transparent with age. But on this statue they are perfect brows, lush and minky, just right for the wide-set black eyes, no, not *black* black exactly, there is the hint of a color—violet? deep blue?, an iridescence that suggests a grackle's impossibly smooth, bright head.

The statue's hands rest palms down at its thighs. Its shoulders are poised, its posture balanced.

Then—boing! The statue parts its lips as if to speak but no speech comes; instead a smile, a bow of the head, a lift of the hands in acknowledgment of her name.

Yes. Merely Solita, is what she says without speaking. The whole of her presence suggests nearly perfect humility. Nearly.

Elnice has never experienced such a presence. She is used to Midwestern matter-of-factness, used to young people who look you in the eye and throw themselves into the world for better or worse. And she is becoming used to everybody in Los Angeles, quick of eye and toned of butt.

However, *merely Solita*. That is who stands before her.

3: The Ripping of Her Heart

"All right! Come in, Solita!" Elnice glances at the driveway, beyond it the brush-lined street. No automobile. She hadn't heard one approach or drive off. No bicycle. Would the girl have walked the two miles up here from the bus stop down on Franklin Avenue, beyond Cahuenga?

"Come in," Elnice repeats uneasily.

The young girl steps in; across the room, Arthur's eyes widen.

"Solita, this is my husband Arthur Coker, and I'm Elnice Coker." Solita nods and smiles. Wow, the teeth too—squarecut and clean. Healthy red gums. Solita's eyes flow over the kitchen and family area.

How old is she? Seventeen? Nineteen? Twenty-five? Her forearms and hands are plump but not soft-looking. Her throat shows no hint of a crease necklace.

Fresco clamors at the French doors. "Oh, and this is Fresco!" Elnice unsnaps the cable and lets him in.

Chuckling, the girl squats to meet the dog as it rockets to her. She speaks a few quick words and massages its creamy fur. Arthur stares jealously. Elnice recognizes Spanish from the general sound of it.

"Do you have a dog, Solita?"

At the sound of her name Solita looks up at Elnice. She scratches behind Fresco's ears, then straightens up. The dog yips and jumps for all he's worth, boy, does he want more attention from this one. In his almost nine years he's never met anybody with hands like that.

"Ty didn't tell us she couldn't speak English! Arthur, how am I going to tell her anything?"

"Just show her. She'll pick it up, eh? Cleaning's cleaning." He is doing a yeoman's job of ogling.

So she takes Solita from room to room, pantomiming and overexplaining everything as if to Fresco. She shows her the broom closet in the kitchen, the cleaning formulas and the rags and sponges, and she trundles out the vacuum cleaner from the foyer closet. Solita caresses the well-maintained Hoover.

"OK!" she says approvingly.

Elnice perceives a liveliness in her eyes, a special vitality. And this is gratifying because Elnice had made a living judging what was going on in people's eyes and acting accordingly.

People? The first-graders she'd taught back in Reamus for thirty-five years? Yes, people. Elnice had been an exceptional teacher, fiercely loved by her students and idolized by their parents, so admired that the city of Reamus declared the day of her retirement Elnice Coker Day.

Bone-deep, she understands that the child begets the adult. Know a child and you know everybody.

"All I do," she confided to Arthur after they'd been teaching a few years, "is give a damn. And I don't let them get away with anything. They have to adapt to a few simple rules in life, and then we can all relax and learn. That's it."

"That's plenty," Arthur had said. He taught high school gym; by the end of their first decade of teaching he could pick out the boys in his classes who'd had Elnice for first grade. "They understand how to get along with each other, and they respect school. The little bastards are just better."

He'd been a good runner in high school and college, briefly held a couple of state records, and track was his favorite sport to coach. "It's a purer sport than football or even baseball," he would muse. "It's you against the clock, you against gravity. You're not trying to hurt your opponents, except their egos. You want to make them bleed inside." And he'd give the kind of happy-dog smile that drove Elnice to ask him on their first date so long ago to the Sadie Hawkins dance.

Elnice looks into Solita's eyes and sees she's a smart person; warmhearted too. But there's an edge there in the tilt of her head, in the one upturned corner of her mouth. This is intriguing and appealing. Is it a frivolous edge? A don't-screw-with-me edge? How without language will she find out? Moreover, how without language will she explain critical things like the ratio of water to Spic-n-Span that works best on the kitchen floor, the temperament of the toilet in the powder room, the imperative of dusting *before* vacuuming? Arthur's lungs require maximum protection from particles. Dust falls to the floor while you dust, then you vacuum it up. She'd never held with "vacuuming raises dust."

She goes next door. Tousled Ty in khaki shorts hauls himself enthusiastically out of bed and pads over on bare feet to help. He listens to Elnice, then speaks rapid Spanish into Solita's seashell-curved ears. Isn't Spanish always spoken rapidly, Elnice thinks, isn't any foreign language spoken rapidly when you don't understand it?—and Solita nods quick nods, eyes lowered. She gets to work.

Elnice offers her neighbor a mug of coffee and homemade cookies, the chocolate drop kind she's proud of. He stands for a few minutes, rubbing one instep behind the other calf and sipping the hot beverage. A short man with a sparrow's chest, he is just a little younger than the Cokers. He's got that smooth-faced Hollywood look they've begun noticing at the Ralph's grocery at the foot of the hills. It's an odd look yet so consistent from person to person, those who have it. A smoothness of the skin, almost a glossiness, as if the flesh of the face had been burnished, somehow, and standardized.

Ty nibbles a cookie. "Jesus, these are good."

"Thank you." Elnice knows it.

"How come," he asks, "you didn't just sell this place and buy a nice condo down in Dana Point, or Del Mar, heck, Palm Springs?"

Elnice laughs wildly at Palm Springs. Arthur, sitting over in his recliner, would laugh hard too, if he could've; a shallow smile is the most he can do this day.

Brandewine is startled.

"*Palm Springs?*" Arthur and Elnice say in unison.

Their shared mental image of the town is one large ranch housing several hundred multi-millionaires who play golf by day and swap wives and shoot up heroin by night. Coyotes around the perimeter.

"Palm Springs *no thanks*," says Elnice. "*Golf*, my God. Tanning parlors."

"We just thought we'd try it here," Arthur adds lamely.

Neither tries to explain the mechanism of their decision to live in Hollywood: the opportunity befell them, they became frightened of everything familiar, they took it. Moreover, even though Ty appears open to unconventional ideas, they cannot admit that they had become tired of their friends and families. So much had been the same for so long.

"I don't think there are any tanning parlors in Palm Springs," Ty says.

"We like Los Angeles," says Elnice.

"Well, the air's pretty good up here in the hills, comparatively." It's true: the Cokers had learned what an inversion was, and they'd noticed that even when there was a terrible inversion, when the smog over the city looked like a pad of brown gauze, the air over the hills was fresh and clean if very warm.

"Call me any time you need help with Solita," offers Ty. "She's here from Mexico—not on the proper side of the immigration bureau, don'tcha know, none of them are. From some godforsaken village in the high desert. Incredibly barren country there, I used to scout locations for Warner's. Her husband's a manual laborer somewhere. She's a lamb! She'll do a good job." He's off, with an extra cookie.

Elnice goes to sit with Arthur. A handball competition is playing on the TV. He watches all sports, and his background as an athlete and his innate sense of body mechanics makes him an intelligent fan. "Wow! See how the short guy gets more speed on the ball by snapping his elbow like that? And keeping it close to his body? The other guy's using his shoulder more and a straighter arm, which's gonna cost him."

She perches on the arm of his recliner. He mutes the TV.

"You wanted multi culture, you'd go to Trevenno's for a pizza," she says, by way of commenting on Solita's foreignness.

"Or Lim's."

"Yes. Those egg rolls."

"You're cowering in here, Elnice, do you realize that?"

Plish-plosh, sounds of scrubbing and rinsing from the powder room.

Men have no idea how things get dirty. After Elnice's hysterectomy fifteen years ago she had been forced to rely on Arthur's housekeeping for hellish weeks on end. One day Arthur had been standing there talking to her then suddenly exclaimed, "There's dust on the TV!"

Elnice asks, "Is she sexy to you?"

He snorts.

Elnice waits.

"She's not my type."

"Good answer."

In fact Solita is for sure Arthur's type—a gorgeous young babe, for God's sake—but even if you stripped her naked and injected molten Viagra into his ass he would have a problem. He could ram it in but he wouldn't enjoy it. It's quite tragic, but his dick just doesn't give a damn anymore.

Elnice listens to Solita working. What is she thinking as she scours the sinks, brushes away the fudgy grime from around the faucets, and prepares to coax dust bunnies from beneath the upholstered furniture? Does she suppose Elnice considers herself above housework?

Elnice could claim to be unwell! She could have a bad back, she could be arthritic! She does suffer from a tiny bit of stiffness in her knees and hands, *but*. Her standards had always been high. She'd insisted on them, for herself and for her little students. "If *I* drop something, *I* pick it up! *I* hang up *my* coat nicely on a hook! Do we tell the truth in this classroom? Yes, we do! We tell the truth here, and we tell the truth on the playground, and we tell the truth at *home*." A lifetime of personal standards, suddenly cumbersome.

Solita is running the vacuum in the living room. Elnice realizes that had she and Solita a common language she

ELIZABETH SIMS

would have talked herself into a corner by now: "My husband's been insisting I get some help! It's all his fault! I'm perfectly capable of cleaning my own house!"

Her thoughts accelerate. Retirement is horrible! You have too much time to think. Regrets, all of them accumulated over a lifetime of mistake-making, plus brand-new ones all the time. Why didn't she keep Doris Saleski's secret? She had been Doris's best friend in college until she blabbed about her abortion to Patty Mellin of all people. Absolutely her worst error in judgment ever. Doris had to leave school after that. In those days that was how it was.

Why didn't she and Arthur ever adopt children?

How did she get so far away from the church?

Who really knows how to welcome old age and its treacherous bastard twins, memory and wisdom?

Solita moves into the family area with the vacuum, oblivious to Elnice's existential crisis.

"Here comes the vacu-saurus!" says Arthur.

It pumps toward them at the end of Solita's energetic arm.

Fresco has gotten so worked up over Solita that Elnice has to cable him up outside again.

It is time for Arthur to move to the armchair in the living room. He gathers himself, gazing at his feet in their jet-puffed athletic shoes, gazing. He takes as long a breath as he can and *ump!* scoots upward, with Elnice giving a shove to the recliner's footboard. If he used his oxygen he'd manage it better, they both know this.

Elnice wanders casually ahead to the living room.

A miler, Arthur was, all-State and slant-six sexy in his wispy singlet and baggy shorts, his spikes and his canine smile. Good sturdy legs, a Tarzan chest, all topped by a rusty-brown forelock you wanted to reach for and tug.

28

CRIMES IN A SECOND LANGUAGE

Elnice was a lucky girl back then.

Emphysema, the smoker's disease. But Arthur hadn't smoked. He'd taught his track and field men not to smoke; at least he demonstrated once a year why they shouldn't.

At the start of each season he'd bring a brand-new white T-shirt into the locker room, as well as a fresh pack of Kool cigarettes, the greasers' brand, and a book of matches. The boys would go quiet the instant they saw the pack of forbidden cigarettes in the coach's hand.

He'd open the package, let the cellophane flutter to the floor. He'd tap one out and light up, puff puff, then suck in a big lungful of smoke, forcing himself not to cough. He'd hold the T-shirt up tight to his lips and exhale through it.

"You think smoking doesn't fuck with you?" he'd say, holding up the crisp new T-shirt now with an asshole-like brown stain in the middle of the chest. In the silence, he'd drop the cigarette and grind it out contemptuously.

Could one deep drag per year for thirty-plus years have triggered this terrible illness? "Hell no," a doctor once told him as he percussed his chest with fat fingers. "It's just like getting hit by a drunk driver. We don't know why it gets low-risk people. Did you ever work with asbestos?"

The doctor had not thought Arthur was dying. With supplemental oxygen he had years to go.

"Indefinite, then," said Arthur. As far as he knew there had been no asbestos in the chemical plant where he'd worked summers in college. No asbestos, but plenty of other perilous inhalants. Who the hell knew? The plant had been shuttered for years.

"Indefinite," said the doctor. "Go have a milkshake."

Arthur takes his pills, does his nebulizer twice a day. The oxygen unit, an unwieldy but amazing machine that somehow boils down oxygen from ordinary air and blows it through a tube you stick up your nose, languishes in a corner of the bedroom. Not yet. Not just yet.

Solita advances into the family area with the vacuum, eyes down and just ahead of its efficient maw.

He hurries to get out of the way, suddenly anxious to get away from the noisy machine.

—and he makes it: he practically jogs a step to get through the living room arch. He flops into the armchair like a clubbed fish.

Elnice wonders whether the ripping of her heart is audible.

She stands quietly for a moment, then leaves the room.

4: A Bona Fide Writer

Rodney the engineer lifts his glasses and rubs the bridge of his nose. His glasses appear ordinary but have safety lenses capable of withstanding the impact of a pea-sized fragment of steel, bronze, or ceramic traveling at 102 miles per hour.

Another man politely watches and waits. His safety glasses are the dorky plastic kind that fit over regular glasses, for people who don't come to the factory floor often enough to justify the cost of prescription safety lenses.

Rodney has never bothered to learn the other man's name, even though it's right there on his security necklace: *Jason.* He has a last name too, there on the tag, but whatever.

The air is cool and somewhat antiseptic with the smell of highly refined machine oil. The men stand on a vast indoor concrete plain. Powerful light pours down on everything from close-packed pods of bulbs and tubes. The building is high and handsome and very clean and it's a factory that doesn't make stuff. It makes machines that will make stuff.

The men stand before a running machine, a ten-foot tower of steel and carbide and electrical circuits with a control console off to the side. The machine thrusts and whirs in a forceful rhythm like a pole dancer dreaming of a Broadway audition. It looks precise and sounds precise and smells precise.

To the machine, the men look like ants.

All around them, buffered by stretches of empty floor, other machines are running, attended by coveralled humans. *Chunka-bizz! Bunk-vunn, bunk-vunn!*

Rodney the engineer settles his glasses and says, "There's plenty of ways to do maintenance on a solenoid. Basically, it's a valve for electricity. You can check the connections, you can check for low voltage with a volt meter. You can inspect for shorts and opens. You want proper resistance."

Jason M says, "If a solenoid fails?"

"Well, they'll eventually fail, everything does. But we're talking the machine probably being obsolete before that happens."

"Oh."

"The key thing for maintenance is the slides." Rodney is a compact guy who goes in for timeless NASA styling: short-sleeved shirt and tie, Twist-O-Flex watchband. "And the bearings in the motor."

"Right." Jason M writes on an aluminum clipboard. This machine will bore holes in aluminum plates, its whirring spindle making the holes while festoons of aluminum curls fly out like party mix. The curls are called chips.

"You want to lubricate the slides once or twice a week under normal running conditions and you want to inspect the bearings about every—"

"Define normal running conditions." Jason M is taller than the engineer but gives it away by not attending to his posture.

"Well," says Rodney, "say two shifts a day, six days. And you've got to clean under the deck, vacuum out oil and chips at least once a month. The chip conveyor's going to carry away the bulk of the waste, you know."

"Right, I know."

"So it's just the strays that are going to get under there, you know, and that's really important, because those chips'll eventually tear up the carriage—"

"Yeah."

They talk some more, and Jason M makes notes. He asks, "How ready is this one?"

"It'll make chip next week if the hydraulics get straightened out."

"Cool. This is still the prototype, right?"

"Yeah, but we could be in production by November. This is what, September fifth? Yeah, we could be in production by November."

"Cool."

Rodney the engineer goes back to fiddling with the numerical controls.

Boonka boonka, says the machine.

Jason M walks three-eighths of a mile back to his cube. He gets his C drive going and types:

See Section P-06.77.m for lubricant specifications.

Lubricate N and P axis slides bi-monthly under full-time operating conditions.

Lubricate T axis slide quarterly under same conditions.

He pulls up another file and types:

Disassemble grinding deck (Section F-10.15.c-i) and clean subdeck biannually under full-time operating conditions.

He's got it down to a science. That's right, he's writing it wrong, writing it precisely wrong.

It's a simple matter of leveling the playing field, that's how Jason M thinks of it. Get that scoreboard evened up.

Good Christ, how else is he supposed to keep from hanging himself?

Jason M is not a computer guy, and he's not an engineer. He's a writer. *A writer, a bona fide writer.* And has the hands to prove it: the slightly bent first joint of the right middle finger, the knuckles generally curled, a byproduct of extended writing, typing, and the general tension of genius. He works in a cube. A small one. A cubette.

The cubette itself hunkers in a room almost as grand and fine as the machine floor, ballfield sized, in a building housing a highly respected corporation which occupies, including parking, some three hundred acres of alkali desert not far from Los Angeles, none too damn near it either. Machinery is produced here, extremely complicated machinery. And it is Jason M's job to write about that machinery.

Can a writer's desk give insight to the writer himself?

Sawdust has taken on new life in today's offices. From the forests of the north come logs—everybody in those northern forest towns says logging is over, yet still the trucks roar by, toting loads of renewable resource—why not admit it, why not celebrate it?—and the logs go to the mills and the best boards from the mills go to cabinetmakers who craft sturdy beautiful desks that get bought by people who give a damn about having a good-looking desk that feels real to the touch. And'll pay for it.

Back in the mills the sawdust is saved until enough accumulates to make a desk. The dust is mixed with a few larger chips for body and some glue, then strong machines press it into boards. These boards are super dense, but if left alone and made into desks, the writers would pick them apart with their nervous energy as parrots pick apart seed bells. So the boards are sheathed in excellent plastic, glued and accurately pressure-bonded. Because it's so easy to add a few drops of tint to that sheathing plastic, it is done, and desks featuring insets of lilac and soft teal find their way to offices across the continent.

Jason M's desk is stronger and heavier than one made of solid wood the same thickness. It is as strong and heavy as a burial vault and it makes him puke.

There is a pit, a forlorn bottomless yet curiously seductive abyss into which English major after English major peers, then plunges, in most cases never to be seen again. It is the Pit of Tech Writing.

Jason M remembers his youth. His favorite subject was English, he loved to read and was a good speller, so his halcyon days were fueled by dreams of being a writer. Poet. Novelist. *Belles lettrist.* Critic-at-large? He held his destiny in his very hands. He scribbled in notebooks, he fell in love with fountain pens, he shyly submitted his work to the school journal, he brashly sent it off to the *New Yorker.* He lived on Spaghetti-Os and M&M's. He applied for grants. The word "corporate" was the vilest of pejoratives.

That was the beginning. He was young.

There was a middle in there somewhere; he possesses a few shards. Standing at the stove affecting raffish noncha-lance as he placed the frozen pot pies on a cookie sheet and turned on the oven as his second-date paramour looked on in open disgust. Stealthily parking his car over a sewer grate in a park where he changed his oil and coolant, allowing the slimy waste to flow into the ecosystem be-cause he didn't own a basin big enough to catch them and *pitying* himself for this. Sweating out essays of abject supplication, trying for a knowing, wry tone of indifference. ("My aspirations might be deemed a bit *too* high. That may be the case. But if I thought less of my talent, I would assiduously be applying to various academies of nuclear physics, economics, and medicine.")

One grim day while waiting for his fortunes to change, he began answering ads on line. *TECHNICAL WRITER. Entry level. Good organizational, grammar skills required. Word, Excel. Must be able to multi-task. B.A. in English or Journalism preferred.*

It never says *competitive salary* or *opportunity for advancement*. There is no hierarchy of tech writers, no Vice President of the Tech Writing Department. All tech writers are peons. But it's better than nothing, and at least it's writing.

And that, regardless of how forcefully he promised himself that he'll Write At Night, he'll Write On Weekends, he'll live like a pauper and save up so as to one day Quit And Write, that was the end. Jason M understands everything. He knows it's not his fault. He understands, and he is moving past it.

Because quietly, quietly, he's found a way to make the work interesting.

On his computer screen he can call up fascinating diagrams of the machines, gigantic mechanisms that will soon create airplane parts from hunks of metal by boring amazing shapes in them. The machines—they are sculptors in the purest sense of the word, the Michelangelos of our time: take a twelve-pound bar of aluminum and cut away everything that isn't a section of fuselage rib.

And Jason M can call up every bit of information about them, all the specifications and tolerances and elevations and *everything, plus* he can swivel away from that teal-inlaid desk and don those attack-squadron goggles and take that three-eighths mile walk to the shop floor where the incredible machines sit in various stages of manufacture and he can talk to the men and women who build them and find out whether the end tanks should be drained every day or every year—which would be best?, most cost-effective?—and he can ask any engineer provocative theoretical questions like what's the worst-case scenario for one of these puppies? I mean, if one breaks down, which system would be the costliest to fix, in terms of expense and time consumption? The electrical?, the hydraulic?, the big moving parts? Like, what trouble will the end user most want to avoid?

The engineers have a pretty good idea of how paltry his paycheck is compared to theirs, which fosters comfortable condescension; he is a time-waster for them, but an earnest one. He's discovered that being a wuss can be an advantage.

Jason M needs to learn everything he can. The machines, these very ones, will be shipped to a factory being built right now in one of the picturesque mountain states, where they will manufacture commercial airliners. State of the art.

He is paid by his company to make sense of the machines, write digital books about them, whole volumes crammed with diagrams and tips and warnings, telling how to run and maintain them. Books way longer and denser than any book you'd ever want to read, picture the U.S. Tax Code, all loaded directly into the software of the machine itself.

But if the counterweight chains should be checked and greased weekly, he writes that they should get the old grease gun bimonthly. It's wrong, yes, but not bizarrely. Not enough to draw attention. (The prefix *bi-* is a favorite.

Bi-weekly, bi-monthly: opinions on shop floors always differ as to what it means: twice a week or once every two weeks? Most guys won't even ask. They'll wing it. Ever heard of a dictionary, morons?)

If the engineers concur that structural damage to the spindle drive screw represents the worst-case scenario, Jason M sits and thinks for days as to how routine operation and testing might be modified to produce, over time, a catastrophic failure. This beyond figuring out how the machines might be coerced into manufacturing slightly faulty parts from day one. He has picked up quite a smattering of engineering principles along the way.

This is the information he writes in his manuals: a little bit of good advice mixed with bad, all presented as sincerely perfectly good! Who's ever gonna figure it out? No one checks his work. His boss would have to follow Jason M around all day every day, hear what he hears, then watch every word he types. Everything gets loaded into the software by IT. Some maintenance directives are designed to pop up automatically.

Jason M opens a drawer where he keeps a stash of fresh data sticks and grabs one. He copies his most recent work onto it, along with as many plans for the machine itself as he's been able to snag over the past few weeks. He turns away from his monitor and reaches for his Mont Blanc and a slice of scratch paper. Carefully he prints, "LEAD BALLOON AVIATION. >20% FAILURE RATE GUARANTEED. DEPOSIT, PLEASE."

It's cute. With a smile he folds the slip and puts it in his pocket.

Mind you, the idea is *not* to make the finished planes fall out of the sky. Not at all. It's to make them so expensive to build, what with all the defective parts and delays from breakdowns—that the company'll falter, ideally go bankrupt, leaving a hideous yawning gap in the marketplace. A gap that might conveniently be breached by a competitor waiting—well, in the wings, one is practically forced to say, waiting in an almost phenomenally coincidental state of readiness.

Once in a while, though—say after a weekend in Las Vegas when Jason M comes home to his apartment hung over and broke—he settles down to sleep with a hot ingot of doubt burning in his chest: What if a defective part passes the last inspection and causes a real crash?

Shorn metal hurtling through the air, screams of the doomed piercing from the depths of the fireball, rows of body bags lined up on some rural football field. The pictures sweep through Jason M's mind, but thankfully only briefly, briefly. He is always able to smother such images, mumbling into the muddy darkness of his bedroom: Simple matter of evening up the score. Nobody hurt, nothing—nothing's gonna—unh. A lone wolf in his den. He swallows and flips the pillow to the cool side.

Thank God for the challenge. For the variety. For the money. The money. The money. Which no one fucking deserves more than he does.

Given his exact specialty, his total income is far higher than any of the engineers'. He might blow it in Vegas on hookers and craps while they comparison shop propane grills and pay the orthodontist and put up Christmas lights, but if they only knew.

5: A Fascinating and Impenetrable Person

Solita comes every Wednesday.

She is just like Los Angeles: fascinating and impenetrable.

It wouldn't be appropriate for Elnice to try to become friends with Solita. She only wants to know more about her, wishes for girl talk if only for a few minutes after Solita's work is finished. She always offers Solita a cold Pepsi or glass of iced tea. Sometimes the girl accepts, and they sit together at the kitchen table. Elnice watches her tip her head back and swallow, the smooth throat moving perfectly, the lips curving in satisfaction.

They smile in womanly solidarity.

Why is California so strange and good?

Elnice loves the warm California sun on her back as she putters on the patio. But does she *deserve* so much warm sun? Does anybody? When she was growing up her family lacked luxuries, but once in a while there would be orange juice at breakfast, one tiny glass apiece. The taste itself was an antidote to the dismal Indiana winters. A few ounces was the standard dose: drinking more would be unhealthful.

Then one morning when they were just married, Arthur opened the refrigerator and poured himself a tumbler full of orange juice and drank it off standing up. She gasped, and he said, "What?"

"You're not supposed to have that much!" They were

both working, though, and could afford all the orange juice they wanted.

It is the same with the California sunshine, except that it just keeps being there whether you feel you ought to have it or not. Nothing you can do about it.

Certain things in California resemble certain things in Indiana but on closer inspection aren't those things. Here Elnice would be driving down the canyon to do errands and spot a bush with yellow starry flowers that at first looked like forsythia but on second look wasn't forsythia. A tall bush with broad leaves and purple flowers that resembled lilac but wasn't lilac; a reddish hedge that appeared to be barberry but wasn't barberry. The conifers look and smell familiar because they are conifers but not totally. They smell somewhat sweeter than the conifers of Indiana. Who would plant bamboo in a pot? And where are the cardinals? Where are the damn cardinals? Why is there so much fury directed toward hesitant drivers?

At times Elnice is a hesitant driver.

Solita. So young and solemn. Why is she cleaning houses? Saving money for school? She attacks her work with such grace and vigor. Serious good worker. She could be running her own business. Perhaps she intends to build a cleaning business; there's nothing wrong with cleaning houses. But not speaking English is a handicap. Elnice's own Finnish ancestors, she'd been told, learned to speak English a week after they got to America.

Elnice has learned that in the Latino neighborhoods of Los Angeles you can live a lifetime interacting only with people who speak Spanish. Storekeepers, the beauty shop, undertakers, TV and radio.

Maybe Solita is happy with her life. Maybe she has hobbies. Children? She's young but old enough, God

knows. Old enough to have goals. Cleaning can be gratifying work, but how many years before she'll want
something more? What's her husband like? Ty said he's a
laborer. Where? Why?

There is so much in Solita. She laughs to herself sometimes as she works, she wrestles with Fresco just hard
enough to show her strength to him. She's got a sense of
humor, a sense of fun in the way she does little dance steps
with the vacuum. If she and Elnice were friends, they could
go shopping together. Elnice could help Solita with her
college applications.

Arthur watches the ESPNs, he stares out the back windows at the canyon, he strokes Elnice's breasts dreamily at
naptime. He is waiting. Drifting toward it.

Once in a while Elnice catches herself humming the old
Peggy Lee hit "Is That All There Is?" As soon as she does,
she stops. What a cliché.

She tries.

She buys bird books and plant books and invests hours
studying the wildlife around their new home. It is troublesome to remember the names of things because she always
gets stuck on "pussy willow" or "spirea" or "yew". She gets
some graph paper and starts working out a new patio
garden.

She invites Ty Brandewine over for dinner. "Bring a
friend!" she urges, but he always comes alone and rarely
speaks of other people, except for a few studio executives
he hates and mimics. Not knowing the executives the
Cokers cannot appreciate the vicious subtleties of the
portrayals. They learn that Ty has two daughters who live
with their mother in Miami, a costly setup, evidently.
There is another ex-wife in New York. In this season of his
life Ty is a loner.

Elnice likes to talk movies with Ty. She likes it that Ty can discuss fine points of movies she loves such as "The African Queen" and "The Misfits" and "King Solomon's Mines." For instance she knew that "The Misfits" was Marilyn Monroe's last movie, but she hadn't known until Ty mentioned it that Gable had done all his own dangerous horsebreaking stunts in it. "I think all that exertion brought on his fatal heart attack,' Ty mused, as if he'd been to the funeral.

Elnice makes overtures to other neighbors, but they are all younger people and very busy, with jobs in the entertainment business, food and beverage, computers, the importation of various goods. Nice people, but busy.

The Cokers observe few small children in the neighborhood. None ever plays in the streets; occasionally Elnice sees children peeking from the back seats of Range Rovers and Hummers, strapped in like quadriplegics. Their well-nourished faces view the world from identically rugged cocoons of safety.

"Listen," Ty says one night at dinner, "you know what kind of lessons kids around here get? Bodywork. They get massages and aromatherapy and rectal cleansings. Kids in normal places take trumpet lessons and ballet. They ride their bikes in the street. I'm glad my kids *didn't* grow up in L.A. Don't get me started."

Elnice wonders why he doesn't see his kids, now teenagers, more often. She is sure trumpet and ballet are offered in L.A., but she is also sure Ty is right about the aromatherapy.

Arthur and Elnice had tried and tried to have children. Their friends griped about birth control, but *their* lovemaking was totally free from worry: passionate, well, frankly frenzied at times. They made love early and often.

But no pregnancies. They accepted this. In those days there were no extraordinary measures of conception, at least none for the likes of them; they never even consulted a doctor, thus they never knew whether the biological fault lay with him or her. It was immaterial. They considered adoption at milestones in their ages: thirty, thirty-five, forty, even forty-five. But Elnice felt that perhaps fate intended for them to pour their energy into teaching.

Arthur made fewer bones. "What if we get a kid we don't take to?"

He had something there, as well as the fact that kids change. All those cute children she taught turned into adolescents, with adolescents' problems and blemishes and crises. She would see them around town, hulking ghost versions of their little selves. It was strange to see Jeremy Denman, for instance, surlily parking cars at the steakhouse and to remember how he cried so bitterly when the class hamster died. Bizarre to note Suzanne Stanko's tattooed neck in light of her early passion for pink tights and Mary Janes. She could still see their faces as they were, upturned to her as she explained the primary colors and the best way to make an 8, all of them miniature and beautiful and losing innocence day by day.

In lieu of children the Cokers had serial dogs, all toy French poodles. This was fine as far as it went. They never overgroomed them or taught them ridiculous tricks.

It's late summer now. Elnice joins a Lutheran church in Los Angeles. This is a solo venture, as Arthur had sworn off being preached to decades ago, after enduring a sequence of imbecilic ministers. "Time for a new set of Theses," he'd muttered one Sunday by way of final argument. The minister at Elnice's new church is lackluster. She prays more regularly but asks around for new church recommendations. Maybe she should change denominations, or do away with denominations altogether and build a little chapel in their backyard piece of canyon.

Arthur's personality is changing.

"Gimme. The mail." He wants to sort it.

She sets the stack of bills and junk in his lap but he says in an annoyed voice, "No. There," pointing to the side table. He says a word Elnice can't catch.

She hears his tone, though, and doesn't like it.

"What, honey?"

Looking at him she is caught by her reflection in the glass over the Emmet Kelly print behind him. There she is: a peachy-faced fireplug with thinning hair, the lines of her skull ever more evident, arms shapely still in her Joel Hannaberry sleeveless knit. She'd never developed the dreaded bat-wing upper arms, but she fears that her neat cheeks frame a mouth that is growing smaller and more worried. At this moment she feels the tension in her face and deliberately relaxes it, letting her brows fall into their natural crescents over her small bright eyes, letting her cheeks go to meet her jawline.

But she cannot help her mouth; it is worried and sad.

"Nothing," says Arthur, but he has already hurt her. He tries to cover up by ignoring himself. "You got a thank-you," he says, sorting through the letters, "from Audubon."

"The membership for Coral?" His niece.

"How would I know?" Annoyed again.

Patiently she holds out her hand. "Let me see."

He extends the envelope, then drops it. "Shit."

"It's all right." She bends to get it.

He says the inaudible word again.

"What did you say, Arthur?"

Both their faces are red.

Solita keeps coming every Wednesday and does a good job of it, but Elnice must always run to get Ty to translate.

"Please tell her I did the kitchen floor already because Fresco knocked a whole jar of jelly out of my hand, so there's that, OK. And the grout in the main bathroom really needs some straight bleach, beyond Tilex. Tell her I'll be in the laundry room, ironing."

Autumn has enfolded Los Angeles, and although the television weather-people keep talking about "fall temperatures" and "good sleeping weather" she can't feel it. The Hollywood hills are a little less hot and a little more brown than in July, all right. Is that it?

As she sprays and presses, smelling the hot comfort smell ironing always creates, thinks of Reamus and how very nearly pretty it looked in the fall. Trees! Big tall deciduous trees are the stuff of beauty in the Midwest, she realizes. Green and full and majestic in the summer, fiery and poignant in the fall, no matter what ugly shedlike house or gas station they might happen to tower over.

The door to the laundry room crashes open and Solita, pop-eyed, is yelling, grabbing Elnice's hand.

Crisis time. Rigid on the edge of his recliner, chest out, Arthur gasps and heaves like a donkey; he must have overtaxed himself trying to get up and away from the vacuum, which lies on its side still roaring where Solita dropped it. A blue circle is forming around his mouth.

"The oxygen!" cries Elnice, veering into the bedroom.

The machine, squat and heavy on tiny casters, came with a special long hose that Arthur could pull behind him everywhere in the house, without having to move the machine. Where is that tube? Only the short original one is looped over the machine. Elnice snatches the plug from the wall and drags the whole thing into the family room, Solita boosting along from behind.

Arthur claps the cannula to his nose and begins sucking at it desperately.

"Wait, it's not on yet!"

How the hell does the thing work, exactly? Solita plugs it in and Elnice presses the switch. One time, just once, the installation man showed Arthur and Elnice how to work it, how to thread the couplings over the tube ends, how to turn the motor on and make the proper amount of oxygen flow from the tube. That was months ago; the man had done it so quickly and easily. Be calm, be calm, what's this little lever supposed to do? She waves her hand over the nozzle but feels no breeze pouring from it. Broken?

She rips the instruction booklet off its plastic tab and now she is panicking, she feels herself losing it, the diagrams and words run together in a red and black blur and Arthur is thrashing at her with his hands.

She realizes the instructions are also printed in Spanish. "Solita! Help me!"

She holds up the instructions before Solita's huge liquid eyes. The girl does not move.

"Help me!" Elnice screams into her face as she thrusts the booklet at her.

Humbly Solita hands the booklet back to Elnice, saying something softly in Spanish. Tears spill down her unlined, healthy cheeks.

She can't read, she can't even read her own language, Elnice thinks as she rushes to the telephone.

"A boring ending, but you guys don't object to that, I suspect," Ty says the next day. Arthur's attack passed as soon as the paramedics got some real oxygen into his system and gave him a shot. They took him in anyway but he was home the next day. After that, week after week, Elnice yearns for Wednesdays with a gut-ache that baffles her. Solita is so bright and eager to please.

One day, however, as Elnice turns from serving Arthur his lunchtime sandwich and Fritos, she catches Solita looking at her with a look she can only interpret as pitying, as if Solita were watching Blanche DuBois put on lipstick.

She thinks about that look the whole rest of the day and into the following week.

Well, it's a good thing growing old happens gradually. If it happened all at once you'd take poison. Elnice and Arthur share equally in the wrinkles, the brown spots, the general skin-flaccidity, and they split up the other stuff: yellowed toenails, hemorrhoids, patchy rashes, dry eyes, eroding fillings.

The next time Solita comes she appears shaken. Her complexion is pale and hard, as if she'd been washed in ice. When Ty finishes translating today's instructions Elnice says, "Ask her what was the matter when she came in."

He engages in a conversation of quite a few minutes with Solita, who snaps her head violently, flies her fists around, and slaps her heart at the end.

"She says she was almost killed this morning. Sometimes she catches rides up here with two other housekeepers. Today they stopped to buy a bottle of Tequila before work—*she* doesn't drink, mind you!—never reeked of it, has she?—and got sideswiped as they pulled away from the liquor store. The driver was drunk already, she says. Aiee! There must be an easier way to make a living!"

Elnice will have to digest that story, but she settles her

waistband around her belly and says, "Ask her if she'd like to learn to read and write."

6: And They Know You

Jason M isn't the only one. He does not know but accurately suspects he's one of several cogs working at the same company at carefully separated levels, working to bring it down so that another may rise.

There are yet others, doing entirely different things in entirely unrelated fields.

Tina G is executive secretary to a powerful man. Such a powerful man that United States presidents stop and listen when he talks, and they positively genuflect when he opens his checkbook. Small children know his name. We all might envy his fame and power as we trudge through the innocent muck of our lives. Is he the head of a mighty banking conglomerate? The holder of multibillion-dollar patents involving junk-food processing and toy manufacture? A movie big shot? Does it matter?

What matters is how hard Tina G, his humble and loyal assistant, works. Man, does she work! While most of her peers are lying in bed slamming that snooze button, *resentfully* slamming the son of a bitch, steeling themselves for the legswing to the cold floor after which they'll let the dog out, match up the kids' clothes for once so they don't look like bums on school picture day, mix up that power shake with 8 or 36 key nutrients, Tina G is already standing pressed and pert at the copy machine in her office. *She's* got an office. An antechamber to where the Great One dwells, admittedly, but four solid privacy-providing walls nonetheless.

Tina G's desk is all premium metal alloy—sleek and functional, a smaller and simpler version of the boss's desk, matched to his in an understated display of design bravura. If you tapped a tuning fork and touched it to his desk then to hers, the desks would vibrate to the exact same amplitude, albeit an octave apart.

That octave yawns wide in an ordinary boss-secretary setup, but Tina G is glad as hell of her lowliness.

She's driven down from her apartment in verdant Pasadena, looking fresh in one of the pastel-hued frocks she favors and she's just copying away. She's copying her *ass* off, she's copying like a bat out of hell. Always the first one in. The security guard glides past her cordially open door in the pre-dawn gloom—handsome devil—they exchange glances—but lacking the nerve to strike up a conversation with such an unattainable creature he coasts off again, marveling at Tina G's plump tits and her commitment to her job.

What's she copying? Pretty much any boss-level document she can lay her manicured little fingers on: memos, financial statements, forecasts, competitor analyses, bound reports that show what an ass-kicking organization this is, always was, and always will be.

The boss's subordinates take the info-tech guys seriously and submit their toppest secret reports in print on special paper that reveals any photocopy of it to be stolen. This does not concern Tina G; she *is* stealing the shit and the people she turns it over to know it's stolen, that's the whole point. They wouldn't want it if they could pick it up on the sidewalk.

She goes for electronic files too, of which there are millions. She keeps a stash of fresh data sticks and packs them with the stuff she copies from the boss's hard drive: emails, attachments, his personal files. He travels a lot, which leaves her time to log onto his computer as him and browse. On any given day she knows what he is excited about or worried about; she knows his thoughts as they develop from someone's suggestion in an email to the final draft of his speech at the annual meeting.

The boss plays everything skin-tight to the belly, especially with the Board of Directors. But is he shrewd enough to suspect trickery from his own secretary? She is so sweet! She knows his log-on and his password, which contrary to the stern advice of the info-tech guys he hasn't bothered to change in fifteen-plus months. His password? studguy. She used to chuckle when she typed it in. Then she got bored and almost felt like changing it *for* him, to something like babyfood or pindick.

She keeps her paper copies and data sticks in a cardboard tray beneath her desk, then transfers them to a wide pocket sewn into the back lining of her lightweight raincoat, between the shoulderblades. This is ludicrously low tech, but digital trails have become more dangerous than analogue. At day's end she either wears the coat or carries it out over her arm.

There is Keith B. He himself is practically a king: senior vice president in the kind of established, happenin' company where the title carries weight. Keith came to the company with outstanding credentials, having been let go from exactly the right prior two companies. The kind of pedigree companies kill for.

Not only that, he's good-looking and affable: broad shoulders, narrow waist, large hands, deep gentle voice. He's no kid, which is good too—his seamed face and silver hair make his lack of belly fat that much more enviable.

Right now he's in conference with the inner circle: the president and all Keith's peers—the other department heads. The subject at hand is the redesign and relaunch of the website, which concerns everyone.

This company is a retail titan with a network of stores, big network. Big stores. You've shopped them. They plunged into Internet commerce back in '99 and got their face ripped off. Debt exploded as they chased market share at any cost, and boy could they spend money. They thought it took talent to spend money, and they thought the more they spent, the more talented they were. When the end came they divested themselves of their own Web business at a near-catastrophic loss—accountants and lawyers slithering from the air vents, a hideous, hideous scene. Name plates ripped off of walls, buckets of blood under desks. The website's been dead in the water for almost a year. Insane.

The organization survived. True, the president, CEO, and roughly half of the top officers had to be sacrificed: fed one by one into the iron-toothed monster that bit off the keys to their leased Ferraris, their country club member-ships, and spit them out naked. Eventually, though, they wriggled their way—every last one—into the washing machine of the career-rebirthing god. They bumbled about quietly in the wet dark, then popped out into the ranks of helluva good executives, spankingly laundered by a bit of absence, a bit of private public relations, a bit of forgetful-ness, and a bit of wishful thinking on the part of other companies casting around for ideas.

Keith B, himself career-rehabbed, knows. Anyone who's gone through the monster is respected as now wise. Wiser even than those who've been wise enough to avoid the monster all along! Such is the level of respect for failure and pain these days. We don't have to worry about those fellows anymore.

It's time for a new president to take the donkey by the dick and get the Internet business back and get it back right now.

The president is a Twinkie-shaped man secretly terrified of the whole prospect of bossing anything in cyberspace but who talked such a good game to the Board that he got the job and the jet. Not that he's a stupe or a coward: He might not have the bravery that ruthless self-examination requires, but he's got the intelligence and guts for bold action. He knows you can't just throw a switch and print money off the Internet.

"So Keith," he says. "Website timeline."

Earnestly, Keith leans forward. "We're gonna need at least four more months to replace Brenner—little traitor bastard—and pick up the pieces. Besides that, we're still ramming down that brick wall—the goddamned data entry software, you know about it. I've got everybody on it, trying to get it to do what we need it to. Not to drop a turd-burger here, but I can't see a relaunch this year. But we'll get the job done."

Other vice presidents, in sotto-voce sequence: "Uff! Unh! Whoa. Pwoo. Shit me?" The president is a man who does not get fake with his language, so neither do the vices, male and female.

The president tosses his blunt head in protest. He is desperately in lust with the idea of plucking billions more retail dollars out of thin air but is scared shitless of making variations of the same mistakes his predecessor made. "That's not good enough, Keith! The Blowback company's *proved* it can be done and they're expanding past any estimate we've ever come up with—they're *doing* it, they're doing it right now, it's there in their stock price." (Blowback isn't the real name of their chief competitor, it just sounds like that when they say it.) "Wall Street's French-kissing money down their throats. We're leaving four and a half million dollars on the table every month! At least! It's the middle of October and you're saying we're gonna miss the holidays with this? What the fuck's the problem?"

Keith (patiently, earnestly, almost tenderly): "I've explained it. It's all in your packets."

(Everyone brushes a thumb against their copies of Keith B's incomprehensible, jargon-laden report.)

Keith turns to face the president squarely; he has learned what works with him. "Would you like to come down this afternoon and talk with my people? We can show you exactly what we're up against, exactly what we're doing. The personality quirks of the mainframe, that's a compelling issue in and of itself."

"Do we really need a mainframe?" breaks in one of the department heads. "I mean, with the cloud and everything—"

Keith ignores him. "All respect, sir, but we're making strides. I don't know what kind of horseshit Blowback thinks its shareholders'll spoon up and swallow—" (runs hand through salt-and-pepper thatch—none of the other male company officers have hair that thick, that healthy) "—I really don't. Man, I *hate* those guys at Blowback!"

President (panicked at the thought of trundling his ignorance of computer technology downstairs): "No, no, I don't have time to come down today." (Bangs fist.) "Maybe we *should* just throw something out there, *anything* to grab some market share, I mean—"

Keith (suddenly slack-jawed): "You mean—not do it

right? (Goes pensively silent.) (Then with a sorrowful smile): "Put a shitty site out there. I guess we could do it if that's what everybody wants. Sure we could! If we're not afraid of taking it in the butt from hackers." (Looks around the table, makes eye contact with each individual.) "Is that what everybody wants? All respect, but are we in favor of taking it in the butt from hackers? I just want to be sure, because—"

President: "Screw it! Just keep working. Let Roberta know what you need budget-wise."

At an upscale sports academy in the San Fernando Valley, two people are getting to know each other. "Spare me the grimy details," says Chantelle W, "and just show me how to hit the ball."

The pro smiles. *With pleasure, baby.*

Chantelle W has to deal with too many details, grimy *and* clean, at her job in the human resources department of an insurance company, one of those mega-ones. She works hard and she pays herself back by playing hard.

Tennis is her game, she played varsity in high school and college; in fact she was a nationally ranked junior player but lacked the tensile ligament coefficient that separated the ones with Wimbledon dishes on their mantels from the rest. But she does love the game. Knows all the angles, she's quick on her feet and strong enough still to blast an occasional ace past the young she-devils at her racquet club. The only downside to being such a good young player was her coach trying to score on her. Until the day she broke him across the nose with her graphite racquet. She was one of the little black girls who didn't know how much power they had until they stopped needing to be liked.

Her detailed series of financial goals includes lifelong passes to the major tennis tournaments around the world, a home in Malibu with a private court, and unlimited time to play. Friendship bracelets from the stars.

But today it's not a tennis racquet she's holding so lithely, it's a golf club. She's standing there in all her athletic cuteness beneath the breezy gull wing that shades the teaching tee, wearing her Club Izod windshirt, her Foot-Joys, and she's getting the feel of that new seven-iron in her hands.

It's been pouring; the cantilevered weather shield groans in the wind but fends off the worst of the rain. The narrow practice strip is sown with real grass. Stray pellets of rain bounce into it, creating a bit of casual water underfoot. The air smells wet-green good.

She needs to learn this game, at least some little bit about it. Enough to get around eighteen holes without throwing her back out, so as to acquire those front-box tickets, that spread in Malibu.

Chantelle W presides over a vermiform array of cubes in the bowels of her company where she figures out things like how much it would cost to add a smoking-cessation program to employee benefits, and how many labor hours the company loses per fiscal in complying with the Family Medical Leave Act. It's a new position for her, with no glamour to it, none. So her strategy for acquiring the high life as she defines it centers on doing a bit of lucrative extra-curricular activity. It might take a while, but she's a determined cog in the system of American commerce.

Insurance companies are rich, everybody knows that. But it's not easy to get hold of that money. Not as if you can sashay in and crack the safe.

Chantelle W, thanks to her prize position as queen of

employee records and buck-stopper on background checks, will be expected to make it possible for *certain* individuals to get jobs there who might not have the best interests of the company at heart. Chantelle W knows why their backgrounds don't qualify them for honest work, but she doesn't know exactly what intramural activities they'll elect once they're on the payroll.

All she knows is, she'll be doing her damnedest to make them look like sterling candidates for sensitive jobs—she'll create documentation, fabricate convincing references and give them an enthusiastic thumbs-up with a big smile to their prospective bosses. She knows how. She's done it before. The bosses, they'll go for it. She'll make their lives so easy. Then she'll sit back and collect generous thank-you packages from a semi-anonymous benefactor. She deserves that much. More, actually. God, life has not been fair. Her parents actually tried to push her toward that drooling coach. They wanted the best for her.

How can a benefactor be semi-anonymous? She's kept from direct contact, but because she's learned quite a bit about the business already, she has a fair idea. No one's going to tell her. But her instincts have always been pretty good. In her spare time she ghosts around the claims department picking up pointers from the inspectors. She is planning a bit of private arson which, if properly done, would help her goals along nicely.

"Ever play before?" asks the pro, unconsciously straddling his driver like a hobbyhorse and rocking back and forth in his coaching shoes. She's a doll, no ring—he managed to check before she slipped her glove on—and he's in the midst of an unprecedented girlfriend drought.

"No. But I was thinking—" her eyes are that luscious melted chocolate color, and she's evaluating him with them, but he doesn't see it, he's looking directly into her eyes but he doesn't see it— "I was thinking I'll be able to pick it up without too much trouble." She hitches her shoulders in a gesture he finds incredibly sexy. "See, I'm already halfway decent at hitting a ball with a stick— tennis—and I figure it all amounts to body rotation through the point of impact, you know—"

"Why are you interested in learning," he interrupts, isometrically flexing his biceps against the shaft of the driver he's about to use to impress the hell out of her by launching one of his fence-busting rockets, "if you don't mind my asking?"

Chantelle W smiles faintly, long-distance. "I think I might be doing some business on the course."

This golf lesson is very important. Her boss—her real boss—has recently made another change in the way she must do business with him. It's interesting and cute really.

The pro bursts out laughing. What a world! It's Christmas Day! Nine times out of ten when he asks that question the lady says, "Because my husband plays and I want to be with him more on weekends." She never says "my boyfriend" because no woman would put herself through the aggravation of learning golf for a mere boy-friend. He hasn't met one yet, anyway. To please a husband who makes good money, yes. Oh, the pert married women he's tutored. They're all fucking pert married women. And they're all white, boringly white like him. He's managed scattered affairs—short ones, women can't sustain the duplicity like men can—then the loneliness again.

But wait! She misunderstands! Her brow is dropping! That beautiful doll brow is descending into little wavelets! She looks disgusted! Wait, see, the laugh was reflexive, a laugh of joy at the possibility that this agile little foxette—

just *look* at that sweet little tush!—might be unattached. But he can't explain himself that way. This golf pro possesses a lifelong jock's solid build and a face that looks as if hewn from a chunk of granite, but he knows he lacks the charm to pull off a literal moment of truth.

"I—I was just laughing at—at"—the flash of an idea!— "see, if you're going to do business on the golf course, you'll have to learn to smoke cigars!" He waits, panting, hopeful smile.

This strikes her just right. She smiles too, squirts out a giggle. She looks up at him.

"Oh, gawd, will I really?"

At times like this, life is nothing but fun.

When reading news of horrible criminals—slasher rapists, acid-throwing maniacs, hostage-taking sprayers of bullets—have you ever wondered whether you've met up with one of them without knowing it? The scraggly man filling his tank at the next pump. The quiet neighbor who likes to build balsa wood gliders. The knee-socked PTA mom. You have. Every American over the age of nineteen has shaken hands at least once with a psychotic criminal. That's a fact: look it up for yourself on the Web.

And if *that's* a fact, then each and every one of us has *also* known humans like Jason M, Tina G, Keith B, and Chantelle W.

At work tomorrow, while you're immersed in peaceful toil, surrounded by your co-workers, your bosses, and perhaps a few strays from the outside world—you can call them externals—just take a moment to look to your right. Now look to your left. You know those people. And they know you.

7: Get Your Hands on Some Words

It is not to Elnice's credit that she has no interest in the Spanish language. She knows *ole* and *ola* and *si* and *gracias* and *macho* and perhaps ten more words that everybody knows. So many California words are Spanish words: Los Angeles, Los Feliz, all the other Los-es and Las-es and Sans and Santas and Els. Those indomitable missionaries and their zest for naming places.

English is what she can teach.

She clears off the kitchen table, fetches a tablet and two ballpoint pens, and starts in on the alphabet. Right away, she works on getting Solita to say the letters in American.

"*I* has to be a real *I* sound, not a little clipped-off sound. Do not rasp when you say *J*. Just say it in a very jelly-like way. You can do it, honey."

Solita had pitied her because she is old and Arthur is sick. But now she is back on equal footing with this girl.

She teaches her the words to the A-B-C song. Stupid fun. Elnice laughs too hard and grasps Solita's arm for support. She is just so happy.

"OK," says Solita. "OK!"

They move on to basic nouns, the names of things all around the house. Table, fork, forks, muffin, crumb, ham, peas, closet, blouse, Buick, house, garbage, dog, dogmess. Solita picks up the words quickly. Elnice perceives a peppery intelligence there in her eyes. And beyond that, hunger.

Elnice is teaching again. She hums show tunes.

Solita comes on Wednesdays to clean, again on Fridays to learn. Over the next few weeks Solita takes to mixing English words with her Spanish. At times Elnice gets the gist from context, but pure Spanish she cannot follow. The common words of Spanish, articles and conjunctions, *que*, for instance, sound like tics, mistakes, not words.

Solita wants to go right into sentences.

"Fresco is on the rug," Elnice obliged. "The slipper is blue."

"The slipper is blue."

"No. Not 'de sleeper'. The. The. The slipper. Slip."

"Slip."

"Good. And the slipper *is* blue. Not es. Not *ess*. Is. Izzz."

"Izzz."

"Good!"

"OK!"

Arthur, his voice a little stronger today, passes by on his way to the bathroom. "The rain in Spain stays mainly in the plain." He is upbeat and nearly ruddy, thanks to more nebulizer drugs and another oral steroid and the doctor's recent lecture about using the oxygen. "On the other hand," he adds, and Elnice knows exactly what is next, "the precipitation in Portugal pelts primarily on the plateau!"

Solita's eyes question Elnice's. The bathroom door closes.

"Silly man," Elnice comments lovingly.

Solita nods in agreement. "Butthead."

"Solita!" Elnice laughs, delighted.

"No? No butthead?"

Elnice pauses. "He *is* a butthead. Sometimes."

Solita did know a few English words to begin with:

Disneyland, Mickey, MTV. Lexus. Pizza Hut. Butthead. Some movie stars.

Elnice says, "I feel like Annie Sullivan. Annie Sullivan?"

A blank look.

"Helen Keller?"

Another blank look.

"Um, Caesar Chavez?"

Nothing.

"Santa Ana?"

Nothing.

"Cortés?"

Nothing.

"Panama Canal?"

Nothing. Nothing all the way through Alexander the Great, Henry the Eighth, Vikings, Great Wall of China, Mona Lisa, Mayflower Compact, Lenin, Aswan Dam, polio vaccine, Mahatma Gandhi, Hitler, climate change.

Solita had heard of September 11th and several U.S. presidents.

"Moon—moonwalk, uh, luna, luna-walk?" Fingers walking on the table, a quick drawing of earth, sun, and moon. "Moon: men walking on it? Like this?"

A peal of laughter. "Silly! OK!"

Others make worse beginnings.

As fall tumbles toward whatever kind of winter Los Angeles gets, Elnice learns the short story of Solita's past via a mix of English words, gestures, and facial expressions.

Solita had been sent to school in Mexico only occasionally and only through the third grade. At the age of fourteen she married a man aged thirty. Her husband had treated her nicely at first, but his business, which was used cars, turned bad, and he took to drinking and hitting her.

She'd been pregnant twice and miscarried because of the beatings. Two years after marrying, Solita bolted across the border to the United States. Her mother, father, and brother are dead.

Elnice is thunderstruck. Solita is nineteen years old, she tells Elnice, and living with a good man who takes care of her as a husband should. But Luis is not her husband. It saddens her that she is still married to the man in Mexico.

"Doesn't Luis mind that?"

"He love me."

"Loves me."

"Loves me, I loves him. Love him! I want to have children in Catholic church. Luis say he get my wedding. Get my old wedding." She stops, frustrated.

"Annulled? He can get your marriage annulled?"

"Yes. He can get annulment but no now."

"Not now. Not yet? Someday?"

"Yes. Some day. Annulment takes money."

"What is Luis like?" Elnice doesn't spend too much time correcting Solita during interesting conversations like this.

"Muy hombre! Strong! He very—" she holds her hands before her as if grasping Luis and looking tenderly into his face.

Elnice says, "Luis is handsome?"

Solita taps her temple.

"Smart too? Luis is smart?"

"Luis is very smart. He read, he write. He is write a movie. Writing a movie! At night he work on her, the movie. He no want me read and write! I look at a paper, he takes it!"

Elnice looks at her narrowly.

"He says I am stupid."

Elnice screws down her gaze even tighter.

"But! He love me. I believe. He pay the rent, he no drink too much. I can wait and show him. I can show English but not now. I can. I can." She stops again.

"Surprise him? You'll surprise him with your English?"

"Surprise him with my English, my English reading and English writing."

"You're disobeying him," it occurs to Elnice. This makes her feel better. "Do you understand that?"

Solita replies with nothing but a saucy shrug.

The girl excels at pantomime: her face is mobile and good-natured, her arms and hands graceful. She throws her whole body into it, jumping up to mime *church*, the steeple, the crucifix, pews, genuflection. The timbre of her voice is as light and charming as a wooden flute.

Luis is a grounds crew worker at the golf courses in Griffith Park, Solita tells Elnice. He is so strong and smart he is valuable to the bosses there. One day, though, he will finish his movie—his screenplay—and the movie will be a hit and he will quit work at the golf course and they will go to Hawaii, or perhaps return quietly to Mexico and build a safe happy home there. They will be rich. Luis must finish his screenplay first.

"Maybe Mr. Brandewine could help him," Elnice suggests.

"Yes! I tell him that! But Luis he no show anyone until she is over."

"She is over?"

Solita makes a frustrated hand-waggle and Elnice says, "You mean he won't show anyone his screenplay until it is finished?"

Elnice wonders how smart Luis could be to reject the help of a Hollywood insider. How smart could he be if all he did was push a lawn mower all day?

Arthur passes by again. "Ask Luis to come clear out that brush."

They take Solita outside into the brilliant southern California sunlight, like cool glass today, and communicate the heavy work of clearing the border of gnarled brush away from the north side of the house. On that side there is no neighbor, only a jagged shard of canyon wall. The next neighbor up is some big movie individual whose house clings to the very top of the ridge like a raccoon on a fence.

"It's because of the drainage," Arthur explains needlessly, wanting to be an authority. "The brush doesn't grow so thick on the steep slopes because water runs off so fast. Everything grows thicker here by the house where the ground is level."

"Yes," Solita says, "Luis come. He *work*. OK!"

"OK," say Elnice and Arthur together.

A spate of rain prevents Luis from coming and attacking the brush right away. In the meantime Elnice and Arthur marvel at Solita's progress.

"If she's this smart, how come she didn't pick up more English before?" Arthur asks one day. "How come she doesn't have a more responsible job?"

"Honey, she's illegal. A regular job, they'd have to check her papers or something."

"Yeah, but half the employees in this town are illegals. I heard they just make up Social Security numbers."

"Well, all I know is she's young and naive and unsure of herself. But...that's changing."

Elnice studies Solita every time they meet, and sees she is right: the girl is becoming quicker and brighter. Solita had never been stupid, no, it was merely that her frame of reference had been so tiny. No one had ever encouraged her to learn for the sake of learning.

It strikes Elnice that Solita is looking to her as a daughter would: she sees the questioning, the *requesting* in her eyes, the search for reassurance, for knowledge, for more of life. The depth of those iridescent black grackle-head eyes thrill and unsettle her.

With the change in the weather they take to having hot tea after the lesson, lingering over their cups and saucers. Then Elnice begins baking elaborate cakes to go with the tea, special cakes strictly with Solita in mind: orange coconut, vanilla mint. Naturally Solita loves the cakes. She loves being with Elnice. The cake-eating extends the tea time.

Arthur is subtly excluded. At around three o'clock Elnice sees that he has a good snack, something substantial—a little plate of rolled-up baloney slices with hot mustard, or two popovers and some cheddar cubes—so he isn't hungry when the girls sit down at three-thirty.

Passing a paperback Spanish-English dictionary back and forth across the table, they talk about good kinds of hand lotion that don't cost too much, argue over whether someone who snores can help it, how old a woman can be and still have a baby, which colors look best near the face when one has an olive complexion—Elnice tries to tell Solita that she would look stunning even in a Purina sack— why it's best to buy a few good clothes instead of many cheap ones, why Windex on the kitchen floor is the best way to keep those little Argentine ants away from Fresco's food dish. Why some dogs sniff your crotch and others don't, why men don't make friends the way women do, mustn't Mr. Brandewine be lonely?

They discuss the California State Lottery. Solita holds

the opinion that the lottery is a wonderful thing, proof of the magic of America, proof that America is a great and rich country. Yet why do her neighbors appear so foolish when they buy tickets? You might as well throw your money into the street. They discuss probability and greed and honest work and satisfaction and the taste of a good cup of tea when you feel so tired.

Elnice adds apple cider vinegar to the rinse water for her hair to make it shine; she has done so since her girlhood on the prairie; Solita has never heard of the practice but finds a place to buy cider vinegar and begins using it too. Her hair looks glossier than ever.

To further help them communicate, Solita draws pictures, amazingly fast. She sketches on notebook paper in a loose, free way, her hand moving continuously, the pencil touching down softly, now hard. One form flows into the next. For fun she draws Fresco in mid-hurdle over Arthur's foot, looking more real and lively than the dog itself.

She tries to explain that Elnice made something break loose within her.

Elnice knows to marvel at this phenomenon whenever it happens, and give thanks.

Solita never misses wiping the lint off the toilet paper holder and the ends of the towel bars. On weeks when a full furniture-vacuuming is not required she nevertheless does a quick job between the cushions of Arthur's recliner, where crumbs collect. She dusts beneath the lace tablecloth on the dining-room table.

Ty Brandewine is enthralled with the tablecloth itself. "To paraphrase Shakespeare," he says, "nothing shocks like convention, don'tcha know."

"Shakespeare?" queried Elnice.

"Mm-hm."

"Surely lace tablecloths are not hard to find in Hollywood homes?"

"Elnice, you're toying with me. Stop toying with me. Would you and Arthur come to dinner at my place tomorrow night?"

After accepting with pleasure and seeing Ty to the door she gives Solita her first homework assignment. "Honey, get your hands on some words—something in print—and bring in five words. OK?" Luis be damned.

"OK!" says Solita.

"I believe Solita and I are very much alike," Elnice tells Arthur as she puts away the pens and tablet.

"Neither one of you's a firecracker," he says.

That's what you think, boy.

8: This Must be the Way Airplanes Land

The terrible scene unfolds like a newsreel pulled from the archives, silent and jerky yet hypnotically today.

Somehow Jason M knows the little girl's name is Pamela and her doll's name is Vicky.

Pamela sips at a cup of milk like a kitten then replaces it on her tray table. Twisting Vicky's head toward the window, she points out the sweep of the land below. A great river swerves through forests and farmland.

Pamela's mother smiles at the flight attendant. The mother resembles the actress Staria Beckwith, while the flight attendant looks very much like a topless dancer Jason M once slept with.

Suddenly the plane lurches sideways.

The pilots yell in surprise; there's no time to make an announcement; they wrestle the controls like crazy men. The plane plummets.

Pamela's mother tries to throw her body across Pamela's but she is pinned to her seat by the force of the dive. The doll disappears from Pamela's hands. The flight attendant hugs the ceiling. Pamela wonders about all this, but after a second decides this must be the way airplanes land.

At impact Jason M screams. His limbs go rigid, sweat spews from his pores, a loop of slobber lassoes his nose.

After a while he gets up and watches a few porn videos. Then he goes back to bed and jacks off resolutely but continues to be awake.

9: The Cokers Meet Ty's Movie

So far the Cokers have seen only Ty's foyer. After naps, they bathe and get ready.

Arthur pulls a Banlon t-shirt with a small embroidered penguin over his head.

"You're wearing that?" Elnice pauses with her bottle of Norell.

"You don't wear a navy blue suit to dinner anymore, especially in Hollywood. I've learned a few things. This shirt's so old it's new." He checks himself in the mirror.

"But you're not supposed to look like you just jumped off the teeter-totter."

"I saw guys in sunglasses coming out of California Pizza Kitchen wearing shirts just like these the other day when you were getting your hair done."

"All right."

Elnice wears a Suzy Kramer sweater set over a Stamenhill Creek skirt with an Anasazi motif and her little beige flats.

Arthur forgets to tell her she looks nice.

"I wonder if I should bring a pen and paper," he murmurs.

"What for?" She looks at him. "I thought we were just going to have dinner."

"Well," he says, "see, he wants to talk to us about his movie."

"His movie—the script he's working on? What about it?"

"He just wants to—tell us about it."

"Have you two been talking?"

"No! Not...not..."

Elnice reads him like a meat thermometer. "What's going on?"

"Nothing!"

She carries their hostess gift, a copy of *Cold Sassy Tree*, which is always appreciated.

Now that she knows more than she did five minutes ago, Elnice expects to find a crowd of people gathered to celebrate Ty's movie. He pulls the Cokers inside, kisses her swiftly on the mouth and pumps Arthur's hand.

But Ty's living room yawns emptily before them as they step through the foyer, heads stuck slightly forward, shoulders hunched, in the posture of humility customary to them when on the verge of meeting new people.

Ty's home is about the same size as theirs, featuring similar herky-jerky steps up and down. But the look and feel is completely different. The surfaces are bright and naked, no patina on anything. Mod, very mod, thinks Elnice. Plush white carpeting and startling artistic items. One hanging piece resembles a collection of turnips arranged in a spiral then spray-painted silver. Arthur smiles at it.

"Cocktails? Hors d'oeuvres?" Ty strolls to the patio doorwall. They see a long tray of snacks lit by hurricane candles on his patio table. Hollywood's clear golden dusk falls over the whole sky beyond.

Elnice fears the late October chill will be bad for Arthur, but he makes a beeline for the snacks. She follows and feels a gorgeous warmth as soon as she steps outside. Ty's patio sports one of those appliances that stream down

CRIMES IN A SECOND LANGUAGE

toasty heat particles as you sit and visit beneath it.

"I like a good margarita, don't you?" Brandewine asks, already pouring from a frosty pitcher.

"Thank you," says Elnice.

The snack tray features rumaki, hot lobster dip, crusty bread rounds, marinated button mushrooms, and a flaked-apart slab of smoked trout. Mighty yummy, plus slim forks and little plates with pinecones painted on them.

As they sample everything their host spurts gossip about movie stars, including a really shocking one involving the most wholesome actress in the world, chocolate sauce, and tarantulas.

"The hell of it for her was," he concludes, "her husband was off in Morocco buying three boys."

"Buying three boys?" Arthur repeats. "You mean, like, procuring them for...her?"

"No. For himself."

"Oh! Holy crow."

Elnice asks, "Where do you hear these things, Ty?"

Ty's head is bracketed by stiff, mustachy growths of stainless-steel-colored hair over the ears. It somehow gives him a more honest look than if he were all bald. Elnice imagines that hair growing all over his head but can't decide if he looked better when he was younger. Ty's eyes are like twitchy bugs tonight.

"Elnice, my dear, in the movie business you get in on everything." He smiles and winks. "You're never ever bored when you're working in Hollywood."

Elnice waits.

The meal itself stars a joint of beef the size of which the Cokers had never seen outside of a wedding reception, with a supporting cast of similarly gargantuan Idaho potatoes, cut into planks and roasted with simple spices, pounds and pounds of well-done asparagus stacked like cordwood, a silver bucket of Hollandaise sauce to go with, as well as an assortment of raw vegetables and pickled garnishes. Good bread and butter.

"What a—Ty, this meal!" Elnice would be overcome if she did not feel something odd in the air. No one had ever fixed something this special for her.

"Good Midwestern food," Ty asserts.

It is all for them and they eat as much as they can hold at Ty's glass-topped dining room table. Disconcertingly, everyone's lap and legs and feet are visible beneath the shadows cast by the large serving dishes. A spaceship-like chandelier hovers overhead.

Elnice notices that Ty doesn't say the kind of things home cooks usually do, the little anecdotes of food preparation, the deprecating appraisals of flavor and texture. And he doesn't *handle* the food as if he'd prepared it, he sort of sidles up to it. The table service feels restaurant-like, especially the heavy linen napkins whose folds show no signs of compression, which they would if they'd been stored in a drawer. Elnice wonders if the meal had somehow been prepared elsewhere and delivered, but that's preposterous. Who would order a catered meal for three people?

Ty pours wine.

"Ty, you probably shouldn't give us your good stuff," protests Elnice. "Because, you know, we can't tell the difference."

Arthur gives her a look but says nothing, his mouth being full of beef.

She peers at the labels on the bottles as if she intends to remember them.

"What are friends for?" says Ty, laughing. "This is just

a cute little cab I found up in Sonoma last month. Picked up a few cases. You can save even more if you get to know the tasting staff!"

After a few sips she must admit that Ty's wine comes across appreciably better than box wine.

"It tastes—sophisticated!" says she.

Ty tastes, then purses his lips, leaving a sheen of wine on them "Mm. Assertive—yet not domineering. A little tannic, but then again, who isn't these days?" Another laugh. "A lovely little table wine. We used to call this Dago Red in my neighborhood."

When Elnice and Arthur are in company, the weight of total responsibility for Arthur eases off the back of her neck. The presence of just one other competent person makes such a difference.

Soon neither Coker has a care in the world.

"People don't eat enough here in L.A.," Elnice generalizes. "I've noticed that." Every woman knows the famous saying you can't be too rich or too thin, but since arriving in Southern California she has seen many exceptions to that. Almost everyone who looked rich in L.A. also looked too skinny. "People go around with concave stomachs. All this wheat germ, what have you."

"Wheat germ is so stark staring passé I can't tell you," Ty remarks, biting a potato plank.

"I saw Maria Crujillo getting a coffee to go. Remember, she was in 'Race to Red Valley'? I love her. *She's* too thin. Especially for her age. And these young girls you see everywhere. These young girls."

"Hm," says Ty.

"This brown sauce for the meat is lovely."

"Thank you."

She pats herself on the back for not calling it gravy.

"And some people look so funny. I mean their faces."

Arthur says, "Like George Remson. It isn't that his *face* is funny, it's just that he looks so sleazy. He was perfect in all those—"

Elnice says, "I think George Remson's attractive."

"You *do*?"

Ty says, "What's wrong with him's that tan. It's too much and too perfect, you know?"

"It makes him look like a gigolo." Arthur forks some more beef over to his plate. "I've always thought that—" he stops, and Elnice looks over worried to see if he is silently choking, but he is laughing.

"I was going to say an actor but I can't remember his name, and then I was going to say who he was married to but I can't remember her name either. Who played the girl in 'Iron Story Love'?"

Elnice and Ty together nail it: "Natasha Porter. Walt Roberts."

"Right. I always thought Walt Roberts should have played more sleazy-type roles, he had that look, like George Remson."

Ty says, "His jaw was too strong for that; it saved him from looking sleazy. May I?"

He tops off their glasses.

"Listen, you two," he says, "I feel we're good enough friends that I may ask you the following question."

Elnice glances at Arthur.

Ty steeples his fingers over his half-eaten dinner. "It's the biggest question in Hollywood." With a sly, cute smile, he asks, "What is your favorite movie? Elnice?"

"Oh! I'd have to say—well, I like anything with Katharine Hepburn in it, you know."

"Favorite movie."

"Well—uh—I guess I ought to say 'Citizen Kane,' you know, like you're supposed to say the Bible when people ask you what's your favorite book!"

"Is 'Citizen Kane' your favorite movie, Elnice?"

"No—no—I—well—"

"Favorite movie. Pick one. You must pick one."

His face is so funnily earnest that Elnice laughs. "Oh, all right! 'Lawrence of Arabia.'"

Ty relaxes slightly. "Good. And why is that?"

"Although I have to say I'm torn between that and 'Dr. Zhivago.'"

"Elnice! Which?"

"'Lawrence of Arabia.'"

"And why?"

"Because it was so inspiring to me! Peter O'Toole and his quest to help people—his quest to do the right thing and give them their dignity. I always feel so glad about people after I see that movie. I mean, his work in the Arab world didn't end well, it's true, but not for lack of trying."

"Yes."

"And the photography."

"Yes. Do you realize that both 'Lawrence' and 'Zhivago' were made by David Lean?"

"No, I hadn't." The concept of being a fan of a director's work, instead of an actor's or actress's, had not occurred to her. The room is quiet but for the clinking of Arthur's fork.

Ty swerves his eyes to Arthur, who swallows beef and says, "'Chariots of Fire.'"

"Of course!" Ty grins hugely, his teeth suddenly Teddy-Roosevelt-big. "Brilliant! Perfect! Athletics, young idealism, spirituality—the whole package."

"The running was good."

"The running was good. Yes. Was it ever. But—could it

77

have been formative for you?"

"Well, I was a grown man when it came out, you know, but I'd say—yes. Yes because—" his eyes mist over "—it helped me realize—that I've made some pretty good choices in life." He clears his throat, smiles sheepishly, and reaches for his wine.

Ty exhales with controlled precision and no haste. "Now for a slight change of subject. Let me tell you about my film, all right? I want you two to hear about it."

Elnice folds her arms at the very edge of the table in a posture of attentiveness. Arthur sits back and smiles.

Ty strokes the stem of his wineglass with a sensitive gesture. "I feel...I have to put it this way: this is my special picture. My magnum opus, if you will, my masterpiece. Though perhaps that's not for me to say." His tone becomes lanky, more casual. "The working title is 'Freedom Lake'." He says it that way to show he isn't *wedded* to it; he is still an artist under the influences of the creative juices.

"Essentially, it's a story of being dead and then being reborn, via the power to love. It's 'East of Eden' in reverse, it's 'Saving Private Ryan' without the artillery—if you'll allow me that—, it's 'Forrest Gump' meets 'Mission: Impossible'."

He can't help grinning, he loves his own imagination, he is unable to hold back his raw pride and enthusiasm. "See?"

Elnice feels quietly respectful, thinking of the disappointments this man has endured. How many screenplays bought and never made? A dozen?

Arthur and Elnice respond that they see. Yes, they see.

"OK. You have this man, this lone man, he's wounded, he's suffering. His wife died of cancer three months ago and he's a mess. Spiritually, emotionally."

"But physically he's a hunk, right?" Elnice guesses.

"Exactly. But a hunk with some mileage on, all right, if you have to know, I'm thinking Buster Jordan for this, he's not getting the kind of work he should be getting these days, frankly his confidence is shot, so my thought is he'll jump all over this. He doesn't *need* a ton of money, he needs the right role, and this role's right for him. His name is Steve Brickman. Brick-man."

"An allegorical name," Elnice perceives.

"Very astute, Elnice! And he's running away from his pain. You know it and I know it. So he comes to this beautiful lake in the Adirondack Mountains, this could possibly be shot in Northern California somewhere, north of Tahoe somewhere. And he rents a cabin and a boat, and he goes out fishing every day. He loves to fish. But not enough to—he's thinking, just maybe I'll commit suicide, tie a rock to myself and just go down."

"Does he catch anything?" Arthur interjects. "The reason I ask—"

"Sure he does, but he does catch-and-release."

"—the reason I ask is, my cousin's got a place up there in the Finger Lakes, and what with all the acid rain they had, the fishing's just barely coming back."

"Well, like I said, he does catch-and-release. *Anyway*, the *point* is, the person who runs the boat rental is this slightly-over-the-hill-but-still-gorgeous-in-the-right-light woman—I'm thinking Laura Dennis here—"

"Laura Dennis is over the hill?" That crinkles Elnice's brow.

"I forget you're new to Hollywood. Just take my word for it. And she has this stunning young daughter, eighteen-nineteen years old. Maybe it's an adopted daughter, whatever. Which could help with casting. Resemblances, you know. Anyway, this woman, her name is Gail Rafters. Rafters, get it, she's adrift, *and how*, she just got out of prison for something, we don't know what it is yet. She falls for Brickman, and they have this tremendously intimate conversation out on the lake where he confesses to her that he feels responsible for his wife's death, because he didn't drag her to the doctor sooner. They talk some more, and he finds out she's a widow too.

"'I'm so sorry. How did your husband die?'

"'I killed him.'

"He waits for more, he's listening, like, 'I know the feeling.'

"'No, I mean I really killed him. I shot him, then I did seven years.'"

"Wow." Elnice decides to keep eating. She helps herself to more asparagus to mop up the excessive amount of Hollandaise she took at first.

"He raped their daughter, you see."

"Wow."

"So the romantic cycle gets going. She falls for Brickman, but here's the twist: he falls for the daughter. The beautiful daughter who insists on being called Butch. 'Butch Rafters.' She's wounded, you see, they're all damaged goods. The girl only wants to be left alone—she thinks!—she hates life, hates men. Steve Brickman brings her out of her shell, as he's coming out of *his* because of her mother. This tomboy, this Butch, her real name is Heather—a pretty name!—and she talks tough, but she's terribly vulnerable and's got a heart of solid gold."

They all pause for breath. Ty swirls his wine.

"I don't know who the hell for that role, it's an incredible ingénue role for the right actress, an incredible opportunity. These kinds of things, sometimes you go for a complete unknown, try to stir up some interest in a beautiful new face. It's fraught, though."

"Fraught," repeats Arthur. "So what happens to Laura Dennis?"

"That's one loose end that'll get tied up at some point, possibly during shooting. Casablanca-style."

"You mean," asks Elnice, "she'll be like Bogie and give up—"

"No, well, maybe, but the shorthand I was using meant I can finish the movie on the fly, the way they did 'Casablanca'."

"Oh."

Ty sketches the minor characters and more action, talking on with effortless intensity. "So actually, I think I could build another twist in there: suddenly a guy shows up at the lake, he's from the mob, sniffing around. Turns out Gail's late husband owed a ton of money to the mob— the Russian Mafia, let's have it, yeah, he was involved in uh, smuggling young Russian girl peasants to backstreet brothels in Rio or someplace, which would've been another motivating reason for Gail to kill him—and she thought she'd bargained all that down after she killed him, but no, they still want their money, now that she's out of prison. Then, let's see, OK, Steve Brickman is forced to kill this guy, he and Gail sink his body in the lake—we could do an *homage* to 'Deliverance' here—then—hm." He falls silent, working his jaw from side to side.

After a minute he says, "You see, there's no way this movie's going to get made unless *I* make it." He rubs his clean tan chin. "The lake heals them all, the beauty of the lake, plus the beauty of their love. I think maybe—that's it! I think Laura Dennis will realize she *must* stay at the lake, while Brickman and Heather leave to start a new life. In the Peace Corps, maybe. Or Greenpeace. They're going to challenge, um." He pauses. "Japanese whalers are a cliché, let's have it be Japanese loggers. No, *Chinese* loggers. *Chinese*. It'll be clear that Gail Rafters is going to be, in fact, *happier* staying at the lake than leaving with Brickman."

"But the mob might send somebody else," warns Arthur.

"Yes, and she'd have to face them," Ty says. "There could be a beautiful slo-mo shootout with her doing some kind of one-up violence to them, Ewok-style, Home-Alone-style. I'll figure it out. I do have some dessert for us later, by the way. German chocolate torte and coffee."

"That's a powerful story," says Elnice, as Arthur nods thoughtfully. He likes anything German chocolate.

Ty's brow darkens. Elnice notices a notch over one eyebrow, a little white V of a scar he'd picked up somewhere. The notch quirks and settles lower.

"Arthur," he says, "what do you think, really?"

"Powerful as hell."

Ty's eyebrows reach up to the gods and the notch opens like a tiny fan.

"Sincerely?"

Arthur is sincere.

"You two are such archetypes. You are Americans. You are America itself. You're so perfect to be talking to right now. I can't tell you what this means to me."

Elnice thinks, then says, "It seems like the kind of movie where anything could happen."

"Tell me why, Elnice." Ty interlaces his fingers.

"Well, because you can start to see that all these characters have choices, and you don't know—it's not obvious what they'll do at first."

"There's a tension there?"

"Yes."

"A sense of anticipation, perhaps, a delicious suspension of time?"

"I guess so. Plus," she adds, "I like when you told us about the cat that's always hanging around the bait tank, and the voice that says what it's thinking. That's cute."

"Cute without being cutesy. The cat as narrator—the one being who understands, the one who interprets for us, the Glinda figure, if you will—I'm thinking Joe Hamlin for the voice of the cat."

"Ty, no, the cat has to be female!"

What are they doing? What are they talking about? Elnice has begun to hope that Ty will offer them small roles in the film or ask them to work behind the scenes. She had always thought the term "script girl" sounded silly but all of a sudden she badly wants to be one.

Or, since the cat voice would be recorded off-camera, she could do that job without getting nervous and blowing it. This is her secret thought.

Arthur could play the old man who keeps coming into the rental shack to bitch to Laura Dennis about the skinny-dippers out at midnight.

"You're right!" cries Ty. "Absolutely. The voice of cat wisdom should *always* be female." He leans forward more intensely than ever. "Arthur, Elnice. So you like it."

The Cokers exchange baffled glances.

Elnice has the sudden feeling that whatever is supposed to happen this evening is about to happen. She looks into Ty's eyes and sees that she is right.

Her adrenaline spikes and, with an inchoate desire to forestall whatever it is, she blurts, "Excuse me while I go to the bathroom!"

Ty's lips go tight, then relax into a smile. Arthur squints at her.

10: The Timing of Money

When she returns she realizes her timing was wrong. The two men are waiting in a state of heightened animation, a little mist of anticipation hanging over their heads. During her absence they had—wordlessly, she is certain—aligned themselves against her. Leaving the room had been a bad move. Ty springs up to hold her chair.

In a tone as fizzy and mood-breaking as possible, she announces, "I could really go for a sliver of cake!"

Ty seats himself.

Arthur says, "I bet it'll be a great movie, Ty."

This is it.

"Elnice, Arthur," says Ty, gravely looking one to the other and back again, "*I* bet it'll be a great *investment.*"

Arthur glances at Elnice, then at his portable oxygen tank, which Elnice had insisted come along to save an extra trip later. He'd started on the oxygen four hours a day plus overnight. Bedtime was coming and they were far from home. That's the way it felt, sitting next door at Ty's table under the spell of Ty and his food and beverages.

"Uh—an *investment?*" Elnice touches her cheek.

"There's never *been* a better time to invest in films," Ty begins.

And it is a beginning, make no mistake. Elnice realizes that while she and Arthur had been eating and drinking and more or less expending themselves socially with him, Ty had been gathering himself.

He explains how it all works, from load-in to production to distribution to payout. "Magnificent opportunity...Incredible market conditions right now, today... Greater than the sum of its parts...Takes money to make money...Literally millions in profits...Income for the ages."

Income for the ages? The Cokers listen as Ty pours more wine into their glasses and spins out sums involving ticket sales multiples and overseas video rights.

"But this film, you see, just isn't going to happen unless *I make it happen!*" He runs his hand all the way around his head, brushing his steel-colored fuzz as if trying to rub off a troublesome halo. "I looked in the mirror the other day and the guy I saw there—" he winks grimly— "said to me, *they're going to bury this one just like the rest.*"

He waits, breathing lightly through his mouth.

Arthur winks back, but Elnice wants Ty to explain why.

"Because it's good! It's truly *good*, goddamn it! And I just can't stand for that to happen. Which it will, I just know it, if a studio buys it. And if by some *wild, miraculous* occurrence it gets made, they'll, you know. Butcher it."

The Cokers well know who *they* are. Those executives.

"Money talks, my friends—"

"—and them that's got the money..." Arthur interjects—

"—calls the shots. Exactly." Ty rolls an olive between his fingers. Elnice notices his hands trembling with emotion from the wrists as if pausing between movements of a piano concerto.

This is not a come-on in the mail. This is not a so-called financial advisor talking about abstract returns in a decade's time. This is not a sly thug on their doorstep trying to convince them their electrical outlets in the bedroom need checking.

It is Ty Brandewine, Mister Hollywood. Their closest friend in Los Angeles.

"I'm sinking everything I've got into it," he tells them, "which, I'm afraid, ain't what it used to be." The wives, the kids, Miami, they know.

"But Ty," Elnice tries desperately for a lighthearted tone, "movies cost so much money to make! Even we know that! You're always hearing—I mean, Ty—we just don't have millions of dollars!"

Ty tilts his head backward at an extreme angle; it splits open at the mouth like a cut can, and a gust of laughter rolls out. "Oh! Hahaha! Ha!"

They watch. Arthur sips more wine.

"You'd be surprised," Ty says, "how much movie a few hundred thousand dollars can buy. Especially using an independent company instead of a damn studio."

They wait, stunned at his estimate of their fortune.

"Arthur, Elnice, I'm not *asking* you to invest in my film, I'm *inviting* you to do it. There's a difference. Arthur, being an athlete, I think you can tell me what it is."

"Confidence?"

"Precisely."

"You're very confident." Arthur's lips stretch back from his teeth in that canine smile Elnice hasn't seen much of.

"Not very. Totally. I am totally confident. Yes. And not only me. Once I begin putting this project together, everyone involved—this thing's going to be as unstoppable as—you won't be able to—in today's dollars? I can't even guess. I'm being perfectly honest with you." His face is like the prow of a runaway bus, swaying from side to side. "The two of you deserve this opportunity. You deserve a reward."

"For what?" Elnice wants to know.

"For *surviving!* For making it this far! My God, Elnice,

you remind me of my dearest grandmother in the world. To her, it isn't gratification unless it's delayed. Haven't you been delaying your gratification in this life long enough?"

Arthur's mind is made up, but seeing Elnice's face he clears his throat and murmurs, "We'll have to think about it."

Ty stage-winces. "Yeah but—see, the thing is, I need to know right away if you're interested, and I need some kind of a token—a, um—"

"When?" Arthur cocks an eyebrow.

"Tonight."

"Tonight?"

"Because, see, I've got several other dear friends who're anxious to get in on this thing, and I want to—well, frankly, I don't want a hell of a lot of fingers in this pie. They'd kill me if they heard me saying this. You're not wearing a wire, are you?"

Arthur laughs warmly.

Ty goes on, "I don't know, it's just that I have such." He stops. "Such well, such tender feelings toward the two of you!"

Overcome, he squeezes his eyes shut and an instant later a tear spills down his cheek. Just one manly tear. Elnice suddenly feels like giving him a hug.

"But what if—" Ty asks, and now his eyes are sharp— "what if 'Lawrence of Arabia' and 'Chariots of Fire' had never been made?"

Elnice had anticipated this question.

Arthur emits a chuff of shock.

Ty goes on, "What would your lives—*our lives*—have been then? Oh, sure, we'd all be alive and breathing, but. *But.* Wouldn't just a little something be missing? Like a piece of our souls?"

Arthur nods breathlessly.

"Not to be too big here." Ty picks up his wineglass, studies the ruby liquid for a few seconds, sets it down. "But out there is a young person just like we all once were, a young person looking for something. A seeker. 'Freedom Lake' is that young person's 'Lawrence of Arabia,' that young person's 'Chariots of Fire.' Who are we to snatch that away?"

Arthur, Elnice realizes, has never been a deep thinker. His wordless agreement with their host slaps her in the face with it.

Ty pincers his forehead with a tense hand. "I have to wrap up the financing tomorrow, I'm going to have to borrow a few dollars of course, and the fellow at the bank, Lou Steinmetz, do you know him over at—? He called me just this afternoon with an incredible rate if I can put a package together by tomorrow. So I'd need, tonight, a kind of—"

"—good faith kind of thing?" Arthur helps.

Shut up, thinks Elnice.

"Exactly."

The look in Arthur's eyes causes her to feel a mixture of excitement and terror. Because he looks as he used to look as a powerful boy at the starting line of a race: poised, determined, eyes focused in the distance, no longer even aware of the starting line.

It's been a long time.

Slowly, he rises from his chair. Ty rises too, cautiously.

"We'd like to be in it." Arthur steadies himself with a hand on the back of his chair. "I mean be in the movie."

Ty licks his lips. "Absolutely. Absolutely." He is breathing very lightly.

"Elnice and I've been looking for a good investment."

She opens her mouth. Shuts it.

Her husband announces, "I'm going home to get my checkbook."

Ty exhales. "I'll go with you."

11: *Every Inch a Worker*

It isn't easy for Elnice to get out of bed the next morning given the monstrous headache that set in around two a.m., but she does because Luis is coming at seven to clear the brush on the non-Ty side of the Coker house. Arthur snores on his back under the covers with oxygen pouring into his nose. She leaves the blinds down.

No time to think about Arthur and Ty.

All the layers of her brain are swollen and sore.

She lets Fresco out. In the kitchen she squishes the juice out of a grapefruit, stirs in half a cup of water, and drinks that. The tartness helps right away. She makes coffee and drinks a black cup. She brushes her teeth and showers, sprinkles powder, combs out her wet hair and puts it up neatly in a polka-dotted scarf. Sighs in the mirror. Walks out to get the paper. The air smells dusty and the dew is already gone. She lets Fresco back in.

She reads the headlines at the kitchen table, which is a heavy plastic-sheathed disk mounted on a white iron pedestal. It and its uncomfortable molded matching swivel chairs came with the house.

The sound of an engine brings her out of her chair; she stands, eyes closed, then open, finding balance. She walks to the front door where Fresco is scrabbling.

Of the dogs they've had, Fresco is the cutest but dumbest. He remembers neither punishment nor reward, and Elnice fears that as he ages he'll more often confuse inside with outside.

A small pickup truck rocks to a stop in the driveway. It is a slant-shouldered Chevy of yesteryear, its yellow paint job pied with rust, making it look like a sickly animal.

Elnice watches Luis hop down from the cab. She perceives that although short-armed, he is a muscular man, thick and solid, wearing beaten-in blue jeans, a checkered shirt, and a short-brimmed straw cowboy hat. The jeans catch Elnice's attention: faded exactly according to the shape of the leg muscles they encase, ranging from ultramarine at the seams to nearly white at the center of the thighs. As a soap bubble or a bolus of mercury looks alive, the pants look alive.

In other words Luis resembles any of the migrant workers she has seen toiling in the orange groves along the highways in the San Fernando Valley.

He stands for a moment looking at the house with a flat expression. (Elnice is invisible behind a potted ficus tree.) His eyes trace the outlines of the house, criss-cross over every detail, from the moss growing under the north eaves to the recently washed picture window to the foreboding fringe of vegetation creeping around the canyon side.

Fresco jumps at the door; Luis inclines his head, listening. His eyes show no sign of humor, his posture hints at neither energy nor fatigue, neither pride nor humility. He is a neutral person.

Looking at him looking at her home Elnice feels a sudden, unpleasant coolness in her arms and legs. She wants him to disappear.

Her inner spell is broken by the man's sudden movement. With a quick stride he covers the ground to the door and thrusts his thumb at the button. *Chime-a-ling!*

She scoops up Fresco, partly out of courtesy, partly for

the meager security of him. Sweat springs out in her palms. Her hand is on the knob: how ridiculous not to open it and meet Solita's manly man! From down the hall she hears the *squee* of the shower faucet. She jerks the door open.

What a relief! The man in the straw hat and blue jeans wears a deferential smile, his eyes bracketed by little mild lines. Suddenly he looks like a toy Mexican man.

"Hello," says she, holding Fresco tightly under one arm, "Luis?"

"Luis Perona Gastello." He takes her proffered hand and shakes it gently, winsomely. For an instant she thinks he might kiss it. His fingers are dry and rough as emery boards. He is clean-shaven and his teeth are somewhat yellow but large and straight. What is his ancestry? Elnice looks into his face unconsciously intently. With his cheeks and temples carved in flat planes, he looks very original peoples.

She introduces herself and begins to speak to him about the brush, but he holds up his hand, shakes his head, and, still smiling, says something in Spanish.

He must know English. Didn't Solita say so? He's writing a screenplay, like everybody and their brother in Los Angeles. He wouldn't be writing it in Spanish, would he? Maybe he is.

She expects some kind of camaraderie to happen between them, something about Solita: my housecleaner, your common-law wife. Isn't she a lovely girl? How is she today? But language is once again a problem.

She goes to the side of the house with him and pantomimes the work. The sun, well on the ascent, pummels them. A few thin clouds diffuse the light so that the sky looks bleached. The air is still.

Luis nods as she talks and moves her hands in swaths.

"I want this and this juniper here to stay. This little tree stays. These Pride of Madeiras have gotten out of hand. Can you prune them or something?—prune? prunya?—to make them more proportionate. If not, they should go. Everything else goes. Cut! It goes!"

To her gladness, Ty Brandewine stumbles out in his shorts and bare feet to the newspaper box. She calls to him and he comes over cheerfully.

"I didn't think you'd be up so early, Ty. Thank you again for such a nice evening. I—Arthur and I will have to talk more about the—the thing." She asks him to help her communicate to Luis about the Pride of Madeiras. "And please ask him how much, and can he do it all today?"

"So this is Solita's grass-mowing boyfriend."

"Yes."

As Ty speaks with Luis she watches the laborer. Something about him is familiar to her, something about his eyes. There is a particular kind of activity there, a pattern she knows. What is it?

Down in her heart she is angry with Luis for being unsupportive of Solita's efforts to read and write. But Solita loves him. Well, she's young and has hormones. Elnice wants to like Luis for Solita's sake, or at least find in him something to admire. She wishes he would realize that an educated woman is a tremendous asset to a man, not to mention society as a whole.

Ty slaps Luis on the shoulder the way a farmer might slap the withers of a dray horse.

"Everything's fine. He can do it all today, it'll cost you seventy-five bucks, and he'll haul away the debris."

"Good."

Luis emits a sound like a giggle, but Elnice can't imagine that is what it is. He readjusts his hat on his head, smiling.

"OK! OK!" his voice is oddly insubstantial for such a solid fellow. Almost a tight voice. It doesn't go with the smiles and the easy strong movements.

Ah! The pattern. She'd seen it hundreds of times before in children who were far smarter than they pretended to be, either to get more attention or to deflect it. The naughtiest children she ever knew had been showcases of this sort of thing. You could see it: the dull looks interspersed with flashes of craft. The dull look was a put-on; the flashes they couldn't help, weren't aware of.

It's unsettling to detect such nonsense in a grown man.

Luis trots to his truck, pulls out a mattock and an armlong pruning saw, and unleashes himself on the underbrush.

She turns to Ty and thanks him again.

"It's I who should thank you, Elnice. No buyer's remorse yet?"

"Haha. Well, you know, I haven't looked in the checkbook register yet to see what Arthur wrote."

"Haha!" Ty rubs his chest.

"You look pretty fresh this morning."

"You wouldn't say that if you knew my mind. I'm half mad trying to figure out who to approach for the ingénue role. It's got to be an unknown, I feel this more surely now than ever. I dunno." He wanders back to his house.

Elnice retreats inside and peeks at Luis through the dining-room window. His back and legs are all she can really see from that angle given the overhanging vegetation. His legs move like pistons, his feet pushing against the earth in worn lace-up boots, *leveraging* the ground, this she can see as clearly as anything.

The strength of men never ceases to awe her. Even Arthur, whippet-like Arthur before his emphysema could lift heavy things—he'd carried an enormous iron-framed sofa bed on his back up three flights of stairs once without getting a hernia—and he could force any tool to work on anything, he could pry and screw and pound with incredible force when necessary, his biceps and neck cords bulging.

Now, his hair wetted down on his skull from his shower and dressed in his red sweatsuit, he joins her peeking at Luis. "They can work, man. Those Mexicans, they put me to shame. One time, my God, I was a kid, remember when I had that damn job with that contractor after the chemical works closed? We were laying these drain pipes and I had to start a trench by hand, the guy was too cheap to rent a trencher, let the college boy dig it, right? Twenty feet long it had to be, and three feet deep. It took me half the day just to make a three-by-three-by-one-foot hole in that clay. I was exhausted! My hands were a mess! These two Mexicans took pity on me. They grabbed the tools and if those bastards couldn't *dig*! Laughing at me the whole time. Man, were they strong." His eyes, hooded, look off into the past.

He goes out and greets Luis, to indicate his place as the householder. Elnice watches Luis straighten up, shake hands, bob his head.

Returning—slowly, slowly—Arthur remarks, "Nice fella. He's about half done already. Pulling out three-inch stumps with his bare hands." Arthur's hand is smudged from shaking with Luis.

"I want to talk to you after you've had something to eat," she tells Arthur. "Would you like some oatmeal?"

"No, I just feel like some toast. I'll make it."

Seeing that Fresco has gone insane with friendliness toward the visitor, Elnice lets him out on the cable. The creature shoots out to the end of the metal cord and strains against it like a sled dog, barking ceaselessly.

Luis pauses, looking, smiling faintly.

"This is Fresco!" cries Elnice. "Fresco!"

The man drops his mattock. He doesn't set it down, he drops it, then he walks over to make friends with the dog. Fresco licks his hands, receives a rubbing. Elnice observes the dog's spine bow downward under the vigorous pressure of Luis's hands. Luis goes back to work, leaving Fresco to bark deliriously at the end of his cable.

She returns to her vantage point at the dining-room window. Then something shocking happens.

Fresco's tether snaps with a *zoing!* and he zooms joyously, barking, toward his new friend. Before Elnice has a chance to react—to turn from the window to go catch the dog—he rockets back the other way, airborne, yelping, having been launched toward the patio by a subtle, sharp movement of Luis's work boot.

She cries out. "Fresco! He kicked Fresco!" She clutches the bosom panel of her Lorna Emberly top. "Arthur, he *really* kicked Fresco!"

"Well, what'd Fresco do to him? Try to bite him?"

"Of *course* not! Oh my God! I can't believe it! Honey—do something!"

"I didn't see it, El. I'm sure he didn't mean anything. Is Fresco OK or not?"

She goes outside. The sun casts fierce shadows everywhere. Fresco limps to her, whining. She stares accusingly at Luis, who stands momentarily straight, like a broad knife stuck into the ground. He merely meets her look with a blank smile.

And she does nothing.
Knowledge is not power, never has been.

12: A Hundred and a Half

As if he'd been staring directly into their souls, Ty had said, "You'd be surprised how much movie a few hundred thousand dollars can buy." In fact, besides their school district pensions and their Hollywood digs, the Cokers' fortune hovers around two hundred and ninety thousand dollars. Children, the traditional money-sump of marriage, had never been a factor; their salaries had been at the top of the scale for years; they'd been fairly frugal not out of discipline but by preference; they'd netted a hundred and five thousand from the sale of their home in Reamus. They'd never craved fancy vacations or gambling or expensive toys. A new car—Buicks worked for them—after a hundred thousand miles.

Correction: they used to take quasi-grand vacations, once every four years. They went to the summer Olympics, planning far in advance, securing the cheapest rates for airfare and housing. Arthur loved to see the track and field events, and Elnice, a competitive tumbler in her day, got her kicks watching the gymnastics and diving. They went to the museums and gardens in those foreign cities too. A two-week overseas trip once every four years.

Half their money is in mutual funds, half in certificates of deposit. Tidy and safe.

Luis is gone, the work done, Elnice will leave for church in twenty minutes.

She sits and watches Arthur eat a buttered English

muffin with raspberry preserves. On one hand the money is half hers, yet on the other, Arthur is sick and needs to feel in control of *something* important, yet on the third hand did that make it OK for him to be a tyrant, or a fool? His face is serene as he chews and swallows.

"Honey," she begins, "you know, we might have to tap into our principal someday." She can all too easily imagine herself unable to care properly for him or herself, the both of them drooling into their porridge while Fresco makes shit-berms everywhere because they're too poor to pay for help. "If I have to be in a home," she says, "I want to be in one where they keep me clean. A good one. Do you know how much places like that cost?"

"Precisely the point," he says, wiping his lips.

"How much did you write the check for?"

"Our checking balance is now two thousand four hundred-some."

"You wrote a check for ten thousand dollars and gave it to Ty? We had twelve thousand in that account. You wrote him a check for ten thousand dollars?"

"I'm willing to load in a hundred and a half."

"A hundred and a half? A hundred and a half?" She can't bring her mind to it. She grips the edge of the table. It tilts slightly on the edge of its curved pedestal. Arthur reaches for his coffee cup.

"We can liquidate," he explains, "the municipal bonds and the utilities and that would more than do it. They're not making us anything; they're just sitting there. Ty can make a lot of movie with a hundred and fifty thousand dollars. That's what I promised him last night when I handed him the check, anyway. So actually minus the ten we're talking one-forty."

"Dear God."

"Are you all right, El?"

"Dizzy. I'm dizzy."

"Very funny."

"I am. I feel like Soviet satellites are shooting me with space rays. I don't know what to do."

"Come on."

Elnice realizes she needs to actually argue this one. "What if the movie *flops*, honey? What if something happens to destroy it before it even gets *finished*?"

"They have insurance against catastrophes," answers Arthur. "And it won't flop."

"Why not?"

"I just know it. Just a feeling I have." He sets the muffin crust down and gets that starting-line look in his eyes again. "I wish you would just trust me on this."

"Arthur, tell me. Why are you so hell-bent on signing our life savings over to Ty Brandewine?"

He gives her the longest, deepest stare he'd ever given her. Longer, even, than on their wedding night. He clears his throat.

"Because he called me an athlete."

He had. Ty had used that noun in reference to Arthur, he'd begun a sentence with "Being an athlete..." and that sentence was about confidence.

So that was what it takes, thinks Elnice. The male animal is in charge of all men after all, all the time. The rest— shirts and ties, the Magna Carta, UNICEF, the Parthenon, "Starry Night", all a hoax. Macho...male animal...prowess. For them it boils down to prowess...It's that simple for them? It's really *that* simple?

She should be glad that Arthur is no longer getting ready to die. Simple.

What does *she* boil down to?

Motherhood is it for so many women. She felt as if she'd parented for decades, teaching, but now, although Solita has been awakening a surge of protective camaraderie in her, she feels empty and confused.

She'd gotten and kept a good husband, one who wasn't a drunk or a hitter.

She'd never burned a bra but never kept her mouth too shut either.

Her way of fostering equality between the sexes was to insist to her pupils that arithmetic was really quite easy, and that boys as well as girls would benefit from learning to tumble and dance. She did not tell them that anybody can grow up to be President of the United States.

She observed the women's movement and concluded that the feminist leaders couldn't decide whether they wanted to take over the world or somehow shame the men into handing it to them. Revolution became irrelevant as the activists transformed themselves from militants to pundits, to theorists, to *insiders*.

Meanwhile, the men had plowed on, living their lives, building, inventing, *getting*, snorting, clubbing trees when the urge struck, their actions governed by nothing more complicated than the notion of *prowess*.

If only she had been born in Los Angeles. The things she would know by now!

As it is, Elnice feels like a dupe. A smug little overweight dupe sitting up in the Hollywood Hills. She feels dazed, she feels embarrassed, but as yet she does not feel wrathful.

That afternoon the Cokers stand side by side on the deck in the rich late light gazing out into the canyon, each thinking. The canyons will remain green and moist for weeks, their vegetation madly converting the carbon dioxide that filters up from the sardine-can neighborhoods below into cheerful little oxygen molecules.

There is a resonance, a synchronicity, to the Cokers' brain waves. It is remarkable how often their thoughts turn, in tandem, toward the bizarre and the dangerous.

They had never been hip, they know now better than ever. They'd believed themselves to be hip at times, as when finding their way around Munich with a phrasebook or experimenting with unlikely sexual techniques. They knew about things like Cuisinarts and styling mousse and futons and Pictionary when those things were just barely catching on.

But what could have prepared them for Los Angeles?

A place where you can rent a Maserati by the hour, a place where people risk blood poisoning in order to get fat scraped from their butts—or added to it. A place where a mudslide or an earthquake or a giant meteorite could strike at any moment, like right when you're shampooing your hair and *smack*! the water main breaks and there you are with no way to rinse, and the kids screaming and a boulder on top of you. A place where the haves really have it, but how they must shiver in their socks whenever they accidentally flip onto one of the black talk radio stations and hear the angry voices for two or three seconds.

And none of these L.A. people know how to drive in the rain.

13: So Very Alive

The FedEx man quits Jason M's cube with a bulky package: the proofs of his latest manual, on the way to the printer. It's a honker: five hundred seventy-eight dense pages of text and diagrams, with a Pulitzer-short-list title if there ever was one: *Operations and Maintenance Guide to the Contrailpoint 3000*. Here's how to run this computer-assisted airplane-making mechanical slave.

Just perfect, the proofs are, every error in place, and a week under deadline. Of course, the dead-tree-based version of the documentation is unnecessary; the version that gets loaded into the machine's computer is perfectly adequate. But the manual must be printed and presented with the expensive machine, essentially as swag for the factory managers buying it. Yes, it shows, we've been thorough. Should the apocalypse come and destroy every-thing digital, you will still have this critically important artifact.

Jason M is not a crude guy, thus what he does is perfect for him: long-term, subtle work. Much corporate sabotage is blunt and immediate, we see it all the time: the destruc-tion of machinery, theft small and large, work stoppages unrelated to union woes. Indeed, blunt events have already happened at this plant, but Jason M's work is like produc-ing a chronic illness. Doctors can rush in and fix an emergency, but a slow progressive sickness is so much harder to eradicate.

Jason M hunkers in his cube, inhaling the manly tang of the multi-hundred-dollar leather briefcase he's recently treated himself to. Within the briefcase nestle a suave goatskin pen case, a calf-bound notebook, and a key fob made from a piece of upcycled bridle leather from an Amish stable. Tech writers are mad for leather accessories, if you didn't know.

Jason M, who should therefore be terribly happy, gazes at a document on his computer screen. Section One. The next manual, for an outhouse-sized machine that will mill intricate slices of metal to tolerances of a thousandth of an inch, awaits him. He blasted through the table of contents before lunch, using as a template the table of contents of the manual he just sent off to the printer. And now for Section One.

Yes. Section One.

He has developed a twitch in one eye.

He turns from the screen and reaches for a scratch pad.

LISTEN, I'M HAVING SECOND THOUGHTS.

He crosses that out.

I'M CONCERNED WE MIGHT HURT SOMEONE.

He rubs his lips with a sweaty finger.

The rest of the world thinks nobody in Los Angeles has a conscience. They think Angelenos talk a good game, but come on: all those hours spent in their car cocoons burning gas, all that water they let evaporate from their swimming pools. Well, Jason M knows at least you're supposed to act as if you have a conscience. But in order to gallop across the finish line first, you pretty much have to get around the conscience issue. He has been getting around his quite nicely for some time, but now it's rearing its ugly little head.

Speaking of ugly little heads, Jason M's pelvis feels as if

it wants to crack right open and spew semen all over his cube, because everybody in the whole world has a girlfriend. Every single disgraced politician has a girlfriend. Guys on death row have a girlfriend. Jason M's own shit-sucking moron of a boss has a girlfriend. Why doesn't he?

After work Jason M looks up gyms. He doesn't want a health club, he wants a gym, a place where guys box and get tough in the company of other guys. He calls one boxing gym and a woman answers. He hangs up. He calls another one and asks the guy if he knows any gyms that don't have websites.

"I don't know what you're talking about."

"I mean, I'm looking for a place that doesn't even bother to advertise."

The guy pauses. "Are you on line now?"

"Yeah."

"Well, Google Neff's gym. It's down on Western."

Jason M does it. "Nothing."

"There ya go."

"Is Neff's strictly boxing and training?"

"Yeah."

"Does it smell bad?"

The guy stops again. "Sure, pal, it stinks like any gym."

"Thanks."

He ends the call and his phone rings immediately.

"Jason. Laurie."

"Yeah, hi. How are you, sweetheart?"

"Listen. Why don't you come over for dinner tonight?" His sister's voice is its usual pissed-off, discovering-a-flat-tire self.

"Well, OK. Is..."

"Is what?"

"Is everything all right?"

"Sure. Why wouldn't it be?"

"Well, isn't Chuck still in Ireland?"

"Yeah."

"Well, fine! I mean, forgive my asking, but will there be anything to eat?"

Laurie says, "Oh. Yeah. Bring a sack of hamburgers, OK?"

"OK."

"And pick up a six-pack too, and a couple of Cokes for Erin."

Laurie holds the door open for him as he climbs the steps under the weight of three sacks of groceries as well as the fast food and drinks. He's got apples and peanuts and Spaghetti-O's and Chips Ahoy. The house is a vinyl-sided colonial in Torrance. Jason M always feels extra hot in Torrance for no good reason unless it's something about the name. Torrance, torrid. Plus there's a high ratio of concrete to grass in Torrance, which will make any place feel hotter. His sister's house has central air, though.

He hasn't even put down the stuff, hasn't taken off his nubuck-trimmed MGM ball cap, and Laurie is whispering feverishly into his ear:

"She's about to self-destruct if somebody doesn't do something, the little bitch's been *stealing*, Jason! She's got a load of shit under her bed, stuff—it's shit from, it's shit from I don't know where, the mall, Walgreen's. I cannot fucking believe this is happening! Chuck's gonna have a shit-fit. And you know who he'll blame." She looks at him impatiently. "Me."

Jason M scrutinizes his sister, who is eight years his senior. She's sweating, her scalp is glistening beneath her chicken-feather hairdo, she's smoking down a Virginia

Slims Menthol Light in deep drags. Her cheeks hang on her face like small flat cakes.

Somewhere in the house a stereo is playing the kind of chaotic sing-yelling that appeals to mainstream teenagers and schizophrenics.

He gets Laurie into the kitchen, pops beers for the two of them. He glances apprehensively toward the source of the music, upstairs and to the rear of the house.

"She won't come down until I call her," Laurie says. The music changes, now a boy's baby-sweet voice is crooning swear words. Laurie doesn't notice her brother's eye twitch.

Jason M reflects on his own adolescence. He went in for the occult: black magic, séances, veganism, and general spookiness, while Laurie went more in the smoking-in-the-johns direction. The occult kids were smarter, reading forbidden texts and arguing metaphysics, dressing monastically in ugly second-hand clothes. Capes. They were crazy for capes. Rebellious, yes, but not as brainlessly self-vandalizing as the others.

Laurie's talking again in a trembly voice. "You gotta help me, Jason." Her hands are small and beautiful; Jason has always admired them. She's wringing the hell out of them. "The tags are still attached, it's all brand-new junk, makeup and brassieres and shit, I recognize this is exactly the kind of—"

Her husband Chuck is a cop in the L.A.P.D. She is a dispatcher.

"I mean, Jason, this is my worst nightmare. Honestly."

This is an overstatement, uncharacteristic of her, who doesn't even well up when Chuck tells about helping the wagon guys spread a sheet over a little kid dead in the street. Chuck does. Jason does.

He wonders how much she's been drinking. Jason knows from Chuck that Laurie is famously the worst dispatcher in the department, hired in haste a decade ago and now unfireable because of seniority. She accidentally cuts off cops in trouble, gets information wrong, and freaks out if she has to handle too much at once, which is about forty times a day. She can't even keep groceries in the house when Chuck is away. Chuck generally does the shopping and takes the hard line with Erin. He's a straight arrow, but not naïve about kids or anything else.

"—like a goddamn little Gypsy," Laurie is saying—

Jason has never stolen anything in his life.

"—and the *point* is, Chuck's ten thousand miles away, God knows when he'll be back."

"How's his grandfather?"

"Well, like, still breathing. I wish the son of a bitch would just die. When it's my time to go, I hope I just go. I dunno."

Chuck's grandfather back in Ireland has begun an end-game with leukemia, which Laurie resentfully seems to consider a particularly Irish disease. Chuck got leave and went there two weeks ago to help the old man meet death; it would happen perhaps in another week, perhaps a month.

"Well, first of all, what were you doing snooping under Erin's bed?" Jason sets his hips against the countertop while his sister braces the refrigerator with her shoulder. The kitchen hasn't fared well in the two weeks since Chuck left. Every surface appears mottled and gummy, and he can smell the garbage can.

Laurie says, "I was *looking* for my hedge clippers."

He asks her what in God's name they'd be doing under Erin's bed.

"You tell me," she says. With grim patience she explains that *whenever* she can't find something she systematically searches the entire house and garage, sparing no cranny; we are merely talking thorough police work here.

"It was purely innocent, then," Jason says.

"Purely innocent, yes, fuck you if you don't believe me."

"Does she know you found her stash?"

"No. I don't think so."

"You're not comfortable confronting her with it?"

"*No,* I'm not comfortable!"

"You want me to talk to her."

"Yeah!"

One time Jason made the mistake of offering to deliver bad news to Erin (the family dog ate a box of rodent poison and went to heaven) and now forever he gets to play the heavy whenever Laurie can't cope and Chuck is unavailable. Being so much closer to Erin's age had helped Jason to get a rapport going with her that Laurie envied but never tried to duplicate.

"You know, Laurie, if she were a boy—"

"Say no more. I know. If I had a son he'd be a thug. He'd be building up a collection of all the knives Chuck takes off the bad guys."

"He'd be our little thug."

"Yeah." She laughs, finally. "Erin's not a bad kid, but I have no fucking idea what she does all the time. If I knew how to approach this, I would," she lies. "Chuck'd know, at least he'd take over and it'd be off my screen. I don't deserve this on top of everything else."

"Laurie, I love you, but you basically suck as a mother."

She shrugs.

The hamburgers are getting cold.

Jason asks, "Did you find any drugs?"

"No, thank God. She's slipping away from me, though."

"Why are you so upset about this?"

"I wouldn't be so upset if it *was* drugs, you know? I mean, I know how life is: a drug bust just isn't the same as a shoplifting bust, it's—I mean, you can get slammed for it, OK, but—it's just not considered as serious. A pot bust, I mean. When you're applying for a job, whatever. She's a juvenile now, but in two years' time! I might suck as a mother, but I've told my kid what's right and what's wrong. Chuck took her to see some kids who've fucked up their lives in Juvenile, but she didn't get it. She's so goddamn bullheaded. Little stuff leads to big stuff. And don't ask if me and Chuck could get her off the hook if she gets nailed. Maybe, is the answer."

They decide to have the hamburgers later, just zap 'em.

Jason climbs the stairs to Erin's room. He taps the door, steps back.

"Uncle Jace!" Erin is joyful for just an instant, then immediately guarded. She turns down her stereo.

Erin was actually reading a textbook at her desk; Jason sees a diagram of the inner ear, with meant-to-be-fun-looking colored arrows. The girl drops into a white bean-bag chair on the floor while Jason straddles the desk chair.

They talk. Or rather, Jason M opens up a line of argument. He's hoping to rely on his charisma, knowing Erin sees him as a cool adult. She has seen snapshots of him jet-skiing in Mexico with a tour group from work.

"Honey, I don't know how to say this so I'll just plunge in." She must have looked stricken, because suddenly the earth splits in half.

"It's Dad! Is it Dad?" The girl's emotional trigger is like a matchhead; before Jason can open his mouth again she nearly shrieks, "He's been in a plane crash! It's a terrorist plane crash, isn't it!"

"No! Honey, no, it's nothing like that! Your father's fine, it's nothing about your father!"

The walls are plastered with rock-star posters the likes of which would have been found only in porn shops in olden times. Clothes crumpled everywhere, clothes in a variety of styles suggesting that Erin is perpetually undecided as to the way she wishes to present herself to the world: big baggy boy-girl or teeny-weeny girl-boy?

But the dominant feature of the room is the unmade twin bed, angled out from a corner. It glows with life and cheer, bathed in the golden wash from the study lamp on the desk. Cotton quilted bedspread, pink percale sheets, it's a rolling landscape tumbled with childhood leftovers: an orange plush Tyrannosaurus Rex, a crocheted clown doll, a Cinderella doll, and four throw pillows with appliqués of ballerinas in various poses. A threadbare but indomitably jaunty Winnie-the-Pooh perches on the windowsill.

It's a bedroom in transition, the harsh equipment of unmodulated adulthood tossed with the dear detritus of infancy. The smell is right, too: four or five different colognes, spices and flowers and fruits mingling in olfactory confusion.

This evening Erin is dressed half-and-half: a skinny leopard-print stretch top over a pair of beefy cargo pants. The sight of her breasts and upper body, slight and willowy, gives Jason M a pang: so young, so pliant.

"Your mother," Jason announces, "snooped under your bed and saw all the stuff you stole. Now OK, the snooping's between you and her, the Ten Commandments do not say thou shalt not snoop under thy daughter's bed. It's because she gives a shit about you that she's so freaked out."

"She's freaked out? You mean this is like the first time she's ever looked?" The girl lightly gnaws her lips, which bear traces of magenta gloss within black liner. "I can't believe she hasn't looked before, I thought she knew all about this."

"Well, what are you up to?"

"Come on, Uncle Jace! It's just junk from stores. They never miss it. Plus it's fun. It gives me a—I don't know, I just feel so *alive* when I'm doing it. For *once*."

This Jason M can identify with.

Yes, the girl's onto something here, the thrill, the risk. Jason thinks about his job, yes sir, no sir, who sir me sir? And he thinks about his second job, which is to subvert his first job. It does make him feel alive, in control, and certainly richer. He isn't merely pushing paper around; his work is creative. He feels a gritty resonance in what his niece is saying.

"But hon, stealing is wrong."

"Is it? Like how?"

"What do you mean, like how?"

The girl twines her long hair around her wrist and says nothing.

Jason M clears his throat. "Well, tell me about it. How do you do it, where do you go?"

"Oh, around." She tells how her 'n' Yin 'n' McKenzie go to the malls and strip plazas— "It's so *easy*, Uncle Jace! They don't even *care* if you take stuff."

"How do you know that?"

"If they did they wouldn't make it so easy! Lifting's fun! We just slip stuff into our pants. See!" And she lunges forward and pulls more stuff from under the bed, shorts and tops and jumbles of makeup and leggings and bustiers and shoes!—the clothes fill the air like Gatsby's shirts, and Erin's manner is similar to that of the great, crooked, unfulfilled man: a little frantic, a little sad.

Jason M notes the bright logos and odd color combinations currently in fashion: brown and turquoise together in stripes, eye-hurting reds and golds jammed next to each other in blobby prints. Of the logos the predominant one is Monkipel, hippest of the hip these days. None but the coolest have even heard of Monkipel. He counts three tank tops plastered with the smirking Monkipel character, half rhesus, half motorcycle. "So what? You need all this stuff?"

The girl squeezes her eyes shut theatrically as her body convulses with irritation.

"*Ugh!* You could say, OK, I don't *need* anything! OK. I don't *need* a thing. Just lock me in this room all day."

"Erin."

"My life is a *pit!* Uncle Jace, you have *no idea.* Half the time I am so bored I could die. I almost *do* die, half the time. Basically—OK. OK." She makes an enormous effort to explicate the obvious. "I told you. I *need* only *some* of this stuff. OK? But what I *really* need is the rush. Something where I feel like I'm *doing* something."

"Whatever happened to throwing water balloons at the school bus?"

"Uncle Jace."

"Never mind. Tell me more, honey."

It was so easy, she tells him, it almost started to get boring. "And then," she breathes, "I got *caught!*" She describes being taken to the manager's office where they tried to scare the crap out of her "but I brazened it out! I didn't have any I.D. on me, so finally they just took my picture with a Polaroid and told me I'm *barred* from the store! They *barred* me, as if that means anything. Whoa, how incredibly frightening! I've been back! In disguise! Twice!"

Jason M's stomach feels as if it is trying to digest a fried sneaker.

He has never pilfered in his life. Never shoplifted, never boosted anything at school or from friends. Even at work he draws a line, won't take home pencils and memo pads.

Erin insists, "This is no big deal. What is so *wrong* with taking stuff where nobody'll miss it?"

In the poster just above her head the nearly nude emaciated guitarist and his blood-soaked logotype scream *sex!* And *sex!* scream the stolen bustiers and face paint. So the girl craves forbidden thrills. Is that so bad?

A contrasting image rolls through Jason M's mind, that of Chuck, Erin's wholesome brave cop dad, sitting in the front room of his grandfather's thatched hut in the Wicklow Hills, smoothing the comatose old dude's coverlet, perhaps learning how to knit from the vicar's wife. Could he really have handled this? Can anyone?

"Uncle Jace, what's wrong with your eye?"

"Nothing, sweetheart."

"Are you doing it on purpose?"

"It's just stress."

"Oh."

"Erin, the point isn't whether the store will miss the stuff."

Instantly the girl takes a new tack: not only is it not wrong, it's tremendously *right* to do what she does!

"These big corporations—they don't care—they're horrible, you know. They use child labor, and they don't pay their workers a living wage. They're death machines in the developing world, but all they want is more globalization.

Everybody knows that. These corporations rip off the poor, so it's only fair for some of us to rip them back!"

From the mouths of teachers and school chums they get it, Jason figures. Agit-prop buzzwords come thick and fast from Erin's raised consciousness: "globalization," "sweatshops," "ethical pollution," "predatory business practices," even "multinational conglomerates" and "the I.M.F."

"Honey, do you know what the I.M.F. is?"

A withering look makes it clear she does not.

"You know," he says, "even if the company's a shit, even if your boss is a shit, there are other ways to...voice disagreement."

"Yeah, well, talk is cheap, isn't it?" Will Erin grow up to be as self-indulgent and incompetent as her mother?

Come on, Jason M, tell her. Ask her if her best friend would miss fifty cents from her purse! Ask her if she plans to cheat on her taxes when she grows up, because the government'll never miss it! Ask her who she thinks pays for her thievery: CEOs? Do you suppose they reduce their own bonuses according to what gets stolen from their corporations? Tell her you can rationalize anything you want. Come on, Jason M! Epiphany now.

But he stares at the chubby Tyrannosaurus Rex perched on the precipice of a ballerina pillow, looming over an unsuspecting Cinderella doll as if about to snap her in two.

He tries the practical approach.

"If you get caught again, you might not be so lucky."

"Daddy'll take care of it."

"Don't be so sure. He isn't."

The girl jounces as if her beanbag chair encountered a pothole.

"He isn't?"

"Honey, being a cop's kid only goes so far. Take my word for it."

Erin hugs her knees, which look like soda straws popping up from the folds of her gigantic canvas pants.

"I guess—oh, Uncle Jace, are you serious?"

"Yes, damn it to hell!"

The girl muses into the middle distance. "Maybe I should tone it down, then."

"For your father's sake. You love him, don't you?"

Instantly teary-eyed, she nods.

"And your mother's sake too."

The girl shrugs.

"Well, they love you. They don't want you getting in trouble for something stupid." Jason M feels as if he's going to throw up, but the sensation passes. "So honey, you'll think about this."

Erin, collecting herself, reflects, "Seriously, Uncle Jace. The key is not to get caught. Right?"

Jason M lets go of his end of the ideological tug-rope.

"Yeah, pretty much. Not to get caught."

And Erin falls back into her soft beanbag with a relieved expression. "I feel better."

They sit together, hands limp in their laps and eyes hooded like monk and nun coming to the end of a midnight rosary, gazing at the comfy little landscape of Erin's bed, the T.Rex licking his chops over the nubile Cinderella while good old Pooh-Bear smiles on vacantly from the windowsill.

14: New Words

The more Elnice sees of Los Angeles, the more she likes it. To be sure, harmful individuals inhabit the city— murderers and people who throw candy wrappers on the floor in movies—and in large numbers, but such people are to be found everywhere. Problems arise when peoples' reservoirs of respect for self and others run low. There are so many interactions involving lane changes and drinking fountains and extra mustard and defective ceiling fans, people get worn out patience-wise, respect-wise. Elnice, however, is not a person who excuses herself very readily. Her fuse is long.

Rude people, she has learned, are more interesting than perfunctorily polite ones. Who remembers the person who spews a vacant *Have a good one*, when later the same day one hears, *Thanks for nothin', lady,*? Elnice thinks about these things while loading and unloading the dish-washer and while massaging her gums with her rubber Oral-B stimulator.

The Friday after the Ty dinner Solita brings with her a list of five words, printed in fairly confident letters on a strip of brown paper torn from a grocery bag. Young children, whose fine-motor control is far below that of adults, naturally produce crooked writing; an adult who has never written before produces a much better result.

"What happened to the yellow tablet I gave you?"

Elnice asks.

The girl drops her eyes. "The tablet I lost her."

Elnice sees this is not the truth. "*It*," she says, " I lost *it*."

"I lost *it*."

"Well, let's take a look at these new words!" They sit right down, Solita's eyes eager.

"*Encryption*," Elnice reads. "That's interesting. I think mostly it means a high tech kind of thing." Solita smiles attentively. Elnice pronounces the word again, carefully.

"Well, literally it means to put something into code. *Code*. A secret way of writing. Where you scramble up the letters." Using the gold Cross ballpoint pen given her by the other teachers when she retired, she prints MEET ME AFTER CHURCH on a new yellow tablet. Beneath it she prints EMTE EM FAETR HCRUHC. "See, this means this. All I've done is taken the letters and reversed them two by two. See?" She speaks slowly and repetitively, knowing Solita isn't picking up everything, but most things.

Solita sees.

"So unless you know the code, you can't make out what this message says. Let's do *gracias*." She prints GRACIAS and RGCAAIS.

Solita gets it.

"Encryption," Elnice repeats. "Now for the next word. *Custom*. Custom. A custom is a traditional thing people do. A thing people do over and over until, until, well, it becomes customary, and then they forget why they started doing it in the first place!" She laughs. "For instance, it's a custom in Japan to take off your shoes before going indoors. It's a custom in America to shake hands when you meet someone. What's a Mexican custom?"

"Cinco de Mayo."

"Well, Cinco de Mayo is a holiday. What do you do on

that holiday?"

Solita flicks her fingers to the sky. "Bango!"

"Fireworks! Yes, it's *customary* to shoot off fireworks on Cinco de Mayo. Custom. Customary. Very good, honey. Now let's see. *Virus*. Virus. It's a bug... no, not really a bug. It's a microorganism. It's a *germ*. Something that makes you sick."

"These two words they were next together."

"They were next to each other? Custom and virus?" Elnice blinks. "Custom virus? Custom virus." Deliberately, her upper teeth capture her lower lip. "Where did you find these words, honey?"

"Papers."

"The papers? The newspapers?" Elnice wonders whether Arthur is listening through the sounds of classic NCAA football highlights on TV.

Solita isn't sure. "In papers of Luis."

"Oh. The things he's working on, his screenplay?"

Solita thinks so.

"All right, let's go on. *Oblivion*. Oblivion. Gee, honey, you sure picked some unusual words."

"I don't know them and many other words I saw."

"Of course. Well, oblivion is, um, forgetting. Like a place where you don't do anything or feel anything. No memory. No remembering."

Solita looks at her.

Elnice is beginning to see what a challenge self-directed learning is.

"It's an abstract concept. We should have stuck with nouns. Well, let's go on. What is this? *Betaine*. Betaine? It sounds French, like a hat or somewhere where they make cheese."

She gets the dictionary. "Um, well! I see betaine is a

naturally occurring compound, like a nutrient. From sugar beets, it says, and it's used to treat neurological disorders. Hm. Let's come back to this word another time, when your vocabulary is bigger. Now what's this?" She reads off, "C nine H eleven N O four."

Arthur grunts suddenly, and Elnice looks over to see a pileup of happy guys celebrating an impossible touchdown. "What a catch," Arthur calls. "It's like there was a ladder in the air he just climbed."

She asks, "Were the letters and numerals mixed together like this?"

"Yes."

"Were they uneven, like this, with the numbers a little below the line of the letters?"

"Yes."

"Well, I don't know what this means. It would seem to be a formula, a chemical formula. I don't know what for. Honey, uh?"

Solita waits.

"What is Luis's screenplay about? Do you know? Has he told you the story?"

"He say the screenplay is a secret. Like encryption!" Solita laughs, delighted with her new command of vocabulary. Her English really is getting better and better.

"Haha," says Elnice.

15: Not as Easy as it Looks

Keith B, the vice president who's having the devil's own time developing a proper website for his company, is a member at a swanky country club, perhaps *the* swankiest country club in Los Angeles. That's a debatable thing, but not too debatable. His membership is a perk of his job as a top company officer.

When Keith plays at the club, a kid parks his car, an old guy cleans his shoes and hands him towels, and boobsome young lasses serve him hamburgers made of chopped filet mignon. The course itself is the place Jesus Christ, away these many years, would pick as the venue for his second coming, no joke, it is that totally transcendental.

Today, however, is not an official golf day. It's an unofficial one, and this is how Keith works it: he peels out of the office at noon, announcing an urgent meeting at the offices of those fellows, oh those fine fellows over at—you know, the hardware men. They want to show him how they've managed to teach their old mainframe model a bag of new tricks, and he must go see. They're claiming it's a completely new machine, but of course he suspects otherwise. Important to have a look at it, though, so—

Off he goes, slumming.

"Ring!" goes Tina G's phone. She is the document smuggler, the photocopying pixie, and she is in her apartment, busy rolling up a bunch of spreadsheets from the boss's inbox as tightly as she can, preparatory to wrapping a plastic grocery bag around them and securing the whole thing with some leftover Christmas ribbon. These particular spreadsheets she was unable to get digital files to.

She tries to make a hasty finish to the job before the phone goes to voicemail, but realizes she's not going to make it. She lets the bundle fall apart; the pages whisper as they flatten.

"Hello?" Her tone betrays the slightest trace of annoyance (at whom? her caller? herself?) which might be detectable to someone in the room with her, but would not be to someone on the line unless it happens to be her mother, which it doesn't.

"I'm *bringing* them," she says, and hangs up.

Whack! goes Chantelle W's clubface against her Titleist ProV1X. The ball streaks off toward a clump of trees.

Jason M has dragged his weedy body to Neff's gym on Western Avenue and begun the process of learning to box, which is a manly thing whether done well or poorly. Jason M needs to feel manlier *now* because he's been feeling like such a piece of dogshit.

Anyhow, here he is, hands taped, shoulder muscles more or less in spasm, legs braced stiffly, anchored in his expensive training shoes. When he got the shoes home from the store they looked so sickeningly clean that he rubbed them all over with greasy soot from his hibachi, took one lace out, cut it roughly, and tied it back together. At least his shoes would not give him away as a neophyte.

Bappety-bap. Bappety-bap. Bap-whing!whing! Shit. The speed bag isn't as easy as it looks.

It's easier than golf, though, which—perhaps you've

guessed—he'd been obliged to take up some time ago. During a round of golf his mind feels as if it were running on a treadmill with snatches of cartoons speeding past him going the other way. You have to think about countless variables all at one time: the lie of the ball, the slope you're standing on, distance, the wind. Plus you've got to worry always about the outcome of your shots, before, during, and after making them.

Not like at the gym. With the speed bag, boy—you don't think, you react. With a sparring partner, the same, only with fear-sweat thrown in. Skipping rope: focus, focus, focus. Your mind gets clear.

It isn't as if Jason M were a stupid fellow who needs help to think a thought. No. You should've seen his SAT scores.

It's just that he's gotten in deep. The whole fake-manual-writing thing had merely started as—well, not a *lark.* He wouldn't call it that. He'd been a cynical young person from the get-go, and this, he felt, was as good as a credo. His ethical framework has always been play along but stick the bastards who think they're sticking it to you. And spend the dough. Above all, spend the dough. But Jason M's dogshit feeling is powerful, it's blotting out his feelings of secret pride in taking a bite out of the system.

Money helps. Money always helps, it's good to have money, it's much better to have money than not to have it, but Jason M finds himself inhabiting a world he never knew existed.

Guys without money or brains get women if they look good. Handsome guys can be the biggest jackasses in the world and have to beat women off with gun butts. Multi-millionaire guys get any women they want: the beauties who know how to wear diamonds, or the brainy tigresses who need someone to finance their first novel, you know?

Big guys who act gentle get women. Scrawny guys who know how to pick horses and unclog drains get women. They really do. Famous guys get women, doesn't matter famous for what.

Every guy Jason M knows is a middle-of-the-pack guy who thinks he's an alpha male. Professional guys, guys with good jobs. Not millionaires. Not bums. College-educated guys. Guys who watch Monday Night Football *and* the History Channel. Guys who golf.

These guys—they are making more and more money, actually edging higher and higher into where the rich guys used to be, only there are so many of them—well, the carrot is receding. See? Jason M had thought that an income of two hundred grand a year would be the living end. And it *is*, if you're going to be happy with a crow-eyed cocktail waitress.

But forget it. The competition's intense. Jason M goes to the clubs and has to chop his way through forests of guys the same general size and shape as himself who dress just like him and make the same amount of money—legitimately!—just to buy a drink for some tense anorexic with dead-pet hair who never even read Camus!

Bappety-bap. Bappety-bap. He tries to control the bag by twisting his right fist as he snaps at it. But he misses completely, popping his shoulder ligaments and flinching away from the bag as it rebounds in his face. He forces himself not to glance around to see if anyone was looking.

The gym smells like fish grease, from the shrimp shack next door.

Still it isn't exactly as he'd hoped. It smelled right, yeah. But he wished for a boxing gym that looked more like the ones in movies: stark and dark at the same time, strewn about with ugly brave guys and ugly old trainers. Look at that guy. He looks like a goddamned aerobics instructor, with that fluffy hairdo and the periwinkle tank top and those white baby shoes. The lights are bright in Neff's and too many guys look like they know how to do laundry.

Why go *through* feeling like dogshit, why go *through* all the nightmares, for this? After $36,000 a year, he thought more than two hundred grand, tax-free, would be his ticket.

Still and all Jason M is learning something valuable: that principles are easier to have when nothing's at stake. There is something not to be traded about getting this first-hand, right between the eyes.

He's had a bit of a dialogue with his contact. At first he'd written out a cautious epistle enumerating his many selfless contributions so far and suggesting they find someone else to take over.

NO, came the reply.

Then he tried to write convincingly that actually, he'd done so much to bring about the future downfall of his company that his work was, in fact, finished.

In response he received another $10,000 deposit into his account. Not that it'll last out the month.

LOOK, I'M OUT, was his next message.

NO, YOU'RE NOT. KEEP UP THE GOOD WORK.

It isn't as if they're being nasty about it.

Bappety-bap. Bappety-bap. Bappety-whing-shit!

After two more minutes his arms are rubber.

He banks in Switzerland, not that he was able to get one of those legendary numbered accounts before they started cracking down. The bankers know who he is, but they're discreet and as long as he behaves himself financially, he'll be fine. The advantage of banking with them is that he can more easily convert his money into foreign currencies and precious metals. Try dealing with your credit union on stuff like that. He wishes he'd hung on to more of his earnings, wishes he had a little pile of yellow bars in a box in Europe, but that wasn't the fault of the Swiss. Often he pictures the bank, a little A-frame perched on an Alp, staffed by clean, earnest European people, innocent of the troubles so many of their customers are roasting in. Drinking chocolate and eating bread and butter. Taking the gorgeous view for granted.

Bappety-bap.

Men don't make little girls fall out of the sky with their dolls and mothers and flight attendants and all the other less attractive yet good people on board, the salesmen and hockey scouts and regional vice presidents—pieces of dogshit do. Men don't cause other men's hands to be chopped off in misfiring machinery, or shivs of aluminum to shoot out from the work deck and pierce their skulls— pieces of dogshit do.

Things are coming apart. They know where he lives. He had made a bit of an error. He had made, well, a threat.

LEAVE ME ALONE OR I'LL UNDO EVERYTHING I'VE DONE. He'd delivered that message just the other day.

It was an empty threat, of course; he'd no intention of blabbing, he could get into too much trouble, good Christ the trouble he could get into. The only way he could undo anything would be to go to his boss, or higher, confess, get all the documentation recalled, then revise it, at untold cost and embarrassment. Although they probably wouldn't let him fix it, they'd fire him. Maybe his boss would get canned too for not having checked his work since leafing through his very first manual, which he gave an A to anyway. Jason M could have inserted the lyrics to the South Park theme song on every page of this one and it would have gone to press unchanged.

Then maybe they'd prosecute him on some serious charge.

Or—he could disappear, and phone or send a warning. But those things are easier said than done. How exactly do you become unfindable? It is the kind of thing he would like *to have done*, not something he wants to *do*.

They know where he lives because yesterday morning he awakened to find a hundred-dollar bill on his pillow. Just that.

He was coming out of a dream in which his boss's girlfriend had invited him over for cocktails, fellatio, and massage until the two of them were levitating, sort of, above a body bag containing his entire output of short stories, all those miserable crappy unpublished pages, it was a double-edged dream, you see—

The bill lay next to his face as if starched and ironed. At first he thought it was a giant flat insect and started up like Sean Connery in whichever movie. But it was a message, to be sure.

I was here in the night while you were chewing on your bruxism guard, asswipe. Do you guess this is all I might do next time? Fuck you. Get busy.

Bappety-bap. Fuck me.

He decides to take a few simple precautions until he can make up his mind what to do. New locks, no pizza delivery, keep working on the bod.

Because that's how they get people, they knock out the pizza guy and take his place.

If you don't leave me alone I'll undo everything I've done.

Why did he tell them that? Why the fuck did he tell them that? Because no one fucks with Jason M, for crying out loud. Is he a sniveling quitter? Christ's sake here.

The fellow who got him into the deal—Don H, a funny happy guy who recruited Jason M from the farm machinery outfit he'd been working for and showed him what to do, a more upbeat guy Jason M had never met—he is gone, man, gone like a coffee lid in a gale. He said he'd scored half a million on two different jobs in four years, over and above his paychecks. He set him up with this blind drop deal and that was the end of Don H. Jason M imagines him receiving a caring blow job from a sweet-faced girlfriend in a snug combination cabin/art studio in upstate New York where they grow organic vegetables and ingest LSD every other night.

Jason M has a hard time saving money. Las Vegas is too close, man, too distracting for a stalk-necked stud with a liberal arts degree and no girlfriend. Too much weekend happiness to be had in Vegas. It's a place he outspokenly scorns, of course, as an intellectual should. But in truth, a comped room at the Palace Station—where the locals come to play the slots in their sweatsuits and bedroom slippers—plus one hooker per night in a desert slut hut is as close as Jason M gets to the feeling of having achieved a goal.

When he gets nervous he rereads heroic literature, and that always bolsters him. *To Kill a Mockingbird, Captains Courageous, Siddhartha.*

By God if a man doesn't have principles he's—

What kind of man does he want to be? What kind of man is he now? It doesn't pay to be a man of principle, yet—

That's the whole point, dummy, he tells himself.

His own mind is the highest power he knows.

16: The Poison Fairy Ring

It's the following morning and Luis Perona Gastello is driving a sputtering mowing machine down the seventeenth fairway of the Wilson golf course in Griffith Park, below the imposing observatory where Sal Mineo made such poignant facial expressions at James Dean. An overnight soaking rain has created soft areas, which he steers through carefully.

The Wilson course, one of the cubic zircons in the humble crown of the Los Angeles department of parks and recreation, is smartly designed, heavily used, and spottily maintained. Here the average golf nut can find a game without blowing a whole day's pay.

The view down the first fairway is an old trivia answer: Where did Tiger Woods hit that gorgeous tee shot in his first television commercial? He smacked it here in slow motion, and we saw the ball flying down the misty wide fairway, his arms stretching after it, his life as a superstar just beginning to spool out before him.

Salesmen and middle managers from all over L.A. sneak off to Wilson or its sister courses in the park, Harding and Roosevelt, to play nine or eighteen on a weekday afternoon, cell phones on vibrate, alibis at the ready. Important championships used to be contested on these courses, but due to cutbacks in city services, you wouldn't dream of taking a top client—anyone you wanted to impress—to play golf in Griffith Park. No, the important golf dates get kept at the private courses, Riviera, Bel-Air, Sherwood, or the expensive public drive-tos of Palm Springs.

Hackers who don't know any better and budget-conscious die-hards who do: these are the athletes who crowd up the tee times at Griffith Park. Luis is one of the few men who actually conduct important business at Wilson, Harding, and Roosevelt.

He finishes his pass down the left side of the fairway and stops next to the green. He looks back toward the tee, not to admire his work, for he is in fact indifferent to the beauty of freshly-clipped grassland, but to see where the nearest party has gotten to. It is a foursome of white old-timers who, if shown their own swings on videotape, would cut their throats. They are searching for a lost ball on the opposite side of the fairway, where one of them had duffed it off the tee.

Luis disengages the mower's gears and sets the brake. He hops off, and, reaching for his zipper, hurries a few yards into the woods. Once out of sight he leaves his pants zipped and kicks aside some damp leaf litter to uncover a small plastic bucket lid set into the ground. He lifts it; the bucket is empty except for two beige spiders, one alive, one dead.

"All right," he murmurs. He replaces the lid and the leaf litter and walks out of the woods toward his mower, tugging his belt as he goes. One of the aging wonders hits a relatively good approach shot; he is only short and left of the green by some thirty yards.

This golfer has chosen his own clothing this day, a pair of burnt-orange corduroy pants, cuffs tucked into his socks against the mud, a nylon Dodgers windbreaker, and a planter's-style Greg Norman shark logo hat. He looks damned good and he knows it.

He walks past Luis without acknowledging him, carefully parks his squeaking pull cart next to his ball, and looks down at it.

"GOD DAMN IT!" The aging wonder's ejaculation is accompanied by a sudden thrusting movement of the head, which displaces his Greg Norman hat sideways. The shark logo makes as if to bite his ear.

His fellows, scattered within a fifty-yard range, barely glance at him. Luis climbs up on his mower.

"God *damn* those Koreans!"

Luis perceives that the man's ball has come to rest in a deep divot gouge.

It is common for the Korean golfers who frequent Griffith Park to take huge hacking divots and not replace them. Luis has seen it happen many times. Divots the size of wigs! Non-Koreans do it too, yes, but it does seem to be a key element of Korean golf etiquette, not to replace divots. Touching dirt is considered women's work.

It is also his observation that the white and Chinese retirees are the most maddeningly slow of all players, next to the young assholes who smuggle alcoholic beverages onto the course. The Japanese as a group possess the fewest actual golf skills, and being generally small, cannot overcome their poor technique by brute force, as the big white and black Americans can. Good young golfers of all sorts can play well and keep up a good pace, but they are often guilty of spitting excessively and making caustic loud comments. Latinos—they're a scarcer breed around golf courses in general, except as workers. Every demographic group that plays regularly at Griffith Park develops a razor-sharp awareness of the faults of every other group, and an utter obliviousness to its own.

Luis has learned all these things over the course of five years of mowing, pruning, raking, and digging. He hates it when Solita uses butthead as a synonym for man, but at times he sees her point. No woman knows how right she is half the time.

He feels sorry for the nice guys.

The man whose ball came to rest in the divot hole nudges it out with his wedge, not caring whether his companions see him cheating. Actually, he is the sort who believes that it isn't cheating if you're just evening up something unfair that's been done to you. Still cursing the Koreans he chunks his pitch shot anyway, leaving it ten yards short of the green. He moves on, passing within a few paces of Luis, unconscious of Luis.

As the white retiree has yet again proved, Latino laborers are invisible. Luis is not presumed to speak English, he is not presumed to be intelligent or aware. He is, if anything, presumed to be especially dim: everybody knows that clever, ballsy Latinos get into the drug trade and stay in it until they make a fortune or die in action or both.

After he'd been on the job a few months he'd overheard one of the starters tell a golfer who was fretting aloud about hitting errant shots with his set of rented clubs, "Don't worry about the guys working out there. If you hit a Mexican, we'll just get another one."

Luis behaves agreeably toward his supervisors and with aloof good cheer toward his fellow workers. He is neither gung-ho nor a slug.

He waits at the greenside until the old-timers putt out, then drives the mower to the equipment shed. Here he collects a rake and a shovel, throws them into the back of a maintenance cart, and drives over to the out-of-bounds region bordering the ninth hole. He busies himself cultivating a patch of poison oak that shields a capped pipe that sticks up about two feet from the ground. He planted the pipe and the poison oak two years ago, and they have proved to be a most efficient little arrangement. In order to find the pipe a person has to enter the fairy ring of poison oak through a gateway, of sorts, of lookalike but nontoxic raspberry cane. If you did it right you didn't get any poison oak on you. Any idiot, however, would stay well away from the patch, and consider a ball hit into it lost for good.

Luis crouches to the pipe, uncaps it, and draws out a rolled-up piece of notepaper. He reads it, laughs softly, and tucks it into his pocket.

17: Learning and Unlearning

"You brought something to read together?" asks Elnice as Solita shakes the rain from her cracked plastic poncho. Showers have been pittering through L.A. for weeks now. Solita's red poncho has tiny white stars printed on it. Elnice realizes it's a child's poncho she must have gotten at the dollar store or even found somewhere.

"Yes!" Solita produces something from the waistband of her skirt with a flourish.

"Ohh," says Elnice. "Oh, my dear."

There, splayed on her kitchen table like an exhausted prostitute, lies this week's edition of *L.A. BackChat*.

Garish, shameless, damp around the edges and im-measurably vulgar, the antitheses of reason, the enemy of taste, the blind date no one wants to be seen with: that's *L.A. BackChat*. It prints all the stuff you hope is true about celebrities and the most bizarre sorry unfortunates in the world.

Solita most likely purchased it at the party store next to the bus stop on Franklin.

Every week at the Ralph's checkout Elnice averts her gaze from *BackChat* and its ilk. If the checkout wait grows long enough, however, her eyes eventually and involuntari-ly come to rest on the poor overweight movie stars and two-headed babies. Then she feels obliged to show the other shoppers and cashiers who might be glancing her way by her expression what she thinks of those papers.

Then she realizes she's tightening her mouth and lowering her lids and realizes she looks like a Dickens dowager. Then she opens her eyes and mouth to show she's not a judgmental person. Then she silently calls herself a fool.

Elnice and Arthur subscribe to *Time* and *Sports Illustrated*, plus lately, *House and Garden*. The guiltiest thrill Elnice allows herself is a few minutes' worth of *Reader's Digest* at the doctor's office. That magazine's packed with enough sensationalism and alarmism to satisfy anybody. Like drinking orange juice, it's unwholesome to want a lot.

Now here on her table lies the last publication in the world she'd want to be stranded with on a desert island. Good God.

And there is Solita, watching her, requesting.

It's her fault; she suggested that Solita bring something she wanted to read, something she wanted to learn. *What was I expecting, a physics monograph?*

Elnice smoothes out the paper, musters a thin smile, and says, "Well. Let's begin right on the front page, shall we?"

A large photo montage of the British princes, laid out off-kilter as if it had been desperately slapped down the second before the page was snatched up by the printer's boy, calls attention to the fact that not all royalty behaves properly at all times. The randy dudes just have too much fun.

Solita's English is coming along so well that Elnice is able to do a decent job of explaining the situation.

But Solita is troubled. "Why are the rules so bad for people? For love?"

"Well, you see . . ." and Elnice launches into a brief history of the British Crown, including pointed comments on the selfishness of Henry VIII, the importance of popular

135

support for a sovereign, and the perennial dangers of scheming courtiers. She draws on her recollection of the film "A Man For All Seasons."

Ty Brandewine pops in to ask if Solita could come over for half an hour when they're done.

"Ah!" he says, "*L.A. BackChat*. Don't be ashamed, Elnice. I subscribe to the pretentious man's version of it: *Vanity Fair*. I'd subscribe to *BackChat* but I don't have the guts. I just pick it up at the store now and then, when nobody's looking."

By the way, it has been done: the hundred and fifty thousand dollars' worth of Coker investments were liquidated, the papers signed, and a bottle of champagne consumed by the three of them. Ty Brandewine and Arthur have been upbeat men ever since.

Elnice is able to produce another detailed lesson from a gossip item about a famous athlete who'd beaten a murder rap. Solita had heard of the man and the charge that didn't stick. She asks Elnice why the police haven't yet brought someone else to trial for the terrible crime. This leads to a discussion of American legal theory and constitutional structure as well as the Los Angeles police department specifically.

Solita's got a few opinions here. "Police?" she says, with a contemptuous snap of her fingers. "Police—they are *not clean* men. In my town, police would find someone else to say did it. Dangerous. Not clean. Mexico police, Los Angeles police."

"I must disagree with you," says Elnice. "The police do a very good job, overall. And in this country we have police-*women* too! Solita, there is such a thing as police brutality: sometimes the police do wrong. But the whole purpose of the police is to protect us. And in general they do! They go to special training, you know, special schools where they learn to do very dangerous—"

Solita laughs forcefully, cutting off Elnice's drivel. "U.S. agents—*pigs!*" Her mouth curves like a scornful scythe and her eyes flash with hatred.

Elnice, who has never been in any sort of trouble apart from one speeding ticket in half a century of driving, shuts up. She knows nothing of Solita's journey across the border, nothing of what it's like to be an illegal in Los Angeles. Of course she knows utterly nothing.

Solita blinks several times and calms down. The tension between them passes, and Elnice moves along with the lesson. Using *L.A. BackChat* as a springboard, teacher and student explore the fields of medicine and geography ("DARING OPEN-AIR AMPUTATION IN STORM-SWEPT NORTH ATLANTIC!"), popular culture ("MEDIUM CONNECTS WITH MARILYN MONROE — MESSAGE TO KENNEDY CLAN: ALL ARE IN DANGER!"), astronomy ("SWERVING ASTEROIDS: LOOSE CANNONS OF THE SKIES!"), and biology and food science ("KILLER CHICKENS CLAIM 100'S OF LIVES EVERY YEAR: EXPERTS PUT POULTRY ON THE HOT SEAT!").

Elnice becomes distracted by a beautiful color photograph of a pot roast surrounded by a glistening garland of potatoes and carrots.

"Oh, doesn't that look delicious? *Delicious*," she repeats, rubbing her stomach, wishing to try the recipe, which involves onion soup mix, raisins, and liquid hickory smoke flavoring.

Solita smiles. "I love to eat."

"So do I, honey. But your figure is so lovely." Elnice has always envied taller women, who could carry more weight but still look slim.

A few pages later Elnice sees a recipe for pumpkin pie, what with Thanksgiving coming up, next to a cartoon of a lovable St. Bernard dog that makes her smile and a quotation that makes her think: "The ultimate measure of a man is not where he stands in moments of comfort and convenience, but where he stands during challenge and controversy."—Dr. Martin Luther King Jr.

Truer now than ever.

It's time for Solita to go home, but they've barely scratched the surface of *L.A. BackChat.* Solita leaves the paper behind. Elnice sits for quite some time in an uncharacteristically fevered state, leafing through its pages rich beyond imagination with information about the world and everything in it.

Over her oven-baked chicken that evening, Elnice wonders aloud, "I wonder if I should take Solita shopping."

"Shopping for what?" Arthur scoops a gob of mashed potato with his bread crust, being a clean-plate man. Fresco sits beneath the table vainly scanning for crumbs.

Shopping. It's a versatile word, but all there is to it is context. If a woman means grocery shopping she says grocery shopping. If she means car shopping she says car shopping. But if she merely says "shopping" she means just one thing.

"For *clothes*, honey. She wears the same outfit all the time, that skirt, I'm sure they're not very well off. If he's only a groundskeeper at a golf course."

"I think that's a given." Of *course* they're not very well off, for Christ's sake. What kind of man would let his wife clean other people's houses unless the income separated them from the welfare rolls? Would women never understand these things? Arthur wipes his mouth and says, "I wouldn't insult her that way, though."

"You think she'd take it as an insult?"

"Uh-huh."

"How come?"

"Because those people have a *lot* of pride. They don't take handouts unless their kids are starving."

"Really?"

"Really."

Elnice has read statistics on the poor of Los Angeles and finds it hard to believe food is scarce in the barrio. "Well, where did you get that?"

"Ty and I were talking."

The way he says it, there is something. He says it in the lightest, most transparently evasive way possible.

Arthur had been a kitchen-table poker champion in his day: His card sense and good memory had easily bested his brothers and uncles in the penny-ante games they played all night at family reunions.

But with Elnice he is the lesser party between God and the greasy bread crust he has just chewed and swallowed.

"When," she asks, adopting a similarly light tone, "were you and Ty talking?" *I'm just asking a question.*

"While you were at bingo yesterday."

"Oh. And what about, besides Latino pride?"

Pause. "You know, I never thought you'd stoop to going to bingo." He does not wink as he says it.

For Arthur to not only change the subject after a direct question, but change it hostilely, this is very, very serious. Elnice feels the slap.

"Well!" she says with audible brittleness, "I've stooped. Should I—You want me to get a job at the United Nations instead? Stooped. I've stooped." Then, "*Stooped,*" on a rising note.

Suddenly she struggles to control her voice. "Well, you know what?" she asks. "I never thought you'd—" She bites herself off. If Arthur had just sat there, eyes down, she might have been able to stop. But he gives her a challenging look.

"I never thought you'd get old!" she cries. "And I never thought *I'd* get old! And I never thought you'd give away all our money to some get-rich-quick huckster! And I never thought we'd be all by ourselves in Los Angeles, which doesn't seem to bother you."

"It doesn't," says he.

"You're perfectly happy here."

"Yes, I am. I've adjusted. You haven't."

She slaps the table so hard it rocks on its toadstool-like base. "What do you think of me? What the hell do you think of me?"

"What are you talking about?"

"What do you think God put me here for? Your entertainment and comfort? There's a life out there somewhere for me! And I want it!"

"Elnice!" His fingers clutch at his knees.

"How happy would you be," she suggests, "if I weren't here?"

He swallows and drops his head, suddenly out of breath.

She notices. "I'll get the—" and leaves the sentence unfinished as she jumps up. Fresco scoots on her heels.

The oxygen unit is in fine working order now, ever since the man came back to adjust it and give Elnice a fresh lesson on its workings.

She activates it and rushes the nose tube to Arthur.

He seizes it, not meeting her eyes, desperate for the oxygen, furious for needing it.

While his cheeks pinken up, the process of which

Elnice actually finds sexy, she perches on the table edge next to him and continues talking. Although the table is heavy, its circular shape and overlarge top make it tippy. Aware of this, she balances carefully on her sit-bones, ready to hop off if necessary. She strokes Arthur's chest while she speaks.

"All my life I've tried to make you happy." She gazes across the kitchen and family room to the drenched, slippery canyon beyond the French doors. "I love you, Arthur. But I know you don't love me anymore." During the period of time it took her to fetch the oxygen tube, she discovered that she can love him and wish him dead at the same time.

He can't look at her. "I do," he insists unconvincingly.

"Well, I'm staying. You don't need friends. You don't need church. Because you've got me. These days, I'm enough for you. And it's true, I don't care how sick and crabby you get. I'll always love you and be here for you. But I'm finding something in church. And I'm making friends at bingo. They're nice women. Three of us, Dorothy and Yvonne and I—we've signed up to make up the monthly food boxes."

Arthur says, "You need church to cope with me. With my—the way I am now." He dares to flick his eyes to her face.

"Honey, I feel the need to give thanks. Sometimes I know I'm not grateful enough." Which is true. Plus she gets a kick out of the new reverend's sermons. The Reverend Doctor Carruthers said he came to L.A. twenty years ago to do standup comedy but wound up leading a congregation instead. He has a talent for telling humiliating stories on himself. "Guess I should keep my day job," is his frequent tag line, to waves of appreciative chuckles.

Bullshit of the church aside, how calming it is to pray. Elnice's mental landscape just magically evens out when she settles down to say the Lord's Prayer. She likes to pray outdoors. She prays standing on the back deck overlooking the canyon. She prays for Arthur. *Dear God if he can't be whole again at least give him something to live for.* And God came through on that one, didn't he?: God gave Arthur Ty's movie. Elnice hadn't thought to put in any conditions. Too late she realized she should have asked it like this: *If he can't be whole again at least give him something REASONABLE to live for.* But she never asks God this: *Let him love me again. Let him at least act as if he cares for me again.* No. God did hear her say, however, *help me keep loving him.* She knows a dreadful shift had occurred, yet she couldn't speak of it even to God. She had prayed on this just the other day while Arthur looked at lumberjack competitions on ESPN2.

For all she knows he prays his ass off in there during commercials.

Arthur says, "I know the score, Elnice."

That is as close as he's going to come to that certain compartment in his mind.

He doesn't need Elnice to remind him that a calamity could befall her and that he would be obliged to care for her, somehow. That thought resides in that dark clammy place too. But for him to take her hand and promise to be there for her as she just did for him, well, he just can't do it. He is angry to have been put in such a position.

For it's just too horrible to imagine, that's all. Too awful to even develop a contingency plan for. Elnice incapacitated!—How quickly it could happen!—A stroke, a fall—his eyelids flutter.

"For better or for worse"—how cleverly that had been

embedded in their marriage vows. He'd said it once, said it easily and stupidly, that one simple word, "worse," who could've known the terrible pregnancy of that word? Just thinking about "worse" is as bad as he'd known so far.

He is sweating and not off the hook yet. If only he'd blurted it out to begin with.

Elnice knows it, she knows what set this conversation in motion. "What were you and Ty talking about?"

Arthur is better with the oxygen but he is unconsciously squirming, his skinny hips shifting his weight in the chair. He gazes out at the canyon, now veiled with thin mist, beyond the French doors.

"Well, it's the movie," he finally says. "Ty's having some trouble with it financially."

"Already? But we just gave him our money, what, a month ago!"

"It's not that! He's doing *fine* financially! I mean, our money's secure, my God, El. You think we're morons for investing in 'Freedom Lake'. But we'll see. Time will prove me right." He sighs. "It's just that another investor bowed out, and now he's a little short."

"Well, we don't have any more money to give him."

"Of course we do. But I was thinking, uh. Thinking maybe we should consider going into an assisted living type of situation, you know, where they—"

"Where they what?"

"Where they, you know, assist you in living. They take you to the ballgame and the museum and things. And to the doctor, they take you to the doctor. You can eat in the dining room. Maybe it's time we started relaxing a little bit." He clasps his hands in his lap, ashamed but hopeful.

"And sell this house," she prompts darkly. He is so son of a bitching transparent.

"Um."

"And give the money to Ty."

"Well..."

"No!" she shrieks. She's never shrieked louder in her life. *"No, no, no!"*

"Elnice—"

"No!"

The next day her throat hurts and he doesn't bring it up again.

18: Darker Dreams

The sky is paint-set blue, the sun a shining egg yolk there in the upper corner, and squat trees form a murky border at the edge. A zephyr stirs the trees' stubby crowns. In the middle of this landscape sprawls a state-of-the-art parking lot with a double fence, cameras, and a security golf cart with a guy cruising up and down. Sounds of the freeway nearby, the kind of ocean roar a freeway makes when no one's really listening.

From a distance the machine factory looks like a pizza box, centered in the parking lot. The parking surface is the smoothest one for miles, having been freshly coated with a velvety substance called slurry seal. Its blackness, its tar-pit smell, gives a feeling of bottom-heaviness to the scene. There is a stern demarcation between ground and sky. You might expect to turn and see mastodons moving slowly and patiently across the expanse, to what sad fate you can only imagine, like Rose Parade floats.

There's plenty of space; much more personnel growth is planned. Most employees nudge their cars close in, but a few holier-than-thous park near the double fence and hoof the half mile in, then gloat about their triglycerides while waiting for meetings to start.

A man whose shoulder muscles are sore but marginally bigger than they used to be, wearing wraparound sunglasses and Scamp khakis hauls an expensive briefcase from the passenger seat of his red Miata parked near that double fence. He twists erect, slams the door, *ca-lunk* go the locks, the briefcase makes him look no more dignified than a Sesame Street lunchbox would, but he's a proud warrior now. He's got something to fight for, something to stand up against, yes, he's made up his mind about something.

Because the dreams have gotten worse. The explicit body parts, the poor little torn heads and butts and bellies of Pamela and her doll Vicky and her mom and everybody fly through space, then swoop down to party in a circle around Jason M's head as he cries and reaches out to try to squish them back together with deep remorse.

19: That Elemental Type

After breakfast the following Saturday Elnice is puttering on the patio in her Dappletree jumper and navy Keds, scooping Fresco's poop and watching a line of ants trudge along the edge of a planter box, when she begins to hear ripping and scraping noises through the hedge from Ty's backyard. *Thuck. Zik. Thuck-thuck.* She listens; the sounds go on steadily, punctuated by occasional grunts. The grunts don't sound like Ty. He'd allowed his yard to get fairly overgrown during the summer, saying that he was going native. Elnice has never seen a drop of sweat on him.

Quietly she carries the stepladder from beneath the eaves, sets it up next to the hedge, clambers up, and peeps over. Just beneath her, Luis Perona Gastello is chopping a shrub with his mattock. He stops to pull up a clump of weeds and toss them aside. He picks up the tool again. *Thuck.*

She clambers down.

Arthur likes chocolate cupcakes. She bakes up a batch and puts some out nicely on a plate with tea that afternoon, then as Arthur goes down for his nap she refills her cup and wanders outside again.

She hears two men talking Spanish on the other side of the hedge. One voice is a tenor drone, the other an enthusiastic, prompting chirp. She clambers up the ladder again. Luis is sitting with Ty at his patio table, the two of them holding cold drinks. Tired from his work, Luis slouches over his glass, but he smiles up at Ty and talks on. Ty sits back with his hands clasped behind his head, his face receptive and amused. He chirrups another enthusiastic remark, and Luis nods and talks on.

Wednesdays are cleaning days, but this Wednesday Solita shows up with another list of words and worry inside her that has stirred wavelets into her smooth brow.

"What is it, honey?"

"Please sit with me," Solita asks, "for minute." Her English is improving so rapidly. "I am unhappy. Do you know these words?" Even when troubled, though, her simple presence is remarkable. She looks as mature and grave as a prime minister.

Elnice guesses that more than a few cups of Spanish blood flow through Solita's veins: the perfect olive skin, the roundness of the features. Luis's face is organized into tile-like planes, Solita's into curves. It occurs to Elnice that their children, if they ever have any, would probably be gorgeous.

Smoothing her blue skirt beneath her, Solita sits right down and draws a piece of lunch-bag paper from her pocket, along with a stubby yellow pencil. "I took a pencil," she says with a quaver, "from Luis."

Elnice receives the paper with thumb and forefinger but before she can smooth it out and read it, her home's special classy doorbell rings, *chime-a-ling!*

"Excuse me." She lays the paper on the tabletop with a deliberate motion that means: *This paper is important and will receive my fullest attention in a minute.*

It's Ty, dressed in his customary day outfit of T-shirt, khaki shorts, and bare feet, returning the empty plate from the blond brownies she'd taken over last Monday.

"Absolutely delicious as always!" he declares. "Hi, Solita."

Elnice has become more solicitous of Ty, as she feels it important to keep track of him, and being solicitous is the best way she knows. With Elnice it's never just-pick-up-the-phone-and-ask-how-the-movie's-going. No. She feels better arranging half a dozen brownies on a plate and running them over but not stopping to talk right then as if she were sniffing around. No. You wait two days until the plate comes back (and Ty is good about returning the plate), *then* you set up Ty and Arthur talking. You insist with your eyes that Ty come in, because lonely Arthur needs some male company if only for a few freaking minutes, you communicate all that in one meaningful look and smile, you shepherd him over to the couch seat next to Arthur's recliner, hoping that *Arthur'll* ask what's going on with that movie, then you quietly go about your business with your surrogate daughter.

Ty lowers himself onto the couch with exaggerated creakiness, out of deference to Arthur. *We're none of us getting any younger, eh?*

"How're you feeling, Bullet, my man?" From Ty's seat he can observe Elnice and Solita at the kitchen table. Solita is such eye candy: the curves of her calves, twined girlishly beneath the table, the outlines of her thighs through the faded fabric of her skirt, her flat tummy. And those breasts under that virginal white blouse—no way can she afford fancy brassieres, those puppies are staying up, up, all by their firm ample selves.

Arthur knows his role. He mutes the TV. "What's the latest on the film, Zanuck?" He had joined Ty in calling it a *film*, not a *movie*, like a serious Hollywoodian.

"I've got my fingers crossed on the financing. Don't worry. It's coming along, the script's supposed to be in

Laura Dennis's hands sometime this weekend, it's on Buster's agent's desk as we speak, but I'm feeling tremendously *blocked*." He utters this with a moan. His slim hands rest limply on his hairy knees.

A football highlight on the muted TV shows a running back dancing into the end zone, flapping his hands and high-stepping. "Why do they do that?" Ty asks irritably. "They look like fags arriving late to a party."

"Blocked how?" asks Arthur cautiously.

"The ingénue the ingénue the ingénue. Butch Rafters. Heather. The *girl*."

"Oh."

Meanwhile Elnice, seated again at the kitchen table, unconsciously adopts her teaching posture: shoulders square, back straight, feet flat, forearms level. Reading glasses in position. As she uncreases the scrap of brown paper and orients Solita's printing right-side up, she notices that Solita's penmanship is beginning to take on its own personality, gradually becoming elongated top to bottom and slightly compressed left to right. Unusual and rather elegant.

Once oriented, the words tumble into her brain rapidfire. DIVERSION. DISRUPT. CLEARANCE. GENEW CORP. EYESONLY. Oh, eyes only. NEUTRALIZE. These words are interspersed with strings of letters and numbers that make no sense.

Half the pills in the Cokers' medicine chest sport the Genew logo.

How can a few words on a page make her feel faint? She licks her lips, draws in a deep breath, looks up at Solita.

Ty Brandewine's gaze tracks toward the French doors and outward to the canyon, which this morning lies under a scrim of yellow haze. "Our budget just doesn't allow for...we've *got* to find that *elemental* type...you should see the babyshit we're seeing from the casting agency...she's *got* to show depth, she's got to show in her eyes that she's got life experience. The way she holds her head! The way she throws a rope to the dock! I don't want some little nitwit out of the UCLA drama depot." He swings his eyes to Arthur. "Huh?"

Arthur lifts his index finger. Ty follows its line across the family area.

Poised in one of the hard ridiculous chairs of the giant-mushroom dinette set, her body projecting supple anxiety, her eyes beseeching Elnice for reassurance, Solita could be Juliet sniffing the poison cup, Scarlett caught with her guard down, Ilsa giving up Rick on the foggy tarmac.

"Where did you find these words?" asks Elnice.

"My God," breathes Ty.

"In the secret papers of Luis," says Solita.

"Aha," says Arthur.

20: Like Kissing Buster Jordan

Elnice jumps up, cramming the scrap of brown paper into the onseam pocket of her slacks. "Solita and I are going out for a walk! You two tycoons, there's tuna salad or baloney in the fridge, you can make sandwiches for lunch!"

The haze is burning away and the sun is slapping down hard shadows from every leaf and house and post. Elnice hustles Solita down the short driveway to the street, then left, uphill toward the top of the ridge. Sparrows and phoebes dart in and out of the bushes, twittering and scratching.

Immediately Elnice's heart pounds and her hips squeak in protest. She doesn't normally take walks around the neighborhood because of the steepness. It's much pleasanter to walk around the flatlanded shopping areas, Beverly Center, the Santa Monica Promenade in spite of the dirty men who pick up and smoke other people's cigarette butts. But she doesn't do it much; Arthur doesn't like to be alone. He still goes with her to the grocery store, though, towing his oxygen tank to linger over the items in the deli case. He likes store-bought garlic bread.

The two women walk along the skinny, crowned road. From the foot of the canyon the mailboxes stand thick along the roadside, then thinning as the road ascends and the altimeter spins higher, signifying the greater acreage controlled by each homeowner. The plants and trees smell hot and resinous, like herbs toasted in a dry pan.

Solita's young legs pump along effortlessly.

"I am sad and afraid," she tells Elnice. "I never pay attention to papers of Luis and the pencils. He say he is write a movie. A screen play. Now I want to reading. I want to learning. The movie he keep her in a little table. I can open the table. I see, like, never same papers. New papers they come, old papers they go. No screen play. I know a movie she is a story. There is no story. The papers they are secret. Where do they come? Where do they go?"

"Have you asked him?"

"No!"

"Why not?"

"I am afraid! I tell you he take away any thing I try to read. Sometime he laugh, but he is angry. It is like—" Solita reaches for Elnice's hand. "I cannot speak. He took away my writing tablet."

"I thought so."

Solita stops, reaches for Elnice's hand, and places it on her stomach.

"Here. You see? I am afraid here."

Elnice feels the warm firmness of Solita.

"Dear, are you pregnant?"

"No! I am trying to show to you."

"I see."

"Luis work four days ago for Mr. Brandewine."

"I know."

"He work one day and now he is Mr. Brandewine's friend. Mr. Brandewine can help him with his movie. Over and over I say, I tell to him this. I tell Mr. Brandewine Luis is write a movie and he want to know about the movie of Luis. But now I know there is no movie."

"Have you exactly told Luis that I'm teaching you to read and write?"

"No!"

Elnice stops and sits down on a pinkish boulder that marks the driveway of the road's topmost resident. The stone is pleasantly warm from the sun. She pats a place next to her.

"Solita. If Luis is doing something illegal, it could be dangerous."

"I know! I love Luis, but I no. I no." The girl stops and chews the side of her thumb. "You will help me?"

"What do you tell Luis about Friday mornings?"

"I tell him no thing. He is at work when I come here and go home."

"Oh." In the midst of her anxiety and confusion, Elnice takes a moment to note to herself the near-perfection of Solita's pronunciation.

"He look at me, though."

"He looks at you?"

"He looks at me and I think he wonders. I would surprise him with my English, but now I no think so."

"Not a good idea now. Solita, I wouldn't let on to anything. Lordy."

Sitting on the stone, they watch a row of thistles sway in the breeze.

"Solita, honey, in order to figure out what Luis is doing, I have to see the papers. Maybe it's nothing!"

"It is something."

Elnice sends up a prayer that she and Solita will be proved drama queens. She pictures Luis shyly showing her his screenplay in progress, a screenplay about spies and terrorists and chemical formulae!—yes, of course! And laughing merrily at her suspicions, embracing her, perhaps insisting that she stay for dinner, please sit down and relax while Solita puts on a pot of polenta and he runs out for a bucket of suds. They all laugh and get drunk and have a riot.

Elnice blinks as the thought blasts out the other side of her brain.

"I bring the papers to you," Solita says.

"No! If he discovers them missing!"

"We go to my house together. Luis he work now. You can read the papers now."

As they walk back downhill Solita steps over a squished lizard in the road.

"Poor thing," Elnice murmurs.

"Poor thing," Solita repeats.

"We're going shopping!" Elnice announces as soon as they come in.

"We are?" says Arthur.

"No, Solita and I. You get to stay home. We have to go right now." Why add any urgency, why not just slip off casually? *Because I'm Elnice and Elnice always says too much.*

Oddly, Ty Brandewine stands in the center of the kitchen like a Navy recruit at the door of a whorehouse, rigid with pent-up excitement.

"Solita. Wait. Before you go—"

Elnice grabs her purse and keys.

"Wait," says Ty, "Wait! I want to talk to you about being in a movie!"

The women stop.

Solita pivots toward Ty slowly and precisely, as if powered by a small motor.

"A movie?" she repeats.

Elnice sees *L.A. BackChat* flash into her eyes.

"Yes, a movie, don'tcha know!" And standing in the kitchen he outlines very quickly what he wants from her and what would be hers in return.

"Acting's fun! You get to do all kinds of things you'd never do in real life! Like kissing Buster Jordan!"

Elnice and Arthur know Ty is big on percentages, but for Solita he paints a picture of petty riches (being able to buy the latest fashions on Melrose Avenue), two-bit fame (being recognized while shopping on Melrose Avenue), and adolescent pleasures (eating pizza at the latest café on Melrose Avenue). Elnice marvels: somehow Ty knew the prospect of chewing up West Hollywood would command greater attention from Solita than buying bangles on Rodeo Drive, guesting on Today, or sipping small-batch gin at the Polo Lounge. Now she understands why he was so successful at writing television for teenagers: his finger is firmly on that pulse, in fact, there is almost no vein wall *between* his finger and the hot blood of self-absorbed young cool.

How he achieves this without leaving his smoky lair, she'll never know.

Solita listens pensively.

"I will think about this," she says at last, as if this were the fourth movie proposal she'd been blandished with today.

"What? You'll *think* about it? Well, sure! How 'bout overnight? I'll call you in the morning. I'd like to talk to you, I mean really get down and talk to you about this. I know you're still learning English, but we'd have a voice coach, a language coach on the set—"

"Elnice could do that," pitches in Arthur.

Ty addresses a few sentences in Spanish to Solita. Elnice can tell he is saying something like, *you'd be perfect for the part! I could direct you in Spanish, if I wanted to! En espanol!*

Solita cocks her head and narrows her eyes. "I have no

green card."

He winks. "No problem. This is L.A., babycakes, and you're talking to Ty Brandewine."

Elnice knows if Solita had played by the rules, she'd be lying in a grave back in Mexico, having sustained one too many concussions at the hands of her husband, or perhaps in jail after braining him with a tortilla iron.

Solita nods. "I will think about this. I am busy now. Now I go. We go." She takes Elnice's arm.

"Shopping," adds Elnice.

"Shopping," confirms Solita.

The guys don't look at them closely enough.

21: Be Expert Like God

The Coker-mobile, a tan Buick, winds down the canyon to Sunset Boulevard. "Where do you live?" Elnice asks her passenger.

Solita recites her address.

"Where's that, honey?"

"Watts."

"I said, where's that, honey?"

"I say Watts. Do I say wrong?"

"You mean *Watts*? Watts?"

Dear God. Every American who'd reached the age of reason by the nineteen-sixties knows of the terrible race riots in Watts, nineteen-sixty-something, the rage of black Los Angeles foaming over like a pot of lye, violence pouring down blindly. What had triggered it? Elnice tried to remember. What year was it? Reaction to the murder of Martin Luther King, Jr?—or some act of police brutality, one more act in a string of viciousness? She remembers the riots in Detroit, too, around the same time, remembers watching television and thinking how can this be? The National Guard battling citizens! Crazy, unbelievable. She and Arthur saw the terror that gripped the hearts of the white people in the nearby suburbs—"a bottle was thrown through the window of a blind pig"—that, supposedly, is what started it all in Detroit one sweltering night.

But Watts. The Gettysburg of urban riots. Watts, for God's sake.

Solita directs Elnice to drive along the surface streets through fierce traffic for a long way. Elephantine buses sap Elnice's patience as they lumber about blocking lanes and spewing exhaust. She realizes Solita must be retracing her bus route all the way through town. She pulls over, consults a map, and cuts over to the Harbor Freeway.

Solita directs them from the off-ramp into a neighborhood. "Aim for the Towers."

Elnice's mind is going very fast, faster than the car. She scans the horizon ahead for looming housing projects. What will the place look like, these many years later?

But all she sees thrusting upward from the flat plain of single-family rooftops is a eucalyptus grove. And what are those spindly constructions next to it—radio transmitters?

"Is that what you're talking about? Those towers? What are they?"

She pilots the Buick down a narrow main drag into a neighborhood of humble houses, some zesty with paint and flower bushes, others shambles. Mostly the houses are masonry, their cheap pebbled walls looking heavy yet fragile, as if you could take a hammer to one of them and be surrounded by rubble in no time. Elnice's bright eyes take in the *de rigueur* L.A. street vegetation, those damned scraggly sword-bushes. Kids straddle bicycles, guys ease their cars into the spaces in front of the beer stores and barber shops. The other essentials of life are there too: barbecue shacks—her nose catches a quick heavenly meat smell—beauty salons, no-brand gas stations, storefront missions, brake shops, car alarm installation, roach control.

Everything, it occurs to Elnice, is an independent operation, not a chain store to be seen. No bank. Everything is guarded by iron bars, burly dogs, and flat-eyed proprietors. Do the nationally recognized stores and services spurn the area because of crime, or are the people too poor to support them? Or both? Yet for every dirty hole of a storefront there are one or two whose owner is trying new things, showing some pride: fresh handmade signs, a swept sidewalk, a rack of merchandise put right out on the sidewalk in a gesture of trust: unrequited trust, perhaps, but trust nevertheless.

Under other circumstances that observation would have influenced Elnice to become almost cheerful.

They roll slowly past the towers Solita pointed out. What a strange place! Someone's little tract lot built into a miniature walled village, of sorts, built of concrete and metal, covered in shards, beautiful shards of glass, pottery, metal trinkets, all cemented into the underpinnings. The antenna-like towers rise up behind the wall, up, up, everything covered in shards of pottery and bottles.

Solita tells her, "This place is Watts Towers."

The place has a combination Moorish and outer space look to it. Elnice thinks of the towns of antiquity she visited on their vacations to the Olympics, their chimneys and spires. Those places were a chore to look at.

But this: a celebration of scraps and beautiful junk! Proud and bizarre and oddly satisfying.

Elnice feels her mind slowing down. It feels good.

"Keep going," says Solita. "Go. Turn left here."

"OK."

"Stop here."

"This is where you live? Then I shouldn't park right in front, let me go down a ways." Already she's thinking like a spy.

The house stands in the middle of a block, it's an itsy-bitsy pink thing with a treacherous-looking overhanging tile roof. The two small barred windows flanking the front door make it look like an angry stucco piglet.

In spite of the paltry windows the house is remarkably bright inside. Elnice notices perfect white paint on the walls, but not the dead cheap white she might have expected; the color contains a wisp of blue, just a trace of coolness. Vivid objects occupy the living room: a yellow vinyl hassock, a rough scarlet clay pot, a white-and-gold filigreed statue of the Madonna on a three-legged table. And on the walls, several striking paintings. She stops briefly before one, a study of Jesus and Saint Veronica on the road to Calvary. Deep blues and browns surround the patient golden expression of Christ, its spooky echo on the torn rag, and the grieving face of the woman who has wiped away his sweat.

Just for a moment, the subtle beauty of the painting soothes her. She barely knows it, but it does.

She smells a conglomeration of Pine-sol and fried meat. Breakfast had perhaps been beans and bacon, then someone had cleaned the kitchen thoroughly.

Solita is watching her anxiously.

She smiles. "You have a lovely home, honey."

Solita leads her past the bedroom—cheap neat bed and dresser, shoes on the floor—to the next doorway. They step into a cell-like room, perhaps eight feet by eight. Solita flips the light switch.

People in the Midwest live in houses with basements and store their extra stuff in them; people in California, land of the slab foundation, have to cram their stuff into whatever above-ground space they've got. Evidently the only windowless room in the house, this one is piled up with boxes from small appliances, old clothes (Elnice perceives a torn paisley ruffle poking over the brim of a packed-full grocery bag), Christmas tree stand and decorations. A small table and a wooden chair crowd together in one corner. No lamp, just an overhead bulb covered by a dish of frosted glass.

The table is actually a sewing machine cabinet, but the machine has been taken out and the table repurposed into a desk. A brass ring indicates that the writing surface can be pulled up to reveal a compartment beneath where the machine used to be.

Solita reaches around her, grasps the brass ring, and pulls up the panel. And there in the compartment are Luis's papers: sheaves of assorted sizes, stacks separated by black clips, a few index cards, some motley scraps, all bearing words.

The two women have been in the house for no more than two minutes. "Solita, go look out," says Elnice.

"But Luis he works today."

"Honey, I know. But if you don't look out, he'll come home right now. That's the way it always happens." Irrational overstatement is quicker than reason at a time like this.

Most of the papers appear to be accounting of some simple kind, on looseleaf paper: one column of dates, one column of initials, one column of numbers that certainly could be dollar amounts but with no dollar signs. The amounts are round numbers in multiples of a thousand, ranging up to 75,000. A typical line runs: 11.8 P.K. 5,000.

The guy's a bookie?

Then there are messages, all in plain English. No salutations or signatures. "We have had a fair working relationship up to now," says one, in block printing on a creased index card. "I'm interested in continuing, but things are heating up. Let me know when I can expect big news."

Another, printed on a strip of white printer paper: "Thank you. The enclosed stick contains a logic bomb that will eventually fuck every local system and I am still working on the WAN. I am a genius." The letters WAN had been circled in pencil. Elnice sees no stick among the papers, however.

She opens the bobbin-and-pin drawer and finds four yellow pencils plus one Bic Stic ballpoint pen. Knowing that spies sometimes hide things in small everyday objects Elnice holds up the writing instruments to the light and inspects them carefully. None appears odd in any way.

Careful to maintain the papers' order, she looks some more, then puts everything back. As she rises, her foot catches the chair leg. She stumbles then rights herself, and in the process notices a small paper wad on the floor, near an empty wastebasket.

She picks it up, uncrumples it, and reads, "THESE ENCRYPTION KEYS WILL HELP YOUR GUYS DO A CUSTOM VIRUS FOR THEIR SYSTEM. OBLIVION NOW! THEY TELL ME NOBODY'S USING BETAINE ANYMORE IN THAT TYPE OF MIX."

The words ring a bell—Solita's first vocabulary words! Elnice puts the note in her pocket. Then she takes it out and recrumples it and tosses it where it was.

She goes out to the front stoop where Solita pretends to lounge, legs crossed, one dying-salmon-colored espadrille pumping up and down.

"We walk again?" asks Solita.

They set off down the little street. Twenty-year-old muscle cars, battered and torn with many a crumpled horn, are evidently the neighborhood's signature vehicle. The women pass a red Mustang that someone has plas-tered with perhaps a hundred decals of the Sacred Heart and Our Lady of Guadalupe. Solita trails her hand over the decals.

"It looks to me," Elnice begins, "as if Luis is involved in... something."

"He no is writing a movie?"

"He is not writing a movie, honey."

"The papers they do not tell a story." She lifts her hand to a young black woman sitting in a wheelchair on a porch. The woman, whose hair has been styled into a smooth bronze-colored cone twelve inches high, does not move but smiles back.

"Well, actually they do. I just don't know how to figure it out."

"I know but, like, I wish I do not know."

Somewhere she'd picked up the universal modifier "like." Elnice feels it makes her sound more American, so she lets it go.

Elnice speculates, "Maybe Luis is involved with drugs, maybe some kind of gambling? Is the numbers racket still a thing?"

"I don't know." Solita steps around a plastic tricycle in the sidewalk. A batch of wispy high clouds draw a veil over the sun, softening the edges of the shadows, which helps soothe Elnice's nerves. "I know the different gamblings," Solita says, "but Luis is no with gambling."

"Not. Not with gambling."

"Not. He is not with drugs, too."

"How do you know?"

A brace of pigeons swoops onto a hamburger wrapper in the street.

"Drugs, gambling, you no do these things alone. Always people come over, always the phone ring. These things—I do not believe."

"There was something about computers."

The young woman laughs quietly. "Luis—one day he bring home a computer. He can not make her work! I can not make her work! He take her away again. But. Luis he is very smart. More smart than like drug dealers."

They round a corner and come upon Watts Towers again.

Elnice stops walking.

When she first saw them half an hour ago she thought the towers looked wonderful yet demented. Who would want to live next door to something like that? Right in a neighborhood. The immediate neighbors of Watts Towers lived in ordinary houses.

But now, up close, she sees the wild inventiveness of the towers, not to mention the painstaking effort of them.

Yes. Pow. Upside the head.

A gear turns inside her chest or perhaps upper belly as she gazes at the funny, humble walls and mosaics. There is a gazebo, a skeletonized ship, countless little shards lovingly assembled into beauty. The cobalt shards of milk of magnesia bottles speak to her! She remembers feeling foolish loving their jamboree of blueness in the medicine cabinet down through the years—before the Phillips company switched to plastic—and here this artist did not feel foolish. He celebrated that glorious blue by cementing broken pieces of it in a graceful arc right into his home. His shrine! He built towers that sweep majestically upward.

It is as if an expert child made these things.

Elnice has got it, she's holding it in her hand right now, this minute. The great paradox of art, the great *demand* art makes of an artist: Be inventive like a child, and be expert like God.

Her heart boils in her chest.

Upward reach the towers, crowned with tiaras made from Seven-Up bottles, upward from the seedy neighborhood into the stale Los Angeles air.

Seeing these things, piled on top of seeing the religious paintings in Solita's home—so simple, so direct—make Elnice realize she has lived a smaller life than she had thought. Something begins to feel poignant and brave in the air of Watts.

Solita stands with her in silence. Elnice looks and looks. At length Solita says, "A man made this a long time ago. A man from—Italy? He is dead."

Elnice observes that the community has rallied around Watts towers, attempting to protect them from decay and depredation by means of signs and fencing. One of the signs tells her that some public money was recently used in a restoration project.

The artist's name was Simon Rodia.

"Simon Rodia," Elnice says slowly.

A sign tells her that he worked construction by day and built the towers by night because he felt like it. "I had in mind to do something big, and I did it," said he.

"When I look," Solita says, "it makes me feel—" She stops. "I no know the word."

"Neither do I," murmurs her companion.

"I wish the fence to be take away."

"Taken away. Me too."

"Taken away. But you see." Solita points to the information panels, which are defaced with illegible graffiti.

"If they write on the signs, then, yeah," says Elnice.

Elnice and Arthur had visited the top museums in the capitals of the world! Why had no one ever told her of Watts Towers?

Her temples feel hot.

This Watts Towers is what Los Angeles is all about, she sees. In recent weeks she has begun to feel the possibilities of Los Angeles. The energy in the air. The purposefulness of the guy who made change at the car wash, the inexplicable cheerfulness of the benoseringed receptionist at the hairdresser's, the alertness of the preadolescents loitering with their skateboards in the shadows of concrete steps. What trouble a shopkeeper will go to to add a creative touch to the façade of his building here in Los Angeles: perhaps an enlarged replica of a sea creature, or a cardboard booth from which the newest employee will entreat pedestrians with free samples, or even perhaps something deliberately ugly—a one-armed mannequin in a torn wig, for instance—that makes a metaphysical statement of some kind.

Being an extra in a movie is a more interesting way to make a living than being a laborer in construction. But even being a laborer in construction is more interesting in Los Angeles than elsewhere because one might be working on a celebrity's house, or the house of someone who does taxes for celebrities.

You don't have to bundle up in L.A. Need to see the dentist? Just walk out and go.

A sound overhead—the buzzing of a helicopter—traffic reporter? the police?—snaps her back to the problem at hand. Should they take Luis's papers to the police? And tell them what? Has a crime been committed? What about Solita?

She pushes wisps of her hair away from her temples. "Solita, maybe you should just have a talk with Luis about these papers."

"No!"

They take seats on a bench in a grassy patch near the

167

Watts Towers information center, which is closed. "No! I feel—I feel talk with Luis will be bad."

"Well, what about going to the police?"

"No!"

"What, then?"

"If Luis is doing bad things, I will find out and stop it. You will help me."

"But aren't you afraid of what Luis might do?"

"Yes."

"Well—the police should get involved. They would protect you and help figure out what's going on."

"Hah! Police would protect no one. They come only when bodies are cold. I no go back to Mexico. I no go to jail here in U.S. or Mexico." She grips Elnice's arm. "I tell you I am afraid of Luis. Yes! But you will help me, we will work together."

"Why not just run away? Solita, my God, you're just a teenager, who could blame you? I could give you some money, you could go away—"

"No!"

"To another city, to Phoenix, or up north—"

"You don't understand! Are you a butthead? I will not leave *you*! Who else would teach me! So kind to me! Mrs. Coker! Like no one!" Solita's perfectly oval face collapses into anguish. Her hands make ropes of her skirt. She bows her head over Elnice's lap, her shoulders convulsing. Elnice feels tears patter onto her thighs.

"Solita, Solita," Elnice strokes the cable-thick hair. "Oh, honey. Shh." *What in God's name is happening today? Whatever it is, it's the right thing.*

"I am your friend," Solita tells her, snuffling, "You know this. You will help me and I will help you. Do not be a man! A butthead!"

Elnice's eyes play over the magnificence of Watts Towers, where a most unbutthead-like man had done his life's masterwork. She thinks of Arthur at home, waiting for her.

22: *Voyeurism for Girls*

"Solita will need to know when principal photography's going to start," Arthur tells Elnice in an efficient tone when she gets home.

Fresco jumps about her ankles. Principal photography, oh brother. "How do you know she's going to agree to be in it?"

"I don't know why you're concerned about that."

This sharpness surprises her. "Well, I'm not concerned, I'm—"

"As if she's got some big plans, some major commitment to get out of the way first."

She observes, "You seem a bit on the muscle this afternoon, dear."

He shrugs, turning inward as he does whenever she calls him on his shit.

She says, "I might as well ask when *will* shooting begin, then? Did Ty say? Get down, Fresco."

Arthur knots his fists in the sagging pockets of his red Adidas sweatpants. "*Soon.* He said, Bullet, my man, I know what you're thinking." His old nickname makes Arthur feel like a winner whenever he hears it. "He said, I know what you're thinking. The mystery of Hollywood."

"Well?"

"Elnice, you can't just wave a magic wand and have world peace. It's the same thing with films."

"But, then, does he have some kind of a budget, you

know, a ledger that says how much money he's spent so far and where it's *gone*?" Elnice dares use the word *gone*. "I mean, he's been talking about casting agents and set designers and what the hell's a key grip anyway?"

"I basically asked him that." With sudden boldness Arthur takes his wife's hand and fixes her with a gaze he hopes she will find penetrating and convincing, and speaks in the flat tone used by documentary narrators when they are about to reveal the *actual* angle of the sniper attack on President Kennedy. "I promise that Ty Brandewine will give us a full accounting of all monies. A full and fair accounting. But you should know by now that you don't do that right in the middle of the production."

"But it's not *in* the middle of production yet, I thought—"

Arthur releases her hand. "Listen to me, Elnice. Ty Brandewine is not in the business of ripping people off. He's our neighbor. We live next door to each other."

"You mean we can't afford to doubt him."

Arthur tells her by a sudden coughing spell that she is absolutely right.

Elnice had viewed television specials and seen the Hollywood movie about the naturalist Dian Fossey. She had been horridly fascinated by the hardships and tests of courage Fossey endured for the sake of the gorillas. The damp. The bugs. The heat. The apes. The local uneducated poachers. The no washing machine!

Now she is experiencing some first-hand wilderness of her own. It is a week since she accompanied Solita to Watts. Creeping behind Solita through the brambles of Griffith Park she's appreciating why the old explorers always wrote things like, "The coarse vegetation acted as an enemy, ripping our clothing and flesh without respect to social rank."

Griffith Park comprises miles of dry jagged hills, wrapped by the mowed ribbons of the golf courses and the pony rides and picnic grounds. You can hear coyotes at night and rattlesnakes in the daytime if you disturb the correct rock ledges.

What kind of plants grow here? Gruff, truculent ones. People like Dian Fossey and Joy Adamson wouldn't have given a second thought to the thorny stuff. To hell with my own hide, they'd say. But *wow, ow,* say Elnice's arms and legs. She'd dressed this morning as ruggedly as possible, smuggling her heaviest slacks in her big purse so as not to arouse Arthur's suspicions, which were, frankly, already somewhat tumescent.

"You'n' Solita going shopping *again*?" he'd asked. "What—how much stuff is there to look at?"

"Yes, hon!" perkily. The simpler the better.

She's wearing a long-sleeved blouse too, but what she needs is a canvas coat, jeans and hiking boots. Sharp sticks are bruising her feet right through the cloth uppers of her Keds. Her binoculars clunk against her breasts. Fortunately the morning is cool.

At every step the odors change: some torn leaves give off a citrusy smell, others smell like gin, others of mold; here the air is musky perhaps from a raccoon's den, here sweet from a wild jasmine vine. The vines curl through the urban trash you would expect: empty wine bottles, used condoms, cookie wrappers. A yellow baby sock inexplicably lies tamped down in the dirt.

Unbelievably, Solita is dressed merely in her usual well-worn outfit: white blouse, blue skirt, those busted-down espadrilles. She pushes through the fierce brush like a grenadier. They haven't traveled this terrain before.

"I figured it'd be rough, but not like this," murmurs Elnice. Solita gives her an encouraging smile.

Elnice has stepped into a different life entirely, and new things are happening inside her. Yes, it's only been a week since she intruded upon Luis's papers hidden in the sewing machine table, seven days since she walked away from timidity and its discontents.

It stands to reason that Luis must engage in all or most of his secret activity at work, as he rarely lingers away from home past his shift hours. Solita skids on some loose twigs down a slope and cracks her elbow on a rock; she grimaces but shakes it off.

One thing going for Elnice is her sense of balance, which hasn't deserted her since her tumbling days. She hops down the slope, still light on her feet, and allows herself a quarter-smile of triumph.

The two women make their way to a vantage point from which nearly all the course is visible. There they separate, Solita scrambling north, Elnice proceeding south.

When present transmutes into past: That's when experience becomes invested in meaning, for most of us. How the past stands before us, gripping our wrists! How it gripped Elnice until now: In spite of her feelings of excitement about being in Los Angeles and her desire to be an active citizen, she had been a servant of the past. But that stopped, that turned around on a dime the day she saw Watts Towers and looked through Luis Perona Gastello's baffling papers.

What would Dorothy and Yvonne think if they could see her now? Her bingo buddies, her church-lady buddies. Dorothy would push up her amber-tinted bifocals and say, "She's gone stupid."

And Yvonne would adjust her bony shanks in her bingo

seat and say dismissively, "She never could play more than three cards at a time."

Aren't these always the kind of things you hear when somebody breaks rank? Ever been called stupid? Ever been called crazy?

At first Elnice attempted to rationalize her actions, *this is the right thing to do,* but she could not support that with the kind of step-by-step thinking that made her so popular with her first-graders. So she simply relinquished her opinions on good behavior versus bad. She surrendered them, and in so doing she banished a certain amount of thought, which coincidentally and totally freed her from anxiety, the result being significant.

She is living entirely in the moment.

That, clearly, would have been the best part of living with the stinking gorillas: living in the here and now, with very little planning and no sense of consequence. Did the gorillas need somebody to keep lunchmeat on hand? Did the gorillas need somebody to pretreat their sweatpants with Spray-n-Wash?

For once not giving a damn whether God is listening, Elnice whispers, "Thank you."

The first time they spotted Luis on their first day of surveillance, six days ago, Elnice's heart seized in the classic voyeur's adrenaline rush: *I can see him but he can't see me. Can he?* But beneath his straw brim his eyes were dull with disinterest. He went about his work. From a perch on a hill overlooking the equipment shed, they watched Luis come and go. For two days, they waited to see whether someone who looked different from the workers would go into the shed to meet with Luis or leave him a package. This did not occur.

They followed him into the heart of the golf course,

keeping to the trees, keeping their distance, avoiding all workers. He roved about the side-by-side Wilson and Harding courses quite a bit during a shift, they discovered, and they found his behavior more and more interesting.

Elnice arrives at a patch of trees on the edge of the course. She's seen Luis slip into and out of this patch several times. Choosing a spot concealed behind some shrubs, she snaps open a plastic grocery bag, guide-floats it to the ground, and sits upon it. She discovered Luis's buried bucket two days ago; it contained a message written on the inside of a matchbook in pink ink: "Waiting for new toner delivery. Be patient already." But since then she's found nothing more in the bucket except a little moisture. Solita split off to watch a hideous patch of poison oak that seems to hold a similar attraction to Luis.

Elnice watches golfer after golfer hack his way past her concealed place, oldtimers, most of them.

Good God, how *do* they manage to play this game without falling asleep on their feet? Then with a little puff of gratitude she watches a foursome of younger, fitter men driving electric carts. They appear to be no better golfers than the geezers, but they're so much easier on the eyes.

Next comes a lopsided threesome of walkers, two Chinese grampas in ratty jackets and one tanned white guy. The grampas chatter to each other in their language, ignoring the other man, who peacefully ignores them in return. Like them, he too is silver-haired but he's turned out richly in dark gabardine slacks and a sweater, a snappy golf bag and spotless club head covers. He smacks his ball smartly, then with a stealthy look around, dives into the woods!

He disappears from her view, but she strains to listen. She hears rustling, then a small plastic *punk!*

The man emerges and hurries to catch up to the others. The early sun makes sparkles in his thick well-barbered hair.

Almost immediately Elnice perceives Luis driving a service cart along the fairway toward the clump of trees. "Damn," she murmurs.

Luis stops his cart and alights.

Suddenly a voice from up the fairway screams, "You bastard!" Luis freezes, his face instantly bloodless. Again the cry comes, louder, clearer, "*Bastards!*" It is a man's burly voice, piercing the last of the haze as the strengthening sun bestows clarity on trees, grass, and people.

Luis takes a hesitant step as if afraid his knees might buckle. He glances up the fairway toward the voice, then back the other way toward the green, where the threesome is putting out.

"Fix your fucking divots!" bellows the man from a hundred yards away. He must be at least two hundred yards from the party on the green, but he is shaking his fist vehemently enough to someone in a blimp to see. Elnice almost laughs aloud.

Luis takes a deep breath and lets it out, glances toward the woods, chews his lip, glances toward the next foursome, then climbs aboard his service cart and speeds away.

Elnice isn't sure what spooked him. She scuttles to the hidden bucket. *Punk!* it goes as she lifts the lid.

The message inside, on a single sheet of white paper folded into quarters, reads, "The board of directors could be a problem. I think H. is approachable. I can discreetly inquire. Yes or no."

She memorizes it, replaces it, and scoots.

Dian Fossey was successful: the gorillas wound up holding her hand.

But Rwanda, it turned out, was a dangerous place. More dangerous than Los Angeles, or less? Wilder? Lovelier? Who could deny the beauty of L.A.'s parks, the vistas from its hills and coastlines, the watercolor wash of morning gold beyond the silhouette of the eastward mountains?

In spite of her fear Elnice wants to take hold of the mischief she knows is in this place. The more it eludes her the more she wants it. She tells herself she wants to conquer it, but maybe it's also true she wants to sample it?

And as, day by day, she abandons rational objection in favor of recklessness, she feels herself growing stronger.

Solita is already waiting at the picnic area near the car. As Elnice walks up, a commotion breaks out among the nearby picnickers that stops Elnice's hurrying Keds on a dime. A group of children with sticks has set upon an effigy of Mickey Mouse hanging from a tree branch. The children, eyes glittering, beat and gouge the lynched figure, cheered on by their moms who are enjoying corn chips and salsa on paper plates.

Elnice's mouth forms a perfect O. The children's thin arms flail with the sticks, their cold laughter rings across the wooded dell. The corporate hegemony over entertainment is being given what for. Suddenly with a *thoop!* Mickey's stomach bursts, and a gout of bright candies spills out. The children dive to it squealing.

Solita laughs at Elnice's face.

"Oh!" says Elnice.

As they drive away Solita describes seeing a golfer, a nicely dressed one but younger than the one Elnice saw, striding along making halfhearted swipes at his ball.

"Angry man, he no care—he does not care about his golf. Swearing, fuck this, shit that! He speaks to himself of beer. The poison oak, he swims into her through the berry plants, I see he go same way Luis go. He golf away again and I find—I found?"

"Whatever," Elnice says wearily.

"I found this paper."

"You *took* it?"

"The paper say a place. We will go there. The man will be there and he will speak to us."

"Dear God."

"We must, like, do something. We must learn more. Why? You remember the policeman." Her tone of reproach scorches Elnice's cheek as she drives along.

Elnice had, against Solita's wishes and behind her back, gone to the police one day last week. She'd just stopped in on impulse at a substation near the park.

She explained what was going on at Griffith Park, she explained it the best she could to a stolid white cop who stood behind the plexi partition and held her eyes the whole time she talked and who finally said, "Did you find any unknown substances or currency in this underground tub?"

"No."

"Any jewelry, cameras, furs?"

"No!"

"Just, like, notes that don't make any sense?"

"*A* note. Yes."

"To your knowledge has anyone been hurt in any way?"

"No. Not to my knowledge."

"Well, what do you *think* is going on?"

She shifted her weight. "I don't know."

He heaved an enormous sigh which rustled the hairs on her forearms through the slot in the partition. Then, leaving his feet in place he turned his torso toward a two-foot stack of file folders. He swiveled back to Elnice, but his gaze sliced through her to the street beyond the doors of the substation. He held this faraway view for a moment, then shifted his eyes back into hers.

Very, very quietly, he asked, "Ma'am, what would you like me to do? Right now, for you, today?"

She understood this to be more than a question. It was a koan. What he really wanted to know was, "Ma'am, what is the sound of my time going down the toilet?"

She apologized and left.

Solita didn't speak to her for a day, after she came clean to her on this. Boy, did she hate cops.

Elnice asks what the note says.

Solita reads expertly, her language arts skills improving all the time, "We have to talk face to face. It's the only hope. Come tonight or it's all over tomorrow." And she reads off an address on Western Avenue.

23: A Profoundly Passionate City

In Los Angeles, today is always more intense than yester-day.

The feeling that has become impregnated into the very concrete of the streets is that ideology may be used to get you out from under moral strictures, but never to impose them. Los Angeles is a profoundly passionate city. This Elnice had not expected. But it's true that the raw souls of humans are what make it so appallingly wonderful: their gristly, growling, insatiable cores. There is much to see, and it is impossible to get tired of looking at it.

And it's not just the loudmouthed movie billboards and the Jaguars and stretch Hummers that flash by on the streets, the price tags on the purses in the boutiques on Rodeo drive, the tour buses. On top of all that it's the indignant guy in the aisle at Ralph's wearing a sleeveless mesh top and what appear to be leather underpants who stabs his eyes directly into yours and brays, "There's too many *people* in this aisle!" It's the feeling you get when the traffic on the freeway thickens like blackberry vines and you cannot even maintain Dallas motorcade pace. It's the nine-year-old girl anxiously sawing an unrecognizable folk tune on her violin at the Santa Monica pier as her cowboy-hatted mother looks on and passes the coffee can, knowing that a begging kid with talent trumps all. It's the razor wire on the overpasses that protects the freeway signs from graffiti. It's the way the clerk at the party mart holds her single long curled fingernail up and away from the cash register keys as if it were a special signal to her inner circle. It's the panicked fathers from North Platte, Joplin, Toledo, Elmira, and Duluth who, having forgotten to keep track of the route back to the rental car lot at LAX from Disneyland stop at gas stations on Manchester Avenue and beg attendants originally from Beirut for help and whose hands don't stop shaking even when they finally sink into their seats in the shuttle vans, their families at their sides silent with shock. It's the palm trees on Beverly Boulevard that turn pink at first light no matter who's looking.

Elnice, who has arranged to rendezvous with Solita later, is driving west on Los Feliz Avenue, toward home. She may be old but she is still a woman; she is resonantly alive. Because of this, she knows she is barreling toward death too. And it doesn't matter.

Her appetite for sex has crescendoed over the past two weeks. Perhaps it's due to the scrambling through the undergrowth of Griffith Park, which reminded her of things she used to do when young. She had been a scraped-knee artist, girl gymnast, lover of Arthur plus two boys before him.

Bullet Coker is old and scrawny but good-looking to her still, with that doggy grin and those strong arms. She thinks about the way he wraps her tight in those arms, the skin flaccid but the muscles firm. She thinks about the way the breeze from the canyon ruffles the white fluff on top of his head.

The jazz in her veins, the juiciness in her lower belly and breasts! This is the kind of desire she felt in her mid-forties just prior to menopause, when she could have had sex with Arthur three or four times a day. Sometimes they did! What is she doing dwelling on sex at a time like this?

She is alive, she is nervous, angry and hungry. Her desire for quiet comfort is obsolete, it's nowhere. What good's comfort anyway, since it invariably leads to dullness? Don't ask Elnice this question now.

When she walks in, Arthur is just coming up from a nap, stirring in his recliner. Fresco is stirring too. She perceives evidence of a prepared and eaten lunch: bread crumbs on the countertop, a smeared knife releasing the slightly sickening bite of stale mustard into the still kitchen air, a red fleck of bologna casing peeping over the rim of the trash can. A bit of creamy coffee dregs in the bottom of his favorite brown crockery cup, and yes, a corresponding sticky ring on the countertop. The refrigerator motor kicks in with a click and a shudder.

Everything is A-OK.

But as soon as Arthur's awake he is talking.

"Honey. Honey? Oh. Oh, Christ, oh shit. I fell asleep. I actually fell asleep at a time like this. I can't believe it. Unh. Honey. Unh."

She sets her purse down. "What is it?"

Clutching his forehead with his fingertips, he jams his brow up and down, side to side. "Shit! The goddamned liar!"

She perches on the recliner arm. "Stop it, dear. You're talking about Ty? What happened?"

"He's going to Miami." Arthur waits in fury for her to react.

"Well, what do you mean? Is he going for a visit because, you know, his kids are there, or—"

"That's what he says. But I—I think he lost our money."

Elnice, of course, knew the money was gone for good the instant Arthur wrote the first check. But she says, "What makes you think that?"

Arthur gives his Nikes a fierce look. "He was out on his patio today, talking to somebody on the phone. I heard him say in that whiny voice of his, 'Just give me another week.' Then he came over and tried to tell me how great these assisted living places are again. He told me he needs more money to add to what he's already got, in order to impress another big investor. 'Investors don't like to be the only ones loading into a movie,' he says. Then he casually announces he's going to Miami for a few days."

"Did he say when he's leaving?"

"Tomorrow night. I think he's blown our money somehow. He owes somebody. That's where our money went."

So she's not been the only hedge-listener in the Coker household.

"Did you ask him that?"

"No! I just know it." He exhales, then looks up at her. "I didn't have the guts to ask him directly." He seizes a nonexistent basketball with his hands and shakes it as if feinting a pass toward her. "Well, what's wrong with you? Aren't you going to say something?"

"Arthur, I knew it wasn't a safe bet. You knew it wasn't a safe bet. I didn't stop you. I signed the papers too. The hell with it."

"The hell with it? What's the matter with you?"

"Look, we have money left. We have our pensions and Social Security. We'll be all right." What else can she say?

"You're damn right we're gonna be all right, because I'm gonna figure out a way to sue his ass, do something, maybe we can get his house."

"It's probably mortgaged to the max."

"Yeah. Yeah."

"I can't think about this anymore right now." She realizes she forgot to change out of her navy Suzy Kramer poplin slacks, now smeared with dirt, back to the regular Joel Hannaberry madras slacks she left the house in. She also forgot to scrape the worst of the dirt off her Keds. She rises and moves to the kitchen, slips her shoes off and tosses them out of sight. He doesn't notice because he is busy rising to his feet.

And he's *up!* out of his chair and en route to her, slowly, slowly, dragging his oxygen hose. To the rest of the world he looks like a zombie with plastic tubing slung about his nose and ears but to her! The apparatus of illness is something she acknowledges, but not as an integral part of *Arthur.*

She moves to meet him.

His expression is a mixture of rage at his own stupidity, relief that she is home again, as well as that certain dry sense of command that returns to him whenever he ceases to be alone.

He reaches her and they stand together before the windows overlooking the canyon.

"I don't know." He touches the glass lightly with his fingertips. "I don't know. I had a sandwich." He takes her face into his hands. Startled, he breathes, "You look beautiful."

It's true: Her face is glowing like a teenager's, her lips are plump, hair askew, a dare in her little blue eyes.

"Get down, Fresco," he says.

"Kiss me," she says.

And with a surge he gathers her into his arms and lifts her to him. She feels his thin worn lips searching her, smells the spice of his aftershave, yes, this is still Arthur, emphysema or no emphysema, and I am still Elnice, fat belly or no fat belly, and, "I love you," she tells him.

He's all there for now, for now, she feels his body, his

thighs, his breath on her neck. Slowly, he escorts her to the bedroom.

Arthur's snoring, she notices, has gradually taken on a different character. In the past it was a regular chugging like a tugboat's engine, low and insistent. But now there's a new note in there, something on the order of a distant chainsaw biting through a tree.

She supposes that had they not made love this afternoon he would have taken the opportunity to press her more about her doings with Solita. But men and dogs are so gloriously manageable.

24: Experts in Revenge

The address the angry golfer had written in his note turns out to be on the meaty part of Western Avenue, more or less mid-town. Signs blur past the tan Buick: *We Buy Gold. Women's Health Clinic. Bail Bonds.* Dusk is coming on, and lighted signs glow against the cooling sky.

Elnice eases the car past the address once. Solita rolls down her window and takes it in.

"The sign she says Neff's. A bar?"

After a block-long hunt, Elnice finds a tight parking space. Western here is an urban strip that coheres a little bit better than the main streets of Watts. As she nudges the car into the space between a decrepit postal service Jeep transformed into an orange-striped pizza delivery truck and a dazzling El Camino low rider in purple metal-flake, she reflects again on the entrepreneurial spirit. Totally unquenchable. If your dream is to open a used tire store, you can lease twelve feet of frontage on Western Avenue and do it. If you want to sell candles and lucky charms and tell fortunes, you can do it. The dream is never out of reach.

Elnice and Solita walk past a row of six roll-up corrugated garage doors. It's a place where you can rent a bay, with or without tools, to work on your car. Evidently for ventilation, all doors but one are rolled up either partway or all the way, exposing people and their vehicles. Solita peers in at each one impassively.

"Hey, chickie!" comes a high voice from beneath a half-open door, in response to Solita's appearance. She straightens up, snorts, and gives a haughty backward kick.

The odors of motor oil and solvents come strong to their nostrils, competing with a sweet smell of frying shrimp from a restaurant ahead.

They walk past another bay, where a trim young white man wearing a white undershirt and torn coveralls wrestles with a piece of automobile as big as he is, a greasy chunk from an undercarriage, he is bent over it, trying to pry off a part with a screwdriver. He looks up as the women pass, and Elnice perceives that it's not a young man after all, it's a young woman with filthy hands, noticeable deltoids, firm small breasts and a sharp chin. Her expression is not womanly. Elnice would expect the face of a woman working on her own car to reflect distaste and anxiety. This one, however, reflects zeal and ruthlessness. Her eyes challenge Elnice. Elnice feels emotion burble up— defensiveness? curiosity? repugnance? In the past she shied away from such women. But now she feels different-ly. *Give me some of that fearful energy.* She lags a step behind Solita, looking.

Neff's gym shares a wall with a shrimp shack, the source of the frying smell. The proprietor of the shrimp shack is draped over the counter like a skinny cat, his head resting on one arm; one eye stares out unblinkingly. Mounds of fried shrimp glow under a bank of heat lamps, ready for the night's first customers. It is a tableau of somnolent expectancy. Heavy-sweet and tempting, the aroma of the shrimp dominates the air.

In the car en route the two women discussed how they would handle things tonight, but it was a short talk as they didn't know what the hell they were going into. What will they learn? They had fallen silent. Out of their silence, though, emerged a connection, something intelligent and unspoken and alive, like that between a battle-tested pitcher and catcher warming up before a World Series game, or between veteran actors about to launch into an improvisation.

Solita asks again, "Is this a bar?"

"No, it appears to be a gym. A gymnasium. Where people exercise."

The block-lettered sign is made of sheet metal bolted into the building's smudged brick front. The door is just a blank steel door. Standing before it, Elnice shuts her eyes, then opens them. She grabs the metal doorpull and yanks.

She yanks again, harder, and the door budges open two inches. Solita reaches in and adds her torque, and together they wedge themselves inside.

They stand in a short dim hallway plastered with photographs of fighters. Elnice notices only that the boxers look intimate, all that bare flesh. Two men hug, one drawing the other to him by the scruff of the neck, as if about to share a light. Another man, joy-eyed, stands spraddling his pelvis wide over another lying peacefully on the canvas.

Then the smell hits her. "Oh, my."

The smell is a deep, many-layered aggregation of old and new sweat, fear-sweat, indignation-sweat, dirty jockstraps and moldy spit, as well as a hefty dose of shrimp fan exhaust.

They move down the hallway to the gym, which is a surprisingly vast room floored with oak boards, with two boxing rings, and apparatus around the walls. Half a dozen men work out, two in one ring, others punching bags or stretching on mats. Most are bare-chested.

A fat man with a horrified expression jumps up from a folding chair where he had been reading a copy of *L.A. BackChat* and rushes over, shaking his head and flurrying his hands at them.

"This is a men's club, ladies," and his oncoming stomach forces them back into the hallway.

Elnice says, "We're here to see somebody."

"Who?"

"Uh, we only know him, uh, as Spike!"

"Spike? There's no Spike here."

"Could we just step in for a moment to make sure?"

Solita moves closer to the man, popping one hip out so that he may better see its curve through her skirt. "Please," she adds with a smile Elnice has never seen and in a tone Elnice has never heard.

"Mm," he says, a changed man. A hard-to-watch shudder of delight courses from his clublike black shoes to the dandruff clinging to his bald spot. "Well, hurry up."

Solita skips past him. Startled guys look around as she passes, a swift pixie searching for the right magic. In a corner, a young man is working the heavy bag, the rough canvas cylinder hanging like something slaughtered, the man's head low between his shoulders in concentration, his gloved fists alternating like pistons. *Chuff-chuff! Chuff-chuff!* The bag sways gently on its chain, its hundreds of pounds of sand absorbing the blows with dead-weight passivity. The man looks up, catches Solita's gaze, and stops punching. Solita quickly moves to the opposite side of the bag and peeks around it like a deer. Elnice catches up to her.

The man was clearly expecting someone, because there is a readiness in his face, a readiness to be caught looking tough, in spite of the fact that his glasses are secured to his head by a black neoprene strip. This is a man's man who called this meeting on his terms and who is too busy to sit around some bar waiting for someone to show up.

But he stands now bewildered, one side of his mouth open. His short, caramel-colored hair lies slick with sweat. His face is pink and slick too, and sweat streams down his pale torso into his shorts.

He speaks first, with an ironic, uncertain smile. "Who are you?"

Elnice answers, "We're here to listen to what you have to tell us."

Very slowly, as if inviting her to end the joke, he says, "I. Was. Expecting."

The women wait. Elnice had told Solita several times, *remember, less is more.*

As the seconds tick by, Elnice perceives that they've scored. This young man doesn't know who's behind the curtain.

Solita says, "We can't talk here."

"I guess not," he agrees unhappily. He had wanted to straddle a bench and talk in a corner of the rugged gym environment.

Elnice commands, "Get cleaned up and meet us at the shrimp place next door."

He looks from one to the other.

The fat man is approaching.

"OK."

Elnice orders three Cokes and Solita carries the waxed paper cups from the counter to one of the booths at the front window. The shrimp shack is a bright cube packed with fluorescent photons and sea-foam fragrance. The frying smell only becomes cloying when concentrated in the exhaust fan chute, and by then it's on its way to the gym and the street. The two women sit side-by-side in one half of the booth.

The man, wearing tan pants and a black t-shirt with the sleeves rolled tight against his muscles, stalks in and flings himself carelessly down. His hair has been toweled and finger styled, spiking down just slightly over his civics-teacher face.

No one is hungry for shrimp at the moment.

"Have a Coke," offers Elnice.

"No, thanks." He's ready. So is she.

"What's on your mind?" She asks.

"Look, I thought—I don't know why I was expecting a guy."

Elnice shrugs. "Just tell us what's wrong."

"I *did*. About ten times already." The cheap fluorescent tubes overhead show his eyes to be bracketed by anxiety lines. Elnice looks in deep. Scared shitless but forcing himself to be brave. He continues, "I want out, and you haven't been all that reasonable. I'm not asking for any-thing. Just to be left alone. I can't figure out if I've been breaking any law. I actually don't think I have. But what I've been doing for you isn't right. I know, I know, why now? I'll tell you why if you really have to know. I left that note so you'd know I was serious. I thought maybe I could give you something in exchange for being left alone."

The women wait in silence. The man becomes aware of the color of Solita's eyes, the remarkable black-violet iridescence of them. The deep fryers make intermittent drowning sounds.

He detects a faintness in his own voice and knows it betrays desire for her. *My God, she's a knockout.* Her smooth plump hands, resting on the plastic tabletop, look as if they could do any kind of specialized massage and do it well.

"I don't suppose you ladies have a pay grade? I mean, there's got to be someone above you, right?"

Elnice says, "I consider this whole racket, as you put it, to be preparation."

"For what?"

"For a better world."

"Oh yeah? Well. I guess you could see it that way. I mean paying somebody what you're paying me to take a Fortune 500 company down the toilet indicates a pretty lucrative result for the—well, your client. And for you. That would be world changing. I don't know about world bettering."

Elnice and Solita nod together.

"I just can't believe two pretty women are running this. Don—you know—when he set me up with this blind drop situation, he said Jason, this is going to be the opportunity of your life. Soaked by the money hose, my friend, that's what you'll be. Then he took off."

A bum squeaks the window with his palm as he shambles past.

Elnice sips her pop. She is glad to know the young man's name. "Actually, Jason, Don still works for us."

"Yeah? Doing what?"

"Similar work."

"Well, is it aerospace again? Because I thought he said he was moving to the East Coast."

"I can't tell you. Look, we're not little church ladies. Men aren't the only ones who get kicked out of the army and off police forces and decide to go a new way."

At this Jason M cantilevers an eyebrow.

"Not the only ones," Solita chimes in a rough voice,

"with needing to revenge."

"We're experts in revenge," Elnice affirms.

"Motherfuck," says Solita.

"Fuckin, man," adds Elnice.

Jason pushes up his glasses. "OK."

Elnice presses, "So no more bullshit."

She's finding this encounter easier than she'd expected. Bluffing's a snap, especially when what you're talking about is submerged anyway. Elnice finds herself calmly thinking ahead, trying to guess what this Jason might say next. What would a fellow like him want out of life? Clearly Jason is a guy who wants something *from* life, he is not a Peace Corps type, not a cancer walkathon type. He appears to be fighting his selfishness, though.

Unconsciously he picks up the third cup of Coke and guzzles it. "There's one thing I want to know: how did you get into my apartment that night?"

Elnice glances at Solita who casts her eyes downward.

"Even more modest than she is tricky, huh?" Jason M allows himself a knowing eye-crinkle. "I didn't even find a window open. Not that it bothered me in the slightest. I know you meant to scare the shit out of me, letting me know you could come in like that. All it did was make me curious."

The thought of the beauty sitting across from him, studying him, slipping into his bedroom to leave that hundred-dollar-bill on his pillow, good Christ, he'd watched enough porn to narcotize an elephant but this was more of a turn-on than a thousand digitally-remastered blow jobs. Had she looked down on his unconscious head with sudden tenderness? Had she wondered at the toughness of his sinews? He licks his lips. Had she bent to kiss him, stealing from him an erotic moment of her own? Had she regretted leaving? Deliciously confusing thoughts, these.

Elnice asks, "Well, what did you mean by your message, come tonight or tomorrow it's over?"

Jason M smiles a rugged half-smile, drawing in his cheeks so that his dimples show. "That sentence is rather open to interpretation, isn't it?"

"Well, are you really sitting here saying all you want is out, or will you stay if a certain condition is met? Or conditions? Your message had that implication."

The shrimp shack man listens. Customers come in and he serves them and they sit in the booths and eat their fried shrimp and shoestring potatoes and drink pop or he packs their food in takeout bags and they pay and he goes back to listening, his head propped on the counter by his thin arm like an olive on a toothpick.

Jason M loses patience. This wrinkle-faced corporate terrorist boss isn't getting it. He leans forward with all the intensity he can command, his biceps swelling to their maximum. "Goddam it! You're supposed to think I'll come and kill you if you keep on my ass about this! I can find out where *you* live." He sits back and twists his right index finger in his left fist. In fact, he has no idea whether his cop brother-in-law would help him find out anything about anybody.

"You wanted to intimidate us."

"Well, you've tried to intimidate me. Yeah! Can't you see where I'm coming from? Can't you just try to see? The money's been great. And for a while the work was fun, it was a challenge. But now, hell, I've got it down to a science and it's boring! But that's not even it anymore! It's that I'm having these dreams! My sleep is getting very interrupted."

A small cockroach crawls along the edge of the booth

behind him.

Solita watches it, then asks quietly, "What kind of dreams?"

Jason M's upper teeth seize his lower lip as tears come to his eyes. Solita and Elnice regard him steadily, their eyes so much softer than any that have gazed on him since he moved out of his mother's house in suburban Cincinnati.

He blinks fiercely.

"My dreams—it's the same dream—it's like this movie of these people on an airplane. This little girl—this same little girl over and over—and her mother and the steward-ess and these other people. And something terrible happens to the plane, something breaks and they start to fall and they all realize they're going to die. Except the little girl. She doesn't know any better." By force of will and shame he strangles a sob down deep in his throat. "I can't stand it anymore. I don't care about the money anymore. This is just a—a human thing. I know I've been useful to you. But I won't be any help to you if I have to kill myself."

"Oh, my dear." Elnice's impulse is to take his hand but she stops herself. He's in trouble, and he's going to be in deeper trouble before he's out of it, she sees. She cannot, however, afford to take on another child at this time. *It's not murder,* she tells herself, *if you're merely abandoning someone to the fate he's chosen.*

Jason continues, "I want to go and work on a charter boat down in San Diego or something. Live down by the docks."

He pictures himself bronzed and savvy, helping green-horn sport fishermen land their marlin and barracuda. Most of them would panic and hand their rods to him. Then the captain would chuckle and turn the boat again to facilitate the capture of the thrashing masculine creature below.

"Plus," he suggests, "what if I tell you something that would help you in the near future?"

Solita, in a girl-gang voice that almost sounds Russian, says, "Like what, man?"

"All right." The young man sucks in a long breath and flexes his shoulders against the back of the booth. The cockroach disappears. "What I've been doing for you isn't going to keep working. The machines—not just for aerospace applications but for everything, every other precision machining thing—they're starting to get so sophisticated that their controls sense and read out what maintenance is necessary and when. They're going to have micro-sensors everywhere, in the spindle heads, on the slides, all tied to the computer. This monkey-wrenching I'm doing for you is gonna be Stone Age in about two weeks. I am not exaggerating." He is, but he honestly doesn't know by how much.

Slowly, Elnice murmurs, "So if we want the problems to go on, we're going to have to infiltrate their computer programming departments. Right?"

"Right. I know some guys who could help...maybe."

Elnice sips her Coke. "To fuck with the software."

"Fuckin'," says Solita, and sips. Jason M looks at her.

"I mean," he says, "I'm already fucking with it, but on a crude level. You get it, right?"

"Well," Elnice says, "you're not a huge concern for us, Jason."

"My God," he says, his voice rising, "don't you understand? People are going to fall out of the sky, and it's going to be my fault and yours! I know that's not the plan! I know manufacturing failure is the plan. But you can't be sure that a disaster won't happen unintentionally."

"There are other ways to run a business."

"No kidding, ma'am."

CRIMES IN A SECOND LANGUAGE

"How would you feel if this business stopped right now?"

"What do you mean?"

"Well, if we came clean to our clients and to law enforcement."

Jason M cuts his eyes to the street and back again.

"You know something," he says slowly, "none of this feels right. Why are you telling me this?"

"We wonder whether you'll cooperate with us."

"You're not making sense. Why would you suddenly find Jesus, sitting here talking to me? There's something wrong here."

Elnice and Solita shrug as one woman.

Jason M goes on, "Why are you looking at me like that? Look, I've got a brother-in-law on the LAPD, and I could ask him to—to try to help me work this out, but I don't want to get into this deeper than I already am. All I want is out. Like I said."

In her frank, back-of-the-throat voice Elnice asks, "Do you think the dreams will stop then?"

He cannot answer, and this angers him and he gets loud. "Who can figure all this out? You've got your racket! Fine! I can't prove anything to you. What a fucking mess!" He glances desperately around the restaurant. "Hey buddy," he calls to the proprietor, "can you figure it out?"

Without lifting his head, the counterman murmurs, "All three of you's lying."

25: New Movie New Life

Ty Brandewine nibbles the corner off one of Elnice's lemon bars, savors its sweet tang, swallows, and resignedly observes, "Elnice, you look troubled."

"Yes, Ty, I am. I'm glad I caught you before you left. Arthur mentioned you're going to Miami."

He is discomfited but not surprised that she has come to him wanting to talk. "Look, I know Arthur's worried too, but I have to ask you guys to just trust me. Remember, I gave you a receipt and then we all signed that agreement."

"Yes, Ty, but I'm—"

"If you're that worried, maybe you should talk to a lawyer about it. To settle your mind. I can put you in touch with the top entertainment attorney in Los Angeles, he's worked for all the big shots like—"

"Ty, no, wait. Please listen to me. I'm not here to talk about the money."

"Oh."

She'd stood long enough in his foyer, holding the plate of lemon bars, that he was forced to ask her in. She didn't want tea or coffee. Now they stand uneasily in his kitchen, where *Variety* lies open, a cigarette stubbed out in an ashtray next to it.

"And I'm not here to talk about your movie."

"*Our* movie. *Our* movie." Bits of ash cling to his cargo shorts where they'd fallen into his lap as he read the paper.

"OK. Just—this. Something very strange is going on

and I want to talk it over with you. Because you're outside the situation and I just need somebody clearheaded to talk to." Impatiently, she brushes a strand of hair that missed getting drawn into her morning bun.

He catches the vibe. "Talk to me, Elnice." You never know when you're going to hear good material. He puts down his lemon bar, takes his pack of Chesterfields from a cargo pocket and lights up, drawing in the smoke pensively. He doesn't think to invite her to sit.

She hugs herself in her Suzy Kramer smock top, this one with a vertical splash of cornflowers that wraps over the shoulder to the back. "It has to do with Luis, Solita's man. Solita and I've gotten close over these months—she's such a dear, you know, and you're thinking about casting her in your—in the movie, our movie, and that's great, I think that could be a good thing for her. Well, you know I've been teaching her English. And I think you're aware that she's poorly educated. So I've kind of taken her under my wing." She tells him about the times Solita brought in vocabulary words that seemed exceptionally odd. "And you know, don't you, that Solita believes Luis to be working on a screenplay?"

"Yes!"

"Well, up until recently, Solita, being illiterate, you know, would have no way of knowing exactly what Luis was doing with this pile of papers he's got. Papers with writing on them, was all Solita knew. But as it turns out, Ty, there is no screenplay."

He gives her a little gleam. "There isn't?"

"No. I went with Solita to their home—my God, Ty, they live in Watts on a crummy street but right near this incredible sculpture one of their neighbors made—"

Ty laughs. "Did you see some garage-door murals?"

"Uh, I'm not sure what you're—but yes, probably. And I snooped into his papers and, well, it was very confusing. No screenplay, but a collection of all these bits of paper that look, well, sinister! There's a list of what could be payoffs maybe, and there are documents from businesses marked confidential, it looks like important information on them, chemical formulas, things like that." She mentions Genew, the pharmaceutical company, and the machine company that Jason M works for.

She stops, her face suddenly pale. "I'm feeling a little lightheaded, I'm a little out of breath. I—I have more to tell you—"

"Come here, I'm sorry, sit down, sweetheart." He draws out a chair.

At once his kindness unleashes sadness in her. "Oh, Ty, thank you." She swallows, exhausted. "Everything is so confusing. I'm sorry."

"Never be sorry for being real, Elnice."

"Thank you." She cries a little.

"Let it out, sweetheart." He fetches a box of Kleenex, fluffs out an extravagant handful and offers them to her. "You relax now. You've been doing too much." And seeing her composure shot, the worry in her small bright eyes, today her temples appear slightly sunken—my God, how easy can it be to manage the endgame for a guy like Arthur? "Is King Arthur being cruel to you?"

"Oh, no, he's—he's just—sometimes he's crabby, and I think sometimes not as—rational as he used to be."

"Yes. Are you eating, dear?"

"Uh—"

"You have to eat. Listen to me. If you do nothing else, you eat. OK? And stay hydrated."

"Uh—"

He brings her a glass of cold water, eases down next to her, and puts his arm around her narrow shoulders. They feel even frailer than he expected, the bones loose and mobile—mouselike, and as she looks up at him with her quick eyes he sees how earnest and small she is, really. With a smile he says, "Elnice, let me tell you something that's going to make you feel a thousand percent better."

She blots her eyes.

"Listen to me." She smells the smoke in his breath, not an unpleasant smell. "Luis," he begins, "really does have a screenplay. Now, notice I don't say he's *written* one. He's been working on one, it's true, he really has. But he doesn't have a finished product. What he has is a platform for an incredible story. It's just a beginning, but what a beginning! My God, the beginning the little bastard's made! You found the scraps of it, all the fits and starts that don't make any sense!"

She looks at him.

Ty continues, "I got Luis over here to do some work for me. I can't count how many times Solita bragged to me he was writing a screenplay. For months and months and months I'm like, right, Solita. Right, Solita. Naturally she wanted me to help him. My expertise and influence can go a long way for a newcomer to the business, and yes, Elnice, everybody! In! Los! Angeles! Is writing a screenplay! There's a lot of desire out there but not much talent, to be frank. But what there is is material! All of those no-talent boobs out there, all of them are sitting on goldmines of stories. They just don't know it. And they spew this crap onto the paper instead of if they really got in touch with what the hell's really going on in their *lives*—but that's another subject entirely. Never mind."

He drags on his Chesterfield, burning an inch in one

lungful. "So the other day I more or less corner Luis about his screenplay, because I'm the kind of person who likes to listen to other people, really listen to them. He was reluctant at first, but then he got this *spark* in his eye and he started talking about his idea. Little by little it came out. And Elnice! I want to shout this from the rooftops! It's pure gold! It's platinum! I'll tell you about it but you have to promise—wait! I gotta go get my notes, I don't want to forget anything!"

Luis climbs down from his mowing machine and slips into the woods. *Punk!* goes the bucket lid. The note inside says, "Just wanted to say thanks. It was great meeting you. Glad we worked it out. Wish we could've met under other circumstances. Good luck to us all. I guess we need it."

Luis's eyes are the color of burnt coffee and much more thoughtful than most people notice. They scan the message once more.

Ty stubs out his cigarette, plucks another from the pack, and gestures with it as he talks. "Here's the setup. You know, Luis is a clever guy beneath it all. He really got a kick out of my reaction to all this. OK, you've got this guy from Mexico. Autobiographical up to that point! Haha! His parents, members of the climbing class in Mexico City, sent him to whatever crappy pretentious boarding schools they could afford, thence to UC Berkeley. His parents think he's going to go from there to being president of Disney! The guy gets a Berkeley education, you know, very counter-culture, and he realizes that people in the States expect a Mexican to be dumb. The only Mexican-Americans who talk like they're from Ohio get harvested to read the news on California TV!"

202

Elnice nods, tissues balled in both hands.

"That would all be summarized in the script. Not at the beginning because it's boring. You gotta have some kind of reference to it though, so some of the later Jungian stuff makes sense. OK, the guy's got a rebellious personality but he's quiet about it. He decides to take a job as a trainee in a stock brokerage firm in San Francisco. He learns you can do wonderful things with computers." Ty taps his cigarette, filter down, on the tabletop. He continues to gesture with it. "OK, so the bosses are shits and the clients are arrogant assholes, and he decides to totally screw over the company by making unauthorized trades on other guys' computers. Nobody catches on until it's too late, and even then they don't suspect *him*, and the place actually goes bankrupt! But no one ever catches on that it was him. So he thinks, hey, I bet I can make this pay, really pay. All you need is one employee in the right position and you can fuck over any company—or *government*. Now, he doesn't really want to be a government spy, if he gets nailed he at least wants a chance to go to jail, not get executed by some CIA asshole and dumped down a sewer. I've written some spy fiction and I know. The best spies are ideologues with low IQs!"

Finally, he lights his cigarette. "He gets in touch with some of his friends from Berkeley—all of them trying to become startup billionaires—and they're finding it a harsher world than they expected. They're a bunch of misfits but have—"

"Hearts of gold?" Elnice queries.

He pauses. "Yes." He squinches an eye at her apprecia-tively. "Anyway, they get together and form an underground corporation! Where they hire themselves out as saboteurs who will learn any job, present phony creden-tials, get hired anywhere, and proceed to either steal competitive secrets or invisibly destroy systems and property. They're mercenaries, see? Who, because of the risks of the work and the greed of those who hire them, command big bucks. They guarantee results based on stock prices—yours goes up by a certain percent or *your competition's* goes *down* by a certain percent—and they do it all cash-based. This Mexican guy, he's the boss, he goes around to prospects and very discreetly offers their services. Or he hires help for this—you can find decent-looking people to deliver messages—single-use associates. And companies go for it! The guys at the top keep it quiet, or they refer it to their security guys, who are not above getting their hands dirty, and then the top guys have deniability. So we've got the basis for a big commercial thriller here, Elnice, see?"

"Yes. I see." Elnice is regaining herself. "And sometimes," she suggests, "they recruit new people into their group? And no one can leave except if they replace themselves first?"

Ty cannot help her, she understands, but instead of dismaying her, the fact gives her dark comfort. If she must act alone, she must satisfy only herself.

"Yeah! Elnice! You are acute today. And this guy handles the contacts and money transfers for the group, in exchange for a cut of everybody's action. Now here's the brilliant thing that'll work so well on the screen, it'll play to audiences like thunder. This guy needs a good consistent cover, right? What's safer than stupidity? So this guy, this brilliant, well-educated, worldly guy pretends to be an illiterate laborer!"

"And he gets a job mowing grass?"

"Yes! Hah!"

"And he mistrusts digital transmission of anything,

even if it's encoded, or—encrypted, is that the word?—because sooner or later people get caught that way? Indelible trails. He only keeps a few written records on paper? And he creates secret drop spots on the golf course for that purpose?"

Brandewine makes a sound like a single corn kernel popping.

Calm now, almost serene, Elnice goes on talking from the back of her throat in her gentle, clear way. "And aside from the original group, none of them ever meets him face to face. So there's a whole web of people doing this secret work. And only he knows them all: The fellow everybody thinks of as the dumb brown guy is the only one who knows them all. And he's biding his time, living humbly, until he can close up shop and retire with millions, and in the meantime he finds himself a dumb, illegal little girl who gives him sex and comfort and good food and doesn't ask any questions. She's part of his cover, too."

Ty looks at her as if she has just taken all her clothes off.

Elnice muses, "It isn't illegal to exchange notes in public. And I would think that if a company uncovers a saboteur they would just quietly let them go. Who wants to let the world—your shareholders—know you couldn't keep your business secure? I guess anybody can hire a thug to throw a shoe into an assembly line, or bribe a union. But these people work in complicated ways. Yes, Ty. A very safe way to do business. Except when somebody finds God. Except when somebody panics and wants to get out. But if you handle it right, nothing will even make the nightly news."

After calling in sick and playing a bit of golf, Jason M runs his car through the wash and returns to his apartment. He throws a chicken pot pie into the microwave. He listens to kids yelling in the pool beneath his balcony. He cracks open a cold Bud 55. Next grabbing a yellow pad and his Pelikan medium, he starts writing out lists of things to do and just things. He jumps up from that and moves stuff around, piling his magazine crates in a more compact configuration, then returns to his lists. Best to make a new start. Elsewhere.

Once in San Diego he'll offer to work for nothing, at first, on a charter boat. He'll do what he's told, show he can hustle, learn the ropes, then get paid some modest amount which he'll use to rent a small room down by the docks. Someplace quieter than this bourgeois complex, which happens to lie right beneath one of the main approach paths to LAX. Maybe he'll live on the beach for a while. That's it: grill fish right out of the sea over a driftwood fire. Steaks right out of the package. Lonely chicks hang out at the beach, especially when they're in transition. Lonely intelligent chicks with long hair and pretty feet. He'll go to work every morning on the ocean. Calm and blue! Stormy and white! He'll wryly accept tips from the pasty-faced suburban chumps who want nothing more than to be him but haven't got the guts. Sure, he's got a few details to figure out like health coverage and what kind of shoes he needs to look like a proper charter-boat mate, but he'll get to all that in good time. Over-thinking a thing is a sure way to kill it.

His buzzer buzzes, no doubt Next Door Dude wanting to cadge another beer. He strides to the door and flings it wide. A sweaty Mexican guy pushes him hard in the chest and stumbles him backward. The intruder closes the door behind him.

"What the hell?" Jason M says.

"There's been a mistake," says the compact, jeans-clad guy in perfect American.

"Yeah! I didn't invite you in and you've got the wrong apartment."

The guy stands there on his color-block area rug like a tree stump. "Did you talk to two women last night?"

Jason M doesn't answer.

"Shit, you did!" spits the man. "I knew it. Listen, those bitches were fakes."

"What?"

"You have to keep working."

"Who the hell are you?"

"You have to keep working."

Jason M's stomach bobbles. "No, man. Hey, I gave notice. I'm gone."

"There's too much at stake for you to do this now."

"That's not my problem." Jason's brain works hard to stay on target. "Everything's gonna be clean, nothing you can do about it."

"How much did you tell them?"

"Tell them! They knew about everything! We talked about everything! Who were they?"

A shout carries up from the pool.

"What's that?" says the swarthy dude excitedly, stepping over to the doorwall and pointing. "What's that?"

"Just kids in the pool," Jason M says, glancing down at them.

The man steps back, pulls a piece of wire from his pocket, wraps it around his hands in a second, and leaps at Jason M, who is just turning away from the window. The wire is tight around this throat, and he barely has time to make fists, barely has time to remember when fighting to flex his knees and watch for your opponent to let his guard down. He barely has time to wish he'd talked all this over with his brother-in-law.

Using his hip as a pivot point, the man yanks Jason M backward and they crash softly to the rug where the sweat-stained worker is able to put perfect steady tension on the garrote. Jason M barely has time for the novelty to wear off about moving to San Diego.

After a moment's hesitation, God gives his soul the thumbs-up, so he wafts upward like a strip of gauze to meet the cherry-nosed cherubs and gold-leafed guardian angels he finds so nauseating on the greeting cards his mother sends him.

An airliner on approach to LAX banks into a turn overhead, the shriek of its engines overpowering the swimming-pool chaos. When it glides off into its final descent, it makes the howls of the splashing kids sound like dead silence.

26: Solita's Story

Luis guides his piebald pickup homeward, rolling the back of his neck against the headrest, letting the hot freeway wind blow the sweat from his pits, and thinking of Solita. What a pepper pot that one's turned out to be. He's been willing to portray a poverty-stricken dullard for a while in order to gain a fortune, but one thing he couldn't deny himself was the love of a beautiful woman. He'd felt lucky to have found the pea-brained little Solita, still covered with abrasions from her flight from the high country of Mexico, wandering up and down Hollywood Boulevard naively looking for a job in a restaurant kitchen.

He'd felt something unraveling with her but had made the mistake of not addressing it. Plain bad management. She'd gone out last night after declaring that she thought she was pregnant. He had accepted her explanation of how home pregnancy tests work: one must go to the store, buy the test, then go to one's girlfriend's house nine blocks distant and do the test. It takes a long time to wait for the results. Angela, her girlfriend, has done this many times before and will be glad to help. Luis asked whether the test could be done in their own home, but Solita said no, it required another woman's help. The way she said it made Luis not want to know more. That was her ruse. A time-honored one, and he'd fallen for it.

He thinks about how the women of his family, especially the ones in the backcountry, exploited the mysteries of their bodies. All women do this, of course. Keeping secrets from their men, cultivating the strange mysteries of menstruation, childbirth, and menopause—this is about the only power they have. If they can make their men shrink from them, appease them, crawl to them, that is something. Out of all this, he knew, grew the tales of the *brujas*, the desert witches. The crones. His aunts and grandmothers—even his mother, who pretended to classi-ness—they all celebrated themselves in this black bloody way.

He coughs in annoyance. Solita is no longer innocent. She is no longer a better person than he is. Good people are stupid people. She is getting too smart.

She fears him still, for he cultivated a firm terror in her to discourage her from ever challenging him. She had presented him with the means to control her, and he had capitalized on it. With women it's so easy. A look. A silence. A sharp word. None of it need interfere with sex.

He's hungry for his favorite meal: a fat grilled steak drenched in red chili sauce, accompanied by a special invention of Solita's, a fried corn-and-potato cake with onions. That and a chilly six-pack. The last meal Solita cooks on this earth should rightly be his favorite. She owes him that and a lot more.

In a way, Jason M did him a favor: challenged his re-luctance to kill. It hadn't been easy, but everything gets easier the more you do it.

Perhaps he should have cultivated trust in her instead. He could have created elaborate warm fictions about himself, he could have come home brimming with gossip from work. This guy's sleeping on the job, that guy told off the boss and quit, bullshit like that. He could have invent-ed troubles, too, troubles he would bring to her, so that she could have the pleasure of knowing him more deeply. *What a good suggestion, Solita. That's just what I'll do.* She would feel she knew him better than he knew himself.

He shudders. It makes him sick to play nice.

He slaloms his truck through traffic, one hand on the wheel, shifting lanes to gain advantage. Distractedly he strokes his penis through the age-softened cloth of his pants.

Things fall into place. Number one, she had been more solicitous of him lately, indulging his tastes for morning sex and steak dinners. Yet number two, she seemed furtive. Somehow she'd drawn the thinnest of veils over herself. There were the unusual scratches on her legs, which she attributed to helping her friend Angela rescue her cat from a treetop.

Suddenly a particular moment springs to mind. He'd come home from work one day and showed her a purple welt on his back where he'd been hit by a golf ball.

Did it hurt! he'd told her, and Solita had said *Yo sé.* I know.

He'd thought she sympathized with the pain, because she quickly turned to the refrigerator to get some ice for it, but now he realized she really did know, she had seen it, had been watching him from a hiding place!

Damn her to hell. Damn that gringa too.

Because Jason M had revealed it. Luis had been smart enough to suspect Solita's new gringa friend, that old lady in the Hollywood Hills, and he had asked Jason M if he had talked to two women last night. He had not denied it. All summer Solita was Mrs. Coker this and Mrs. Coker that, but recently she'd shut up about the old lady. It was all so obvious.

He's worked like a mule to get to where he is: a mere

year, perhaps, from a life of ease in Brazil or Spain. Far away from the lost revenue, trouble, and damage he and his associates would leave behind.

Well, he could make good on his standard threat and deliver Solita to the men who want her back in Mexico.

Yes, she had stupidly, trustingly, revealed to him the name of her home village in Mexico as well as what happened there. When you possess something valuable in Mexico, it's easy to hook up with the party with the strongest vested interests. Indeed, he's found that to be the case in the United States. Land of vested interests. People always pretending to be idealistic! He thought of his fellow students at Berkeley. He spits out the window. So sanctimonious! Covering their selfishness with trivial idealism, all of them, except for himself and his friends, who actually knew the score. The billboards of Los Angeles fly by: movie stars looking tough or funnily hopeless, plus pitches for sports cars, retail banking services, malt beverages.

He's tried to keep things simple.

His father used to sit in the easy chair, where he would twirl his eyebrow hair and say, "Just remember: there's nothing a woman can do to you that would make you have to hit her. A woman can't hurt you." His father had never struck his mother; Luis had never really hit Solita or any other girl or prostitute. He had grabbed Solita roughly once, that was all.

His father didn't know Solita, though.

Luis had hated to see his parents running after money and status all those years, hated them for prompting him to be an actual big shot as his father was a half-assed big shot: owner of two motels on the outskirts of Mexico City! He despised them for being fake. If they only knew the direction their pretensions had driven him to. They would see him as dishonest, but would gladly overlook that once they saw evidence of his net worth. Then too they would understand his joy in pitting gangs of consumerist whores against each other. If he helps bring down the system, it serves everybody right, even his parents. He converts most of his money into gold. He loves gold, the look of it, the feel of it. He once bought Solita a fine gold chain, which she wears on Sundays. He too would like to wear gold, a big thick rope of it around his neck. And he will someday.

Someday Luis will really be a father, a good one. He'll walk down the street to the local café showing off his son, who will deliver soft kisses to his mother's cheek and tiny punches to his father's palms. Luis will have easily found a new woman, a beautiful one with Solita's fire but none of her careless malevolence.

They will all live in a fine city, enjoying the good things and excitement it offers. A beach house, too, on a serene ocean coast. He will buy up property in the city, buy and sell property and become a significant man. The politicians will do what he says and he'll have fun proving to them how stupid they are. He'll take his family to the movies, perhaps to see Ty Brandewine's version of his life story, and Luis will laugh himself sick. He will educate the boy himself, so that he grows into a young man with no scales over his eyes. The woman will look after them. Luis will be happier. What's not to be happy about, such a life? More kids! No work, no bosses. He will grow fat. Paradise!

It's getting late.

Arthur sucks at his oxygen like a twelve-year-old runaway who's just discovered toluene.

"Can't sleep?" Elnice asks from her side of the darkness.

"We went to bed too early. It isn't even ten o'clock."

Fresco is restless too: he roams and chatters in his can't-decide-whether-to-bark-or-whine way. Arthur gets up and lugs his oxygen hose toward the kitchen. Flipping on the hall light, he catches sight of himself in the oval mirror there: crimson track suit, hair like wisps of milk-weed, leaden stubble, eyes glazed with anxiety. Why does he feel so nervous? The poodle's bowl is empty. He opens a can of Powerdog and dumps it in. Fresco doesn't even give him an incredulous look—two dinners in one night?—just dives for it.

Arthur watches the dog's jaws squish up and down in the food. The doorbell cracks the silence causing both of them to aspirate small amounts of saliva which they have to cough out. Fresco flings himself at the fortress of the front door. The bell rings again, *chime-a-ling!* Arthur hears Elnice creak out of bed. He pads in his slippers to the door and puts his ear against it. Someone is crying outside.

Tina G awakens to a small sound. She listens. Nothing. She feels the weight of her current boyfriend's arm slung over her hip; he is sleeping deeply, having forgotten nothing on his packing list. Their all-night flight to Singapore had gone well: pretty piles of Asian food and tasty Australian wines, plus free sleepwear and lotion. A nice kickoff to a weeklong vacation. The shopping she'll do! She's thinking silk, she's thinking pearls. Big whopping pearls in futuristic settings. They'll hit Tokyo too, then spend a few days in Bali just relaxing. Knowing she's loaded and hoping to marry her, the boyfriend has schooled himself in her favorite sexual routines, which he performs with a mini-mum of rest breaks.

But no way is she gonna settle for a doorknob like him. Tomorrow she will do a little business at the Suisse Bank.

Imagine! Little Tina G, little Berkeley drop-out who traded her Birkenstocks for Prada, in Asia kicking up her pert heels and making sure her nest egg's doing what it's supposed to be doing. Of course she'll find everything in order, those Swiss are so tick-tock dependable. Perhaps she'll meet a coolly handsome Swiss banker with a hidden passion for snorkeling.

Chantelle W is drinking cosmopolitans with her golf pro at a posh bar in Laguna Beach where they've seen movie stars. The pro says, "I've given lessons to every action-movie star in the business and believe me, those guys could not win two bucks off of you."

Keith B, vice president at the Internet retailer, abruptly left the company just as the president was getting up the guts to challenge him on his bullshit timelines. He received a smallish golden parachute from that hapless dumb company. His new assignment turned out to be—get this—chief operating officer in a frighteningly up-and-coming independent media company, with plenty of established rivals. One or more of them will pay handsomely for his special talents. They have ways of quietly moving money around for such purposes.

Life is good.

It is Solita standing there crying, gripping the doorframe for support. Arthur steps back in surprise.

"Please, Mr. Coker."

Elnice is at his elbow now. "Come in, Solita," as if she'd been expecting her. "I'm glad to see you."

The girl sinks into her customary chair at the kitchen table, gulps down the glass of water Elnice sets before her, and speaks well enough in spite of the split lip that leaves a kiss of blood on the rim.

"In Mexico I see a murder. I saw a murder. Thank you." Arthur hands her a damp paper towel.

"Yes?" says Elnice.

"Three years ago," she says clearly enough around the paper towel, "a police man kill my brother. My brother he knew the police man was big in the drugs, a big shot. The police man wanted money from my brother, but he no—he would not give it to him. He was a bad police, you see?" She wads the towel in her fist.

"Yes."

"My brother he insults him. He says his mother was *puta fea*—ugly bitch? He do foolish business, then he run to my home. The police man comes and shoots him. I take a picture! He close the door and thinks no one can see him shoot my brother. I see it and with my husband's camera I take a picture! A photograph! Insta-matic! This man and his gun and my brother lying bleeding from his chest. The police man is very surprised, then he turn to shoot me, and I jump out the window, I run to the mountains."

"Oh, my dear." Elnice's hands tremble slightly on the tabletop. She has on her pink waffle-cloth wrapper. The wide sleeves make her wrists look frail.

"I should kill him instead of take his picture but I have no gun and no knife. Then I come to California. Alone. I did it. I know this police man will kill me if I go back. He is friends, too, with many police in Mexico and police in Los Angeles. I will no enter a jail in Los Angeles or Mexico. I will die before that. This man is alive and I know he will always look for me." She gazes calmly at Arthur, then at Elnice. "Luis will come here soon."

Elnice reaches out and touches a finger-grip pattern of

bruises encircling Solita's right forearm. The elbow is swollen and red like a mango.

The girl says, "I get away. Luis he wants to give me to the man in Mexico."

"No, honey, he wants to kill you."

"The same."

Arthur asks, "What happened to the picture—the photograph?"

"I meet Luis in Los Angeles," answers Solita, "near here. He helped me. When I know I love him I tell him about my brother and the picture. I carry the camera to Los Angeles from Mexico. I tell Luis I want to send the picture to the governor of Sonora. He come—he came to my village once. I think he is a good man and will make trouble for the police man who shoot my brother. My brother, his wife go away. She went away." The strain of speaking so much English shows in Solita's face and in the tension in her hands as she talks, but she plunges on. "I want to kill the man who shoot my brother. He wants to kill me and I want to kill him. Luis send the picture to the governor. He go to post office. I want to know what happens when the governor sees the picture. A month later Luis say he find out. He *found* out what happened. The picture made trouble, but only a little. The man he is angry and will kill me for revenge if he can. We must leave now."

Elnice says, "How do you know these things for sure?"

"Luis told me them."

"He lied to you."

"Everything is the same. Luis has become that man."

Elnice considers. "So the story about your husband abusing you in Mexico wasn't true?"

"Oh it was true! My friend Elnice! My husband would have turn me over to this police man for, like, ten U.S.

dollars. For nothing! This police man would be a good friend for him," she spat. "Hah! Buttheads!"

"Is your name really Solita?"

Elnice and Arthur wait.

"I have forgot my old name," says Solita, finally.

"Well," says Elnice, "what do you want me to do?"

"Oh, Elnice." The girl scoots her chair closer to Elnice's and rests her head on her shoulder. Elnice smells her spicy hair. "You are my friend." She lifts her head. "Luis want to kill you too. We three must leave here now. Luis will come soon."

Arthur says, "We should call the police."

Solita says, "The police will do no thing."

Elnice says, "I'm not afraid of him."

Twin cones of light sweep across the front picture window and dart into the kitchen.

27: Arthur Races Again

"Don't open the door," says Arthur. He swallows and fondles his oxygen hose.

"Nonsense," counters Elnice. What she said a minute ago is true: she is no longer afraid of Luis. She welcomes seeing him, in fact.

Fresco remembers the look and smell of Luis; he does not caper in his usual nutty way, *touchme touchme touchme*. Elnice gathers up the slinking dog and opens the door.

"I am looking for my Solita," Luis is deeply concerned, furrowed brow, but—friendly! Smiling shyly, he steps in.

Elnice shuts the door. "She's here."

He drops the friendliness. "Good."

With barely a glance at Solita, Luis seats himself in Arthur's spot at the kitchen table. Arthur joins him, taking Elnice's place. He holds the cordless phone handset at his side. Surely Luis sees the phone, but he's unconcerned. Elnice moves to the empty chair. Solita sits in silence, her eyes down.

Everyone knows what is about to happen.

Luis appears relaxed. Though a foot shorter than Arthur, he seems bigger, with his frank wide face with its tile-like planes, his brown hands, his work shirt and soft blue jeans, his boots. Arthur's face is the color of cold oatmeal.

"What is that?" says Luis, pointing.

Slowly, Arthur answers, "I need this contraption to breathe."

"Ah. Goddamn thing, eh?" He drops his eyes to take in Arthur's spindly legs in their red pants.

"Yeah! Wait—I—you know, I didn't think you could speak English!"

There's that shy smile again. Everyone suddenly becomes aware of Luis's right hand. The knife must have come from a sheath strapped above his work boot, yes, his pant leg is still hiked up, caught on a tab of leather, and the hunting knife gleams in his hand. No matter what the knife, doesn't it always gleam when it is turned upon you. Damn, it *sparkles*.

Arthur fiddles with the phone, but Elnice grasps his wrist and he stops. He knows his power is limited, and he must choose his moment carefully.

Luis's burnt-coffee eyes are quiet, just like his hands. After a moment, though, the hands begins to move, the hovering knife making tight figure-eights in the air above the table. His hands might be dealing cards. His face beneath the kitchen light looks capable and perceptive. It might be the face of a movie star in a modern-day western where the Mexicans are the good-looking ones and win in the end.

He speaks, his English crisp and sure: "We're going to have a little discussion."

Arthur, Elnice, and Solita sit cornered in the dining alcove, as Luis, his back to the business end of the kitchen, hardens his eyes on them.

At last Fresco senses disaster and yaps ferociously from the safety of Elnice's arms.

"Give me that dog."

Elnice stares, catching on increasingly quickly. "No."

Just in case the knife and his immersed fury aren't enough, he yanks little stupid Fresco from his mistress's arms and dangles the animal by its leather collar. He has become Elvira Gulch in drag taking Toto to the sheriff, and he steps to the sink! To the *sink* for the sake of neatness, perhaps, but before he plunges that knife into the dog's body, the animal twists with desperate athleticism and sinks his short fangs to their hilts into Luis's wrist.

Little Fresco! Had he ever before harmed a flea? Outdoors in the canyon Luis's scream resounds as a faint high note, interpreted by the few people who hear it as a distant gull keening over garbage somewhere.

Luis had killed chickens with a hatchet at his grandfather's house, the recollection of which unfailingly impressed his university classmates. The chickens had never succeeded in biting him, though. Blood oozes from the puncture marks. He briefly drops the dog in preparation for regripping it this time around the throat, but Fresco bounds out of the sink like a Russian gymnast and rockets down the hallway to the place beneath Elnice's side of the bed where he always goes when the chips are down. Cursing in Spanish, Luis rinses his wrist in the sink, then shakes it. This takes but a few seconds.

The three other humans have remained motionless as if already bound and gagged.

The dog thing didn't work and Luis is breathing heavily but he's still in command. "All right, look," says he, turning to them, "What do you know?" His eyes switch back and forth between Solita and Elnice.

Arthur pipes, "Know about what, know about what?"

Solita speaks in a steady voice. "I have seen my brother killed in my home. Do you think I am afraid of you?" She allows herself a triumphant look. "Yes. I speak English."

Luis's mind is racing, careening around a curve of paranoia.

He knows that other men kill for a few basic reasons: 1) hot blood (Bitch, if only you hadn't grabbed that last slice of pizza); 2) demented sport (Let's see how many women who look like my ex-wife I can find and strangle); and 3) for a living (Sorry, punk, you shouldn't'a held back that five thousand you owe my boss).

He is different; he kills only for the purpose of risk management. This can all still work.

Elnice speaks. "Luis. You're the one who should answer questions. Why are you letting other people use you? The people who put messages in that bucket in the woods and in the tube?"

No answer from Luis but a small smile. He towers over them, standing at the table as they sit.

"What is your reason for that?" Elnice tries again, simply.

"Elnice my friend," says Solita, "We are fools to ask for a reason. There is no reason! For the people in the bucket and the people in the pipe in the ground. Buttheads! All buttheads!" Her voice strengthens. "Buttheads do secret business that hurts people. I find blood on your shoes, Luis! Bloody shoelaces! I have keep the shoelaces for the DNA! You will tell me nothing. I see this and I say ha!"

Her nostrils flare like a buffalo's. "You depended upon me for being dumb! Now I am smart in English! I learn to read your secrets! You think I would always be only Solita, only the same! My friend Elnice is a good teacher. And I see the answer is for money. Money," she spits. "If your secrets—if the secrets they are because of something good, an idea, if you stand for something, fight for something, I would know this. Your secrets are for money."

Elnice perceives that Solita has absorbed several useful lessons from *L.A. BackChat.* She thinks this as she continues to watch Luis and wait for an opportunity. Had he killed Fresco Elnice would not have much minded, she suddenly realizes. Everybody dies.

For some reason Luis endures this scolding. He sits still for it, cocking his head, gazing into the middle distance.

He was not a poor child. He was not an abused child. He did not begin by stealing cars. Even he is surprised to see himself doing what he is doing. When he first thought of building a secret society of corporate tricksters, he did not include murder in his plans. Murder is only for people who have much at stake. He could not foresee then how much he would have at stake now. If he were to quit now, he would possess a certain amount of money. But he would also be saying, *I was wrong. I wasted my time.*

Not all principles are equal. Luis's work is ultra principled. When you aspire to certain standards—when you hold certain ideals above all others—it is also possible to prize them above individual life. It is possible. But only when you have devoted great portions of time and mental and emotional energy to them do they begin to breathe on their own and *demand* that you prize them above individual life.

Boundaries become paper targets.

He accepts the fact that his captives cannot understand, will never understand him and the importance of his goals.

It would be better for things to go back to the way they were before, when he was living the life of a quiet, conservative cheat, and no one was the wiser. But they cannot go back, and his fury builds. Nothing must be lost tonight.

The three hostages sit behind the screwy giant-mushroom table and watch their terrorizer stand there thinking. And the longer he thinks, the bolder the girls grow in exchanging glances, their voiceless dialogue kicking in.

We will—

Yes.

Elnice knows that neither Dian Fossey nor someone like Katharine Hepburn would hesitate.

Arthur sits, concentrating on possibilities.

One more eye-flick from Elnice to Solita. Eye-flick back. *OK.*

And Luis just this instant is making peace with the fact that he will commit a triple homicide within the next ten minutes, when over goes the table, slamming down on his feet, and two panthers, teeth bared, leap at him.

He doesn't feel the impact of the table edge through the steel toes of his work boots, but he loses his balance and falls hard backward. *"Huh!"* he grunts, and his feet come free but he is on his back like a beetle, and he slashes with his knife, *whik-whik* in the air, let them try to take this away from me. Lacking a shotgun under the counter, Elnice seizes the woman's weapon, a steel frying pan, and she's about to swing when Solita steps in *with the barbecue fork* from the hook next to the stove, the one with the walnut handle and fire-tempered tines, and runs him through with it like a Cossack.

The canyon registers this one as well: unmistakably the bellow of a guy who's just been stabbed with a big-ass fork.

Arthur takes the opportunity to call 911.

But Luis is not run all the way through as he would have been had the two hard tines not converged, he is merely stabbed, a few inches of fork into the right-hand side of his chest. Solita pulls out the fork smeared with blood.

Arthur shouts the address.

Luis holds onto the knife and slashes and feels the blade meet something and that something *give*, it must be part of Solita, and the old lady bangs him directly on the crown of the head with the skillet, it hits like a hubcap hurled from a great height, colored stars swirl, *get up!* and he doesn't know how but he regains his feet, and his non-knife hand gropes for somebody and his fist closes on the soft flesh of the old gringa's upper arm, and in a twinkling he's back in command.

His knife is poised at Elnice's neck, it's touching it. Now it's not. Now it is.

He takes a ragged breath.

"Solita, run for Ty and call the police!" commands Elnice in a clear voice, forgetting her vulnerable larynx, forgetting Ty's trip to Miami. And Solita is gone through the hallway before Luis can utter a threat. Elnice sees a crimson snake slithering down Solita's calf as she disappears.

And you know as sure as anything that he is doing the wondrous, incredible guy-thing that Elnice and Solita have lately adopted: *act this instant, justify everything later.* The impulse that alternately builds and destroys civilizations.

His bony hands grasp the table's vertical edge, and in a tenth of his normal time he's standing. His eyes glow like a werewolf's.

Luis wavers. Cut her throat? Then what? Get nailed, most probably, for murder? He's already thinking through a possible arrest. Don't kill anybody here. Not here and not yet.

A mere five feet separate Arthur from the crazy bastard holding Elnice; the countertop stretches away to his left, the refrigerator to his right, he has no weapon, all their knives are safely dull in their slots. His only choice is to take Luis's knife away from him, and so, unleashing a surge of adrenaline his body actually complies! Airborne, he makes a silent lunge for Luis's arm. The oxygen hose flips behind him like a fishline.

And he takes hold, manages to wrap his fingers around the knotty muscles of the man's forearm, and the knife flicks away from Elnice's throat.

During the long instant that follows, the eyes of husband and wife meet. Their faces are, for a fraction of a fraction, merely inches apart. Condensation clouds the oxygen tube beneath his nostrils.

This is it, her eyes contend.

No, it isn't.

Convulsively, Luis releases her and rams his fist into Arthur's chest, sending him toppling back into the overturned table.

"Come on," Luis grunts, retrieving the knife, and Elnice finds herself propelled into the hallway toward the front door.

"Elnice," Arthur rasps from behind.

The cold line of the knife again presses her throat and her right arm is twisted horribly behind her, between her shoulderblades, and she hears a *pop!* from that shoulder and almost passes out but now they're at the door, swinging around to open it. Luis yelps and Elnice opens her eyes to see Arthur up and moving. His oxygen cannula has come loose from his face, and Elnice feels Luis's body stiffen in horror against her back, he twists her around again and steps behind her, now she's being dragged backward on her feet, she is skipping to keep her balance, the rubber of her Keds squeaking on the paving tiles. The knife tip beneath her small wattle stings her now and again like a wasp.

Luis scoots her along, but Arthur is closing the gap, and Luis cries out again as if pursued by a flesh-eater.

The street is deserted and very dark. A half moon throws down a glimmer of light, however, which is all anybody needs to see exactly what's going on.

In fact Arthur could easily pass for a zombie: even the beige oatmeal color is gone from his face and hands, his skin is stark white, every red corpuscle in his body is rushing to his muscles, his face shows the preternatural concentration of Bullet Coker overtaking a savagely talent-ed opponent, gutting it out down the stretch.

He is *running*, his toothpick legs pumping like pistons, and his nemesis is running backwards, shielding himself with Elnice, scrambling steeply uphill, toward the top of the canyon road. Arthur is running, showing the world that there is still something he prefers to life itself.

Elnice skips in a continuous rhythmic recoil from the knife blade.

The lifeless oxygen hose falls away.

Arthur catches up to them, his eyes again meeting hers, his fingers stretching for hers—there is blood now, drib-bling from his lips—blood and pink froth—his fingers snatch at Luis's sleeve—

Luis makes guttural sounds of panic but doesn't let go. The three people, entwined, jostle together uphill.

Elnice understands that Arthur is dead already; the light has gone out, she sees this as clearly as she sees the jut of his jaw in the moonlight, despite the fact that he is still upright and moving.

He stumbles, makes a last lunge, then falls, his hand grazing her shoe.

28: How Long a Bad Thing Can Last

Elnice allows herself to be crammed into the small space between seat and dash almost indifferently, her mind having entered that state of detachment experienced by soldiers suddenly ambushed, or passengers in a plummeting jet. Arthur's body lies splayed in the middle of the moonlit road; Luis runs the truck right over his arm; she does not catch a last real look, though she might have seen a smudge of red sweatsuit flash past a dark hole in the floorboard.

The truck floor smells of motor oil and dirt.

The pickup truck yaws violently as Luis struggles to control its flight down the canyon road. His boot alternately stomps on the accelerator, in fear, then the brake, also in fear.

Elnice's mind is fastened, in depth, on a single memory.

On the second afternoon of their life together as husband and wife she and Arthur loaded fishing gear, a basket of sandwiches, and a vacuum bottle of coffee into a little boat and set off from the dock of their rented cabin on the shores of gorgeous Lake Margrethe, in northern Michigan. Arthur pulled on the outboard motor, and they plowed through the water to a spot he knew, in search of northern pike.

They caught fish! Boy did they hook into the pike, casting treacherous red-and-white lures made to look like mortally wounded minnows—Dardevles, they were called, and Elnice loved the reckless sound of it, and she loved fishing, and she loved being married at last to Arthur, and she loved the world and everything in it to bits, even the things that were not Arthur or Arthur-related, and in her giddiness whenever a pike hit her Dardevl she would shriek, "Arthur! Arthur! Oh, Arthur!" and he would laugh and coax her through the playing of the fish, then lean over and scoop it out of the water and expertly remove the barbed lure from its lip or gullet. He tried to shush her because another man was fishing the lake half a mile away, but gave up after a while. Love, love, love.

When they returned to the dock, the man was cleaning his fish on a board under a tree. He looked up as they trudged happily past with their heavy stringer.

"Guess your name's Arthur, huh?" said he.

That day on Lake Margrethe was the nicest memory she had, though she wouldn't have necessarily come up with it in a nicest-memory contest. She would have been obliged to say the day *before* that (their wedding day), or their vacation in New York City, or the first Coker family reunion she attended when everybody buried whatever hatchets they were wielding at the time and Arthur's ancient great-aunt made the best apple dumplings you ever ate. But that's the way nicest memories are: they don't ask for your input.

A heavy jolt, a collision, actually. *Cabam!* again! and Luis curses in a hoarse voice, and she hears the roar of another vehicle just behind them as they approach Sunset Boulevard. *Bam! Ca-whump!*

Solita, she realizes, is behind them, driving the Cokers' Buick! *Dear God.* She'd found Ty Brandewine's house empty, run back to the Cokers' and grabbed Elnice's keys from their spot on the counter, gotten in and given chase! Not knowing how to drive wasn't stopping her. She knew enough to turn the ignition and pull the transmission lever into drive.

"Crazy! Don't hit me! Goddamned slut!" cries Luis, who had given Solita one driving lesson a year ago then thought better of it. He pants and coughs. Elnice had forgotten about the barbecue fork puncture.

Luis's thoughts after being stabbed did not cohere well. Wanting to remain in control, he grabbed the first person to hand, Elnice. By good luck, Arthur had got eliminated, Elnice is cowering in his truck, and he realizes that as long as he has Elnice, Solita will follow. The twists of fortune!

He knows a quiet spot in the San Gabriel Mountains, north of the metropolis.

He'll be fine, just fine, after all.

He would never call a woman brave. Crazy yes. As they pass beneath a lone street light he catches Solita's face in his side mirror, her eyes like wild gems, her mouth a ferocious gash below them.

They encounter no traffic all the way down to the main road. However, a sudden stream of cars coming along Cahuenga forces Luis to slow down as he careens around the corner, attempting to merge.

Horns blare, and Elnice seizes the instant to reach up, grasp the door handle and swing out.

She holds on just long enough to glimpse the ground as one does when executing a twisting vault, gauging the landing, then she lets go, tumbling on feet and hands, tucking her head. A car swerves so near her head she hears its tires sing, and she flops to a stop at the edge of the roadbed, eye-to-eye with a gorgon-like tangle of rusty wire.

Solita bucks the Buick to a stop. "Hurry, Elnice!"

And Elnice leaps up, sprints to the driver's door, shoves Solita into the passenger seat, and drives.

Her body feels like hell but not bad hell. The shoulder that went *pop* under Luis's grip: not a dislocation after all, maybe just an old adhesion letting go. The pain is buried beneath coursing adrenaline. Hands and knees—scrapes, road rash, no matter. She'd taken hard falls on the gymnastics floor, jammed her neck a couple of times, no, she's all right.

Solita's leg bleeds steadily. She rips a strip from the hem of her blouse to bind it. She knots the cloth while looking tensely over the dashboard.

The piebald pickup makes an abrupt U and gives chase.

For Dian Fossey, her gorillas were everything. Therefore in any given crisis, she had everything to lose, and this motivated her to do the fierce things she did. But Elnice now understands that having nothing to lose is just as good.

Heading west on Sunset, Elnice wrenches the steering wheel drastically, she exceeds posted speed limits, she briefly plows along a sidewalk to deceive Luis into thinking she is about to crash and stop. Other cars *waugh* their horns and veer away like magic. When you drive crazily you suddenly have the streets to yourself. She cuts north on a canyon road, then another—is Luis still back there?—the women can't be sure—all the way through the hills, miles and miles, into the San Fernando Valley. On the shouted advice of Solita, Elnice off-roads into a wooded park. A tree stump jumps up in the headlights, then a horrible sound, the car coughs and shudders and rolls to a stop and goes to sleep, and the women get out and run. They dash through thorn bushes and mowed zones, gulping air, snapping branches. They run and run and when they stop in a pool of shadow at a concrete retaining wall behind an apartment or condo complex, the world is quiet. No Luis. No police sirens. They laugh savagely, shocking themselves, their teeth flashing in the night.

After a brief conference, Elnice boosts Solita over the wall and waits. The ground is damp-cool. It is a good place to be, with just enough light to see by from the apartment complex's security lights. Soon hunks of corrugated cardboard drop down on her.

Solita follows, her springy young legs balancing her weight as she hops from the top of the wall. "It was like you said—much card board in the bins back there."

Elnice announces, "We're going to camp here until morning. We need sleep."

"Camp?"

"Sleep out—you know—this is as good a place as any. You did it when you left Mexico, right?"

"Yes. I am not afraid of snakes."

"Well, good."

"Hell with the snakes."

Elnice gets busy laying cardboard in overlapping rows on the ground. "Yes, good, Solita. Hell with 'em."

"We have no thing."

"This is a minimalist arrangement, I'll grant you. Give me that piece, will you?"

"Elnice—I am sorry." In the shadows Solita's face looks older, the lines from nose to mouth deeper.

Elnice, kneeling, stops working. "Well, I am not."

"Mr. Coker—"

"Solita."

"You had no chance to say goodbye!"

Elnice takes a long slow breath. "We've been saying goodbye for months." But Elnice's grief comes upon her sharply. She lets out the first sob, and she knows it's the first of a thousand, and she chokes her husband's name over and over. She sinks to the ground and Solita silently lays her hands on her back.

After a long time, the women fashion a coffin-like shelter, crawl in, and go to sleep.

At sunup a breeze stirs a tree next to their campsite. Agitated cheeping overhead suggests a pair of songbirds arguing or having sex. The morning is pleasantly cool. On the other side of the retaining wall people are retrieving newspapers, starting their cars, and going to work. Traffic copters chop overhead, above the hawks and pigeons and housefinches. L.A. is exactly like the deep forest or the open ocean: you treat it right, it'll treat you right. The women relieve themselves in the bushes and, though very thirsty, hunker on the flattened cardboard of their shelter and talk.

Finding herself violently widowed and in a vagrant-like situation has driven the last bits of extraneous junk from Elnice's mind and heart. She will manage her grief. She gathers up her hair. "We have work to do. I wish I had my purse." They inspect each other's wounds and do what they can until they should find water. "Do we look a mess," Elnice mutters.

"I cannot make Luis a different man," Solita remarks, rubbing dried blood from Elnice's neck. "He will kill me and you, my friend Elnice. We will walk over these roads until we come to a church. A church of the Catholic faith. They will help us there. I will stay and serve the Church. I no can take vows—I can not take vows, because I am married in law, because that I am not a virgin. But I can serve. And—I will help you, my friend, return to the state of Indiana. We must no longer, like, stay together. In the church I will be safe."

Elnice blinks. "Wait a minute, honey."

"No. Luis has won."

This flat statement surprises Elnice.

"He has not. I'll bring him to justice or die myself. I'm going to ask the first person I see to call the police for me."

Solita comes slightly up from her squat. "Then you will die. You have learned nothing."

"He killed Arthur!"

Bent forward now at the waist like a grappler, her scratched red arms swinging, the girl hisses, "Luis he no touch your Arthur! Who else see Luis at your home? No one. Mr. Coker go for a walk and die!"

After a moment Elnice says, "Oh."

In a softer tone Solita continues, "The laws of men are no for me."

"Not for me."

"Not for me. Luis he has many U.S. dollars. You know this must be true. If the police arrest him, he will not stay in the jail. I know enough of these things. Luis can become invisible and he will wait." The sun, stronger now, warms their backs.

"You know," Elnice says, "he must have gone and killed Jason."

"He killed him or he will kill him."

"What about the bloody shoelaces?"

Solita twists her hands in her skirt. "They are in our home. Luis will never find them but I will not find them also if I never go back there. He said no thing when I said bloody shoelaces. The blood might be his. A cut. I do not know. Use your brain, Elnice my friend. Do not think like a butthead. Do not be a stupid. The law of men can not help us. Law written on paper can not make justice happen at all time. You have seen this!"

True. The breeze shifts, blowing Solita's hair across her eyes. Elnice watches her tuck it behind her ears.

"Solita. Help me understand Luis."

"What do you mean?"

"There must be more to the man than I know. More— substance."

Solita shakes her head with a sad smile. "There is no more and less substance than what you see. We found a thing hidden by Luis. A thing—a thing—"

"A mystery."

"We found a mystery. But it is only a thing hidden. Luis wanted money like any man."

"Yet he wanted to accomplish things, too. You know, honey, he wanted to destroy things, buildings—people. He wanted to destroy something he was against. That, to him, was an accomplishment." Elnice feels no pity for him; she wishes to have a colder advantage over him.

"He did not know what is real. No—" Solita is dissatisfied with that remark. "He did not know how long a bad thing can last."

Elnice gets it. "A bad thing can last a long time and get bigger after you've finished with it."

"Yes!" Solita's eyes shine in the morning brightness. "My friend! Now you see."

Elnice pictures Bullet Coker lying in the street, his blood coagulated, his spirit hanging about wonderingly. He would have been discovered by now by the uphill neighbors or the paper boy. En route to the morgue. Police seeking her for questioning. Fresco still cowering under the bed. Well, his water dish had been full.

"What we need right now," Elnice decides, "is some cash."

What does it take to crack through belief? Belief in the essential orderliness of the universe, belief in the worth of a culture, belief in nature as cozy bosom, belief in reason itself? Whatever answers we might make, one thing we do know: The beliefs of Elnice Coker are lying in the soil beneath an evergreen grove somewhere in Van Nuys. They are lying cracked and dry like bits of discarded snakeskin, useless, no longer juicy, no longer vital, about to dissolve back into the litter of great yearnings.

A new Elnice kicks the cardboard out of her way and goes off in search of water and other resources. An Elnice who sifts right and wrong through her own sieve.

Two women emerge from a gauzy thicket of wild fennel next to the parking lot of a newer shopping plaza. Having washed themselves in a stream they do not appear particularly wild, at least at first glance.

The clothes have been rinsed and wrung out and dried on their bodies, causing them to fit like skins, like the clothes of the poorest field workers: the shoulders curving, the limbs clearly outlined. The cuts and abrasions have been bathed and soothed with clean leaves, the blackened blood gone.

They carry nothing in their hands. Their faces are composed.

A woman wearing sunglasses and slim pants slams the door of her polished Lexus. She is the kind of woman who names her cars; this one is called Chandon because of its champagne color. She walks past an empty shopping cart on the way toward the grocery store, as she is, furthermore, the kind of woman who will return a cart after she has used it but not take a cart someone else has left in the parking lot.

As she walks she's roughing out a timeline in her head for that night's dinner—Vic and Laraine are coming over—starting backward from eight-o'clock-on-the-table: pour the water, light the candles, take out the roasted squash, it can hold for a few minutes while—oh, don't forget to bring the aioli to room temperature, neither of us remembered that last time—

And as she cuts between two minivans, feeling in her purse for her list, suddenly a friendly face pops up right in hers.

"Thelma, *hello!*" A short grandmotherly woman, looking oddly worn—somehow—takes her arm. In a cheerful, fragile voice the woman asks, "How have you *been* since the cruise?"

She's a kindly little thing, so the woman in sunglasses answers kindly in return, "No, you've mistaken me for someone else. My name isn't Thel—hey!"

And before she can comprehend that she's being gently mugged, she's sitting on her butt on the warm asphalt, shoved there by the odd, strong little woman, while a bigger, younger gal came out of nowhere. A girl? A pretty brown madonna—she came out of nowhere, seized her purse—where did the other one go? She must've—her *purse!* her *goddamn purse!*

And there open-mouthed she sits, clutching the list of ingredients to roasted summer squash with stuffed pork medallions and wild rice, watching two curvaceous rear ends disappear fast into the bushes. Chandon, nearby, is unharmed.

What did the little creature say? "We'll send everything back! Don't worry!"

29: Never Freer Than Now

A girl with blackidescent eyes and a serious expression, wearing a secondhand navy blue sailor's tunic, desert-camo army pants, and essentially demolished pink espadrilles, and listing slightly under the weight of a massive cheap knapsack, marches away from the Army-Navy surplus store on Sunset near Hyperion, heading west.

She passes two other girls, a few years younger who, sideways, study her. They've gotten themselves up this day in midnight-currant lipstick and dark stiff blue jeans, and little Monkipel tops.

They don't know it, but it is the expression of purpose in the oval face—the firm mouth, the level gaze—that holds their attention.

Baffled, seeking the key, they continue to scrutinize her as she recedes up the street.

"It's the espadrilles," says one, finally.

The phone rings inside the house that looks like a small pig in the spindly shadows of Watts Towers. It is late afternoon.

Luis is lying in bed making plans and worrying. The mental percentages are about eighty percent plans and twenty percent chest wound. His sweat has soaked through his clothes and the sheets and even the thin quilt. He is ignorant of first aid. How could this be, an educated man like Luis?

CRIMES IN A SECOND LANGUAGE

It just is. A healthy man with goals does not need to think about these things, much less stash a Red Cross manual in his dresser just in case.

The blood worries him more than the pain and the sucking sound as he labors to get a full breath, the blood just keeps slowly bubbling out despite the wads of paper towels he's plastered to his chest, and he's resorted to the peasant remedy of drinking red wine in order to replace that vital equally crimson fluid.

How bad can it be? A fork in the chest? It's not so easy to die. How tough it was to squeeze the life out of Jason M!

His phone rings.

He ought to cut his losses and throw a few more belongings into the duffel he began packing a few minutes ago before he had to lie down feeling dizzy—then—

Ring.

He knows he shouldn't answer it.

But the impulse of a man at a disadvantage prompts him to reach out and grab it.

"Luis?" an expressionless female voice meets his grunt, but he knows who it is, all right.

"Meet me at your bucket at seven-thirty this evening. All right?"

He makes no reply.

"Your bucket at the golf course. All right?"

A healthy, untrammeled Luis would have snarled fuck you and beat it out of town or stayed put, depending on his confidence level.

The portion of his brain that was planning to flee begins to rationalize a rendezvous.

Sure she could be waiting there with some thug she knows. But why didn't she just come for me here? Because she doesn't know any thugs.

Certainly the police are not yet involved: no cop could be talked into staking out some maggoty place in the woods when she could lead them right to this address.

She's got big plans for him. She wants to bargain with him; she and Solita have figured out he's got money. What a pair of geniuses. Of course Solita will be there too, they're together against him just because they know about the bucket and the pipe. They think they're God over him. They think he'll crawl toward the bosoms of two women because he's hurting and afraid.

"Hah!" Forcing himself into steadiness by squeezing his shoulderblades together, he rises painfully.

The knife: yes, it's secure in its ankle sheath, he feels the stacked leather handle with his other ankle, and he turns toward the door.

It's Saturday at Griffith Park, and a day of the week hasn't been invented yet that lures more golfers out to the greenways. The grass beneath their eager feet meets the morning with a good attitude, but as the day wears on what with all the stomping and gouging, it begins to whimper, you can put your ear to the ground midday and know it for yourself. The flags droop, the hole edges sag, the tee markers go wobbly, and bets get upped to double or nothing.

Eventually the sun wears out and dips behind the towering dry ridge to the west and the air becomes chillier than anyone anticipated five hours ago. It's winter in Los Angeles after all.

The golfers smell the chilliness before they feel it.

And the light wanes and still they tee off, the desperate ones at the bottom of the tee-time totem pole, they've convinced themselves that nine or twelve holes'll be all right, 'n' even if it's pitch dark on the eighth tee we're playing in, fuck it.

OK, but finally no one's left to tee off, and in the gloaming the course empties out, hole by hole. Peace descends, the healing power of dew and silence. The swallows swoop for supper just above the weary ground. The very tree trunks relax, those flourishing cypresses reaching into the fading sky and fading out at the tops themselves more beautifully than any Disney beanstalk you've ever seen. It's about half past six.

"Give it back, Jack," says one golfer to another on the eleventh green, hand out.

Luis makes his way down Wilson's seventeenth fairway, stealthily and slowly on the near side, opposite the thickest of the undergrowth where his bucket lies buried in the ground. An hour before the appointed time should be enough.

His feet know the terrain as well as they know the route between his side of the bed and the bathroom. There's plenty enough light to see by, though from time to time clusters of black bubbles rise up annoyingly inside his eyeballs and he must peer over them.

He crosses the fairway at an oblique angle about fifty yards from the green, for the dual purposes of making his body less obtrusive to anyone watching from that point and to retain a better view of the flora surrounding his bucket.

His legs feel hollow. Not weak, but odd, as if the bones had gone somewhere leaving his strong muscles to support his weight.

A doctor later, yes. Get this fixed, goddamn fork in the chest. What'll I tell the guy? I was horsing around with my kid. Horsing around with my boy.

The wound has stopped dripping blood, but his upper belly strains against his shirt front as if he'd just gorged himself, which is funny since he hasn't eaten since last night. His shirt clings to him uncomfortably, sticky with drying blood and spilled wine.

He has accomplished a great deal already, and all will not be lost if he can simply get his hands on Solita and the gringa.

Even at his stupidest he hasn't given them much to go on. He'll be all right. A few more steps on his hollow-strong legs bring him to the curtain of greenery. He parts a branch, peeks through, and seeing no one, steps into the clearing.

Elnice made her call to Luis from a quiet spot near the clubhouse. She purchased an iced tea at the snack bar and walked thoughtfully away, sipping. She carried a paper grocery sack in one hand, lumpy with her one small necessity.

Swarms of golfers brushed past, the logos on their caps and shirts shouting force and fire. Some were careful of their wide golf bags slung over their shoulders, others heedless, expecting anyone coming along to give way. Occasionally two such golfers would bang bags and scowl but not look back. The air seethed with a mixture of hearty anxiety (those yet to tee off) and resigned relief (those returning from eighteen discrete and forgettable little wars).

No one paid any attention to her as she slipped into the greenery beyond the practice green.

Have you ever wished someone dead? Oftentimes, we must admit, such wicked thoughts spring up after a slight injury. "The guy cuts me off, then *he* flips *me* the bird!"

Yeah, man, if anybody needs killing it's that asshole.

But sometimes the injury is not slight. And you imagine: the rat-faced boy who tormented you all the way through elementary school, through grades and grades, you see him lying at the bottom of a lake somewhere with his penis cut off and clamped between his teeth.

Or you see yourself swinging a sledgehammer into the cranium of that rotten cheating gorgeous first lover, you see that sledgehammer crushing bone and brains and eyeballs until blood coats the floor and your soul finally rocks peacefully in the warm hammock of revenge. Of course we've imagined such things. Those who have been wounded still more grievously—violated by a parent or malevolent stranger, or deprived of a loved one by catastrophic evil—how seductively thoughts of murder come then!

As our brave agile old girl moved about the city that day, on foot, by bus, on foot again, she held a war council with God. She raised issues she'd never raised before; she demanded dialogue.

Her views of right and wrong used to be clad in ironwood, but *God* himself was far less protected. A macro presence, to be sure, but without the distinct edges and specific gravities of rights and wrongs. Her question, her nut, could not be cracked simply by employing religious science: The full presence must be consulted, because uncertainty lurked there beneath the wings of the seraphim, and the back-and-forth should have taken longer than it did.

Could the absence of Arthur grow into something bigger and crisper than the presence of God?

Elnice knew what we all know: Religion is there for when the chips are down. Going to church, giving thanks and praying, learning the doctrine, writing the checks, filling the food baskets, all this is to cement our affiliation, supply us with spiritual dog tags. Will we do the right thing when the phosphor showers begin?

She acknowledged that her chips had never been seriously down before. How easy it had been to make the right choices when the choices were idiot-proof.

Arthur was going to die anyway. He might've died that very day, all by himself. At best how long might he have lasted? Six months? Six weeks? Certainly nothing like six years. How much did it matter, even to Arthur, that he was dead now? She became aware of him near her, and if she looked peripherally she could see him, bundled in his red track suit murmuring something unintelligible to her.

In fact he'd been spared! His slow death ended with a quick one. No more pain for him: no more fretting about the lost money, no more dismay over the betrayals of Ty Brandewine. No upset, even, about missing the Olympics, because they're not on until next year.

What would he miss? Their occasional big hot breakfasts. Sports on cable. Elnice's breasts and stomach.

His suffering at the hands of the quite ordinary murderer Luis was short.

But the intensity of it: running, running toward death as if it were a beacon. Could Elnice bear the memory of it? What about *her* suffering now? Arthur's eyes gripping hers beyond the point of that knife would be like a barbed-wire longline girdle, gouging and insistent for the rest of her life. She's supposed to forgive that? Even revenge won't erase that memory.

Arthur turned into a jagged star tumbling in the air above her on the street; he screamed something insistently, but she couldn't make it out.

She'd been a preacher herself! "If *I* drop something, *I* pick it up!" Responsibility. Fairness. Poetry memorization.

A responsible preacher has a right to ask God for one specific thing, one thing once in a lifetime, and her moment was now. God seemed to listen—no, God *did* listen, this she felt rawly but surely.

A deal was struck between God and Elnice at the intersection of LaBrea and Pico and their discourse ended. She came away not faithless, but with a temporary suspension. That was the understanding.

And her spirit was grim in sudden, irrevocable knowledge of herself.

She thought about the battle to come. *There should be at least a split second when I can redeem myself.*

In fact, she'd never felt freer.

She waits in the spot she and Solita discovered weeks ago— decades ago. A stump forms a discreet overlook; sitting upon it she can hear the smallest sound.

The gun, a massive .45 semi-automatic manufactured by a reputable South American company, rests in her lap.

The man who came to meet her in the alley behind the liquor store showed her everything she needed to know. He had a long white face and a red hillbilly Adam's apple. She had thought she wanted a revolver for simplicity, but as soon as he drew the heavy blued .45 from the grocery bag she knew it was the gun for her.

"See this little lever? D'just flip it down, then take both hands and aim it. Hold it tight, now. Line up this little thing with this notch here? D'just get good and close to whatever you want to hit. Pull the trigger. That's all there is to it. There's a round in the chamber, see? You're all set, plus you got a full magazine."

She understood, having fired handguns before, at a girls' camp the summer she turned fifteen. They learned how to hit paper targets and empty cans with .22-caliber Rugers. Needless to say, this was in the Pleistocene era when shooting sports in the United States were widely considered to be as healthy as red meat packed in heavy syrup.

She can hear everything: the soft crunch of a sparrow hopping in the leaves, the sigh of a branch being pulled back and then closing again.

Through a tunnel in the leaves she sees him.

Her legs respond to the command signal from her brain and she leaps from the stump like a champion and *bounds* into the clearing, weapon raised, revealing herself.

The sight of her a mere four paces away sucks away what little wind is left in Luis. The black bubbles again rise up mountainously inside his eyeballs and he attempts to peer over them, to assess his assailant, yes, she surely has something in her hands, but it couldn't be, no. And then the strangest of things happens to him in the slowest of motion.

He falters! Just as he reaches for his knife, his knees buckle. Shit! Get the knife, get it you imbecile but he finds himself *just kneeling there!* Going blind. Unable to bounce up to his feet or finish drawing his weapon.

And then, projected onto the massif of black spheres inside his eyeballs, a movie starts up. The movie features rain drumming onto a tin roof—small shack—the high country after a drought—yes—and there's a little boy watching the torrent collecting itself into rickety gutters, draining into a barrel at the rear of the shack, precious water. Precious rain. Precious boy.

Elnice instantly understands that Luis has turned coward on her. He's begging for his life! On his knees, mute with panic. His eyes bore all the way through her head, oh he knows what's about to happen, sure enough. He raises his arms in a futile gesture of supplication.

And although she is surprised by his reaction, she permits herself an atrocity: she takes an instant to *savor*. Her stomach relaxes and she feels more powerful than ever. Cooling, grass-herbed air swirls over the golf course like a balm. She gathers the air into her lungs and feels the goodness of it.

The darkness gathers faster as it deepens.

Luis has no choice but to watch his movie, to be absorbed by it. *I am drowning in this rain.*

And a tremendous flash of lightning blots out the picture, and a thunderclap deafens him.

The recoil drives the gun from Elnice's hands into her chest, but she doesn't notice.

Her enemy remains there kneeling for a few seconds, then collapses flat forward. His mouth chews the ground, then stops.

And what of the bullet? Well, it went exactly where the bucking barrel of the .45 sent it: whistling past Luis's upraised left biceps, ripping through a thick, pretty patch of evening primrose a hundred yards away, then patting harmlessly into a mighty cypress trunk.

Pent-up air flows from the nose of Elnice Coker.

She had expected Luis to attack her—to stab or shoot her—at the moment she confronted him. She knew his reflexes were quick. But hers were quick too, and she would be able to pull her trigger in self-defense as soon as he moved on her. God should have been all right with that type of symmetry whether she lived or died.

But Luis did not attack her and she fired anyway.

In spite of that, her breath comes evenly and calmly.

No one hears the gunshot clearly enough to wonder about it, diffused as it is by the trees and shrubs. To the last lingering shoe-clappers in the parking lot it sounds like the crack of a large dead branch.

Elnice walks swiftly away from the golf course and boards a bus at the park's south gate. People are leaving the park with their hampers and sweaty children and going home. The city is friendly and beautiful.

30: The God Thing

Dawn breaks with a fine-grained light that filters through the eucalyptus trees and gleams on the satiny dew.

The first group of the day sets off, just able to see. It's a power foursome: A couple of telecom salesdudes whose wives have threatened mutiny unless they're home by noon to take the kids to Magic Mountain, one spry old cap'n who regularly broke par here forty years ago, and Tina G. Good old Tina G: back from Asia, minus the boyfriend but plus a whole raft of duty-free stuff *and* some cozy feelings about the Suisse Bank and a few handsome men in a certain hotel bar who were more than glad to discuss the ins and outs of discreet expatriation with her. She is very happy.

Hidden in her golf bag is a thick roll the likes of which we've seen before: a collation of all those fascinating (to somebody!) documents from the bountiful desk of her gentle boss, some two hundred pages tied with red crinkle ribbon.

That other boss, whoever he is, 'll be glad to see this stuff. Her Dri-Joys fend off the sopping dew nicely as she and her companions break trail, their speed-eaten Egg McMuffins digesting unevenly.

Tina G has mastered the fundamentals well enough to make her ball go where she aims, if only for a hundred and forty yards at a time. The dew evaporates. On the seventeenth, Tina sets up and *thwack!* Right on the money.

"You know you were aiming right *at* those trees?" asks

one of the com-link salesdudes helpfully. His voice is honking and self-important; it has actually been his greatest handicap in business and he knows it but cannot bring himself to modulate it. "You've got a problem *aiming*, you're setting up with your shoulders way off line. Your *clubface* was square to the pin, but the way your shoulders were, made you come over the top and . . ."

She walks quickly away from him and into the thicket with its little hidden clearing.

Her scream brings all three men running.

They look down at her ball, nestled in a fold of Luis's pant leg, near his buttocks.

"That's an unplayable lie if I ever saw one," honks the com-link salesdude. The others will remember that line for the rest of their lives.

Elnice tells the police a story, part real and part horseshit, about a combo home invasion-kidnapping-carjacking. She had thrown the gun in its paper sack down a storm sewer halfway between Griffith Park and home. The police sense the horseshit but are unable to separate the threads of it. Motorists had reported a white woman driving a tan Buick insanely, but no one had gotten the license number. The Cokers' Buick was found in a wooded park, its front axle, oil pan and manifold in smithereens. Would she know anything about that, they courteously wonder?

She experiences memory lapses. The men who kidnapped her as Arthur chased them had driven her around then pushed her out of the car and she had whacked her head. Talking about it is very upsetting. The police go away, having taken Arthur's body for autopsy and so on.

She opens a can of Powerdog for Fresco and cleans up the kitchen.

The next day she rents a car and finds Solita at the hiding place behind the Van Nuys apartment complex they agreed upon before stealing Mrs. Joy Silver's purse. Solita would not have parted from Elnice had she known Elnice expected to die; convincing Solita that she would return was the only way Elnice could work it. And now Solita would never know.

Elnice does tell her enough, however. "He won't bother you anymore, honey."

"Good," grunts Solita, tossing her knapsack into the rented Kia's backseat.

Elnice returns the purse anonymously by post, including a replacement of the one hundred ninety-three dollars, plus a batch of chocolate cupcakes to make up for Joy Silver's trauma. She changes the sheets on the bed in the spare room and lays out a set of towels for Solita.

The day after that Ty Brandewine returns home and Elnice hits him with the news. She cuts through his horrified reaction to announce that he and she are in the motion picture business together and they'd best raise more money to get this goddamned movie made after all.

"Ty," she says, for the first time in her life not reluctant to exploit her own pain, "I'm a widow. I've been cheated, and you're going to help me. It wasn't your fault that the money got lost. I know that." She totally knows otherwise—any nitwit would—but it wouldn't be advantageous for her to rebuke Ty. He's got know-how she doesn't have yet. "We're going to make this 'Freedom Lake' and get a return on our investment, just like you said in the first place."

She will raise funds all by herself—obviously this is necessary—and strictly control the money and oversee the production. Ty obviously has talent but no drive, no sense of responsibility. He'd wasted all this time diddling around and probably gave the Cokers' money to his divorce lawyers or spent it trying to buy some love out of his kids. But the script is damn good. It really is.

And Ty, he's not stupid.

Sitting at his dining-room table with Elnice and Solita over a mellow little meritage from Livermore, he says, "Elnice, I never would have dreamed. There are many things I never understood. There are many things I regret."

Solita advises, "Don't look back. It will kill you." She had easily enough given up the idea of going into a convent. Life is safer now.

Elnice adds, "There's really no reason for any of us to look back, is there?"

Ty asks, "You liked my script from the beginning, didn't you, Elnice?"

"Yes. But it does need work."

Ty's smile recedes. "What do you mean?"

Elnice clears her throat and says, "We have to tone down the New Age-type crap in it, don't you think?" Her tone is unflinching.

"Uh."

"I mean, that stuff is so pedestrian these days."

Solita breaks in, "Pedestrian?"

"Ordinary," Elnice explains, "boring, to be found anywhere. Unremarkable."

Ty is silent.

"For one thing," Elnice goes on, "the talking cat has to go."

He sits forward. "But I thought you loved the idea! Besides—"

"I don't anymore, now that I really think about it. The idea's ridiculous, Ty, it doesn't go with what you're trying to do in the movie. It feels tacked on, like you're trying to put in something that everybody will see and say oh, that's so appealing, when in fact it isn't appealing or humorous or even wise. It's just forced and, mm, I guess self-conscious is the best way to put it." It's almost as if she's learned a new way of talking.

"Well!" A mixture of shame, fear, and respect flow into Ty's eyes. "Well, well!"

"And a great movie requires great music. Did you put music in the budget? We have to get with it, don't you think?" Elnice sips from her stemmed wineglass. "This movie is about realism, what happens to people when they stop pretending. I want you to think about that, Ty. Who wrote the script for 'Chinatown'?"

"Uh, Robert Towne."

"That was a good movie, I saw it again last night on Turner Classics. Maybe we can get him to consult on our script."

"I think he's dead. But I'll look into it! Elnice, I have to tell you—"

She looks at him.

He smiles effervescently. "I'm feeling my energy coming back!"

"Good. And we need to talk to some other people, get some other investors."

"That would help."

"We need ideas on who to approach. Let's invite your agent to lunch somewhere nice as soon as possible, OK?"

"OK."

"You'll call tomorrow morning?"

"Yes, Elnice."

"Make it a place that's not old Hollywood. Pick a new place and talk to the manager in advance."

Ty laughs, delighted. "I can't wait!"

After he sparkles his way home, Elnice and Solita fix a dinner of baked chicken, sliced tomatoes, and fried corn-potato cake for themselves. Elnice eats with gusto. Solita, no longer childlike, sips a glass of Ty-supplied wine. She sits easily, taking up more space than she used to, arm draped over the chair back.

"Lots of movie stars," Elnice remarks, "dump their friends for new ones once they get big."

Solita smiles. "Buttheads do such things. I will not do that. Maybe I will not get big any way."

"You will."

"Then we will get big together."

Elnice touches Solita's warm arm and knows anything is possible.

Old friends and relatives come and go by plane to Los Angeles, paying their last respects to Arthur and committing varying percentages of their life savings to Elnice's movie. Who can refuse her at a time like this? And how well she looks in spite of her grief, in the outfit Solita helped her pick out at Neiman-Marcus: a rather expensive but simple midnight-blue dress, new heels slightly higher than she'd worn before, and a slim purse to match. She'd bought more clothes there too, for everyday, things she'd never thought of wearing before, like an interesting scoopneck sweater with cocoa and pink squares on it, wide-legged slacks, and new driving loafers to replace her Keds. The elastic-waisted Joel Hannaberry knits and wash-n-wear Suzy Kramer smocks are shunted into the back of the closet, because Elnice doesn't need to be anybody's cheerful little chubby harmless companion anymore.

There are thousands and thousands of unsolved murders in Los Angeles.

Half a day after Luis was loaded into the coroner's wagon, his contacts began regrouping, bumping around Griffith Park and elsewhere, sniffing, calculating, coalescing, dissolving, coalescing again—loosely—just as a robust nest of rodents does after being disturbed. They're not about to allow the business they love to slip away. Chantelle W, in fact, is considering leaving the insurance biz—her modest private arson job went well, nobody hurt and almost two hundred grand in her pocket, tax-free—and becoming a golf teaching pro: going through PGA school, tutoring eager students at some pretty course in Arizona, perhaps, building a little empire of her own on the side, keeping up the tradition Luis so adroitly developed.

Tina G has hired a private investigator to try to find out what happened to Luis, and is convincing herself it would be advantageous to take over his role as manager for a while, just for a while, until she's got enough money put away. Surely Tina G can be trusted to know when enough's enough.

Solita, after breakfasting with Elnice, lies on her stomach in Ty's clean-lined living room selecting a new name from a Ty-generated list of suggestions, and he is handling the delicate job of acquiring the proper documents for her. Elnice had bought Solita some new things to wear, too: slim young fashions with chunky belts, fun shoes, and so on. Solita extends one leg and taps an electric-green sandal on the marble fireplace surround, feeling the cool stone with her toes.

Ty is on the phone, speaking to someone in a kittenish tone. It's hard work, this little pas de deux with corrupt authorities. He's good at it, though, and it lends an appropriate amount of spice to the overall venture.

Elnice is next door in her dining alcove, marking Ty's script with a red pencil, Fresco at her feet. At her elbow is a professional-looking brown notebook containing a business plan in progress. The script needs restructuring by someone untrammeled by sneering studio executives; the characters need releasing. She is making a beginning on her own. She slashes her pencil through, "GAIL: I've struggled with my body image most of my life. Until now, that is. Being held by you here in this place, so near to the time of solstice." Beneath it she jots, "GAIL (TO STEVE): Do you like an ice cream soda on a hot day? It's like a little poem you drink."

Los Angeles is her real home now, because she's got history here, and a purpose here. She feels of a piece with Los Angeles, and nothing will ever daunt her again. She loves the creativity that bursts at you from every angle: dishes in restaurants, movie marquees, the very clothes on peoples' backs. Thoughtfully, she fingers the sleeve of the creamy jersey blouse she'd chosen for today.

Solita will star in the movie, and with her serene beauty—a Latin Ingrid Bergman, *Variety* would be prompted to call her—the film will interest all those jaundiced Hollywood people who refer to themselves as independents. Solita has not returned to her home; she no longer sees Watts Towers every day, but she is reading a history of Western art she found on a shelf in Ty's house.

Elnice thinks and thinks about the Buick-vs.-the-pickup-truck chase she and Solita led and won and wonders how such a sequence might be worked into the film.

She wants to fit in Watts Towers, too. Perhaps she can devise some kind of Californian subplot including a villain who ends up hanging from the towers, or an abused Latina housewife who uses them for inspiration, or a sweet disabled boy who designs and sells T-shirts to raise money to protect the Towers' humble potsherds and mortar, in defiance of an uncaring world.

Solid, rough-hewn ideas tumble from her like logs from a millrace.

Although she misses the corporeal Arthur, she must admit that it is easier to have merely his ghost around. True, the ghost cannot open a tight jar for her, but neither does the ghost require spaghetti and haircuts. The ghost does not leave the TV on loud and coffee rings on the counter.

Arthur's ghost is one of those gently implacable ones—not angry, once he'd settled into it, but insistent. This is all right with Elnice. She knows what he wants: their money back plus interest. Nothing makes him happier than to see Elnice ordering Ty around, and nothing will thrill him more than seeing her make it all work.

Elnice has not had a chance to do much praying.

Working over Ty's script with her red pencil, she lifts her head to observe the sunny canyon beyond the French doors. A harrier swoops low past the deck, its wings like black blades. Elnice feels a degree of discomfort about the God piece. They made a deal but the deal did not go as planned. What is her obligation at this point? Things are not quite right; unfinished business; the God thing needs to be clearer. But like many suddenly busy people she reasons that God will wait. She will work him in again somehow. She bends her head again to the script. It might take a little time, but she'll work him in.

SPECIAL NOTE

Did you know that people who recommend books are among the most intelligent, respected humans on the planet? If you liked this book, please spread the word to your friends via social media or over the beverage of your choice in a companionable setting. Your opinion is very important!

THANKS

I'm grateful to my family and friends for their love, support, and belief.

Special thanks to the Los Angeles Police Department and Ute Kegel.

Above all, as always, thanks to Marcia, for everything.

Read on! Here's the beginning of *The Actress*, the first in Elizabeth's Rita Farmer Mystery series.

Chapter 1: Rita in Peril

I screamed.

I filled my lungs with the stale, coffee-smelling air of the dungeon and let out a ragged howl that ricocheted off the cold walls. I closed my eyes and screamed again as every cell in my body writhed in a futile attempt to deny the horror that was being inflicted on me by the guy in glasses holding a small cardboard box that said DEATH.

The guy, who had introduced himself as Ned, stood to the side and brandished the box in his freckled hands. I decided to scream once more, this one a sharp, convulsive type of cry.

"OK," said the casting director, a thin black woman named M'kenge, with expressive hands. "OK, Rita, please do it again, only"—she cupped her hands as if to suppress a flower growing—"this time don't shrink down. Get all taut and tall, like you're going to break out of your skin." Upward release of hands.

I did so. I stood at attention, remembering I was supposed to be tied to a pole, put my hands behind my back— behind my butt, actually, which looks more like natural bondage because your shoulders aren't all hiked up—and arched my neck like Joan of Arc at the stake. Ned shook the box at me and I screamed.

When you take a breath to do a scream, you don't just grab a gulp of air and let go. You need to take the time to load your lungs all the way to the bottom. You need to pull all the slack from your diaphragm like you'd pull a bowstring in archery, and then and only then do you unleash that scream to its target, which is the red beating heart of every human within four miles.

I screamed, and it felt good. I was screaming well today. I ululated in the middle of this one—nothing fancy, just another jolt of emotion, just another ripple in the violent fabric of my horror. I'd warmed up carefully.

This was a job I wanted. A job I needed. This was Evan Granger Jackson's new teensploitation movie, *Fingershredder II,* sequel to *Fingershredder,* the low-budget instant-cult terror film you've doubtless heard about or seen. If you're a male age thirteen through seventeen, you've seen it three times.

The role I was trying for was Student Teacher Who Gets Her Fingers Shredded Halfway Through the Script by the Evil But Understandably So Because of Childhood Abuse Sadistic Killer. The fingershredder.

So I screamed. I screamed my ass off, discharging the screams through relaxed vocal cords but tight external throat muscles as Sam Wojczyk had taught me in his acting class at UCLA.

I was lucky to have Ned standing there holding the cardboard box, because at least he was human. In case you've never auditioned for pictures like this in Hollywood, you often don't have anybody playing opposite you. You're just there all alone in front of the casting director, maybe possibly a producer, an assistant with a clipboard who might also be running the video camera, and the empty coffee cups and scone wrappers of the day.

The cardboard box was a stand-in for the fingershredder device audiences came to know and love so well in the original. See, the fingershredding guy figures out pretty early in his career that paper shredders don't work well on fingers: they jam quickly, even the heavy-duty, government models. Plus he likes to shred other body parts too, then eventually the victim bleeds to death in terrible pain. So he invents this gadget using parts from a vacuum cleaner, a Cuisinart, and a walkie-talkie. Works great on the screen. A fiendish device, of course you've seen stills of it in *People* and *Teen* and such. I'm surprised they didn't license miniatures of it for inclusion in Happy Meals.

"OK, stop," said M'kenge. I had not met M'kenge before today's audition, but I'd carefully learned her name because that's what a professional actress does. I feel unusual names are more critical to remember than ordinary names, because people with unusual names have a bigger burden in life than the rest of us, in a small but important to them way.

An unusual name practically *invites* you to forget it. M'kenge pronounced her name *Em-ken-gay.* On the page M'kenge looks as if it might be pronounced *Ma-keng-ee,* which would make it sound Scots, which her parents surely could not have intended.

So M'kenge said stop. I looked at her attentively. She blew a breath down at the tabletop, then ran two fingers along the side of her skull as if trying to unzip a headache and let it out. Her head was one of those beautiful short-cropped African heritage ones, large smooth cranium, narrow jaw. She did not bother to smile. She was looking at me with intensity and thrilling dissatisfaction. Thrilling because she clearly wanted to help me get it right.

I so wanted to get it right.

"Rita, can you do it again, this time full-face to me. I know in this scene you're supposed to be watching your student Melissa's fingers getting shredded, and then her tongue and all that, but now I'd like you to scream as if *your* fingers were getting shredded. You were given pages for that scene, so let's try it, just the screaming part." She clenched one hand on her stomach and reached skyward with the other. "Bring it up from your gut, but not totally from there. Give me some highness, I guess what I'm trying to say is can you make it more piercing?"

Piercing.

"Yes," I said, my heart singing because she didn't say, *Thank you, next!* If they ask you to do it different ways, they think you might be able to deliver exactly what they want.

"Make the hair on the back of my neck stand up."

"Yes."

I thought of the most horrifying thing in the world to me right then, which was getting my credit card declined again at the grocery store, which would mean I would have to sell Gramma Gladys's diamond brooch to buy cereal and juice boxes for Petey and to prevent the landlord from evicting us.

So I imagined walking into Adil's Pawn America with that diamond-and-sapphire brooch, and all that it meant, and I felt not only frightened but angry, and I set my heels into the carpet of the soundproof audition room which was doubling today as a bloody dungeon, and I screamed and screamed again.

Plus usually for a film role you're doing it in somebody's office, not a casting studio, the studios being the cattle chutes between the herd of actors out there and the yearned-for slaughterhouse of TV commercials. The company that made the *Fingershredder* movies, Half Fast Pictures, however, rented studio space for these auditions because everybody in the offices would have gone insane listening to people screaming for days on end. Evan Granger Jackson liked to have lots of first audition tapes to look at.

We had already done an earlier scene with dialogue in it, not that there was lots in those movies. Which is what makes horror movies so much like pornos. There's not that much difference between "Please don't! Stop!" and "Please don't stop!" The scripts are interchangeable, it's only the action that's different. Really, just listen sometime.

"Thank you," said M'kenge with finality in her voice, and I could tell she was disappointed. She crunched up one cheek wistfully. To me, an acting professional, it was the worst kind of disappointment, that tone that says, Man, this one *just missed.* Missed by *that much.* Next!

Of course they rarely say anything at the moment, they leave that for your agent. But I was experienced enough to know that tone; I'd heard it so often.

Was my life's ambition to play supporting roles in teen horror flicks? No. But give me credit for not having stooped to doing porn, not that I have the body porn requires anyway—the Macy's-parade tits, the lion's-mane hair. I'd had breast augmentation, but only one cup size, up to C from my God-given B, which I felt was necessary for the movies, but no way could I ever compete in porn.

I was a serious actress, and I'd long known acting was the best path in life for me. But time had become my enemy: at this point I was twenty-nine and grimly fighting the concept of thirty. Thirty is what you never want to turn in Hollywood, let alone forty or worse. Time, frankly, was running out. My agent was getting me lots of auditions, because she still believed in me. But if you could convert auditions into car payments what a butt-sassy world Los Angeles would be.

I thanked Ned, I thanked M'kenge, I thanked Ellen the coffee-stained assistant. Thank you, thank you, they thanked me back and Ellen flipped my head shot to the bottom of the stack. I caught a glimpse of my face, spritely and wholesome above the collar of my crisp white blouse, then—flip—there was the next actress's face, spritely and wholesome, possibly just what they were looking for.

I passed her on the way out. Her head was high, shoulders back, confident smile ready. We exchanged friendly glances, because you never know who you might be asking for a job someday.

That night Petey and I ate the last can of Campbell's tomato soup and the last of the rice, which came to three-fourths of a cup before cooking. I mixed it all together, put salt and pepper on it, and called it Spider-Man's Mom's Special. God bless my boy, he was so hungry he ate it.

Petey was a Spider-Man maniac. He was four now. When he was three he was a Curious George maniac. When he was two he was a hit-the-rainbow-xylophone-until-Mommy's-ears-pour-blood maniac. I watched him eat and wondered what five would bring.

Precious boy. I saw his father's face in his miniature one: there were Jeff's gorgeous marine-blue eyes, Jeff's touchingly dimpled cheeks, Jeff's contemptuous upper lip. Would he take after his dad? Marry the cute girl next door, move to California for a dull job and start drinking a fifth a day and slapping her around?

I asked Petey that question with my eyes. He looked at me, swallowed a mouthful of the disgusting dinner I had prepared, and answered, "Noah at school? He pooped on the piano."

I hugged him. It was a quiet night.

[End of Chapter 1 of *The Actress*. There's no time like the present to get your own copy!]

ABOUT ELIZABETH SIMS

Elizabeth Sims learned the art of fiction by listening to tall tales on her father's knee, and reading all sorts of books brought home by her mother, a teacher. (These ranged from Grimm's Fairy tales to the Canterbury Tales, from Laura Ingalls Wilder to Ernest Hemingway.)

Today, Elizabeth is the author of the Rita Farmer mysteries and the Lambda and Goldie Award-winning Lillian Byrd crime novels, and she has written articles, short stories, and poems for numerous publications. In addition, she is an internationally recognized authority on writing. She writes frequently for Writer's Digest magazine, where she is a contributing editor. Through her articles, in-person workshops, and online teaching, she has helped thousands of writers find their wings.

Are you a writer too—or would you like to be one? If so, you might find solid guidance and inspiration in Elizabeth's book *You've Got a Book in You: A Stress-Free Guide to Writing the Book of Your Dreams,* published by Writer's Digest Books.

Elizabeth earned degrees in English from Michigan State University and Wayne State University, where she won the Tompkins Award for graduate fiction. She has worked as a reporter, photographer, technical writer, bookseller, street busker, rand hand, corporate executive, and symphonic percussionist. She belongs to several literary societies as well as American Mensa.

BOOKS BY ELIZABETH SIMS

Nonfiction:
You've Got a Book in You: A Stress-Free Guide to Writing the Book of Your Dreams

Fiction:
(It's not necessary to read either series in order.)

The Rita Farmer Mysteries
The Actress (#1)
The Extra (#2)
On Location (#3)

The Lillian Byrd Crime Novels
Holy Hell (#1)
Damn Straight (#2)
Lucky Stiff (#3)
Easy Street (#4)
Left Field (#5)

Crimes in a Second Language

I am Calico Jones: Four Short Stories

For up-to-date everything about Elizabeth and her books, visit **elizabethsims.com.**

Made in the USA
Columbia, SC
12 October 2017